FOR THE LOVE OF A GHOST

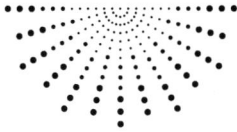

ALSO BY JACKIE NORTH

The Love Across Time Series

Heroes for Ghosts

Honey From the Lion

Wild as the West Texas Wind

Ride the Whirlwind

Hemingway's Notebook

For the Love of a Ghost

Love Across Time Sequels

Heroes Across Time - Sequel to Heroes for Ghosts

Holiday Standalones

The Christmas Knife

Hot Chocolate Kisses

The Little Matchboy

Standalone

The Duke of Hand to Heart

FOR THE LOVE OF A GHOST

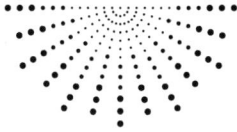

JACKIE NORTH

This book is dedicated to...

All those who know that love is love...

*And my passionate readers - thank you, every one of you, for joining me in
my time travel romance journey*

We only part to meet again. Change, as ye list, ye winds; my heart shall be.
The faithful compass that still points to thee.

"Sweet William's Farewell to Black-Eyed Susan"
~~John Gay (1685–1732)

CHAPTER ONE

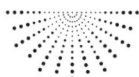

F inn laid out his ghost hunting equipment on the bed: the EMF meter, the motion sensor, the infrared thermometer, the motion camera, the copper divining rods. Most of it was not new or even that expensive, but he was always careful to pack everything in a small padded chest of his own design, which he had lined with high-impact foam that squeaked when he put anything in or pulled anything out.

The EVP recorder was new, as his last one had broken when he'd dropped it the week before in the middle of a ghost hunt at Pioneer Cemetery in Old Town Harlin. Of course, ghosts didn't haunt grave-yards—everybody knew that—but he'd been invited by the Spirits of Harlin group to be an *expert* during a ghost hunting party made up of a busload of Japanese and Korean tourists.

The hunt had been a blast, and he'd enjoyed the tourists' enthu-siasm and curiosity, so while the whole evening had been more laughter and chatter than quiet attentiveness to the spirit world, it had been great. That kind of experience, *ghost cred*, would go a long way towards when he would finally be able to submit his audition package to Ghost Force, a growing Youtube channel with thousands of followers.

The audition package was why he was staying at the Harlin Hotel, only half an hour's drive away from the house he grew up in, and *still* lived in, much to his own dismay. He'd taken English Lit as a major without really thinking about where it would take him. Now, college was over and he had the summer to figure out what he was really going to do before he packed up his bags and boxes and moved on with his life.

Everything felt like it was standing still, waiting, holding its breath. The only thing moving in his life were the ghosts, or at least the search for ghosts. Nobody had proof and everybody wanted some. Finn aimed to be the guy who got it, though he half-suspected that the hunt was the thing, the excitement of the chase. Just like the guys on that show about the bottomless pit who were always looking for evidence that there was buried treasure, there was always tons of evidence, but nothing that proved anything. The chase itself was the thing.

When his cellphone blared out the theme of *Grim Grinning Ghosts*, he answered it.

"Hey, Dad," he said, flopping into the old-fashioned looking armchair in the corner. He grabbed the EVP recorder to heft in his hand, enjoying the sleek, new feel of it.

"Hey, Finn," said Dad. Finn could hear the smile in his voice and smiled back, as he usually did.

"How are the bees?" he asked.

"They're still buzzing," said Dad. "How are the ghosts? You set up yet?"

"Not yet," said Finn. "Thank you again for the loan to pay for the hotel room."

"It's not a loan, son, it's a gift." Dad sighed; they'd been over this before. "I just wish I could have afforded a room at the Stanley Hotel for you."

"That's not it, Dad," said Finn, sighing right back. "They didn't want me up there. Didn't want me messing with their predetermined level of spookiness."

"Is that what they said?"

"Not exactly." Finn traced the On/Off button on the EVP recorder with his thumb.

It had been hard to swallow his disappointment over the Stanley Hotel's refusal to let him openly hunt ghosts in their hotel. Sure, he could have snuck his equipment in and pretended he was an ordinary tourist. He could have skulked around, joined the Haunted Tour group like he was just anybody out for a lark and a scare, and not who he really was: a real ghost hunter.

"They just didn't want the intrusion, I think. You know, Stephen King did his thing up there, and now the hotel will never be the same."

"I think it's the better for it," said Dad, stating his mind as he always did. "They'd not have half the business they do if not for him."

"You'll meet him one day, Dad," said Finn. "I know you will. Just keep writing those letters."

"That was one time," said Dad, his voice rising in mock self-defense. "One time, damn it, one time I wrote him, and it was a letter that needed writing."

"I know, I know. Elba is a god, and the movie was a dud." Finn laughed. "*The Dark Tower* should never have been made into a movie."

"That's right, son, and don't you forget it." Dad chuckled, soft and low, letting Finn know that all was right with the world. "Well, anyway, the Hotel Harlin is plenty haunted, isn't it? You could get a brand new scoop rather than pacing in Mr. King's footsteps."

"He would be honored to have me pace," said Finn, pretending to be all serious about it. "But yes, I've got three lovely ghosts to find and capture on film. I think they did the lobby up since the time you and Mom stayed for your anniversary. Did you hear about that?"

"No," said Dad. "What'd they do?"

"They've got a little, I don't know, tableau with three portraits in these fancy wooden Victorian frames. There's a little table with a notebook for each ghost with articles pasted in, and newspaper clippings, and letters from folks who stayed at the hotel who say they've had encounters."

"Nice. Did you take the tour yet?"

"That's later," said Finn. "It'll probably be one of the cute kind of tours, you know, so as not to scare the residents overly much."

"Not everyone enjoys being scared," said Dad. "Just us'ns."

"And Mom," said Finn, laughing a silent laugh. "Even though she won't admit it."

"Mia's the only hold-out," said Dad. "All *My Little Pony* and not enough *Scooby-Doo*."

"She sullies the Keating name," said Finn, laughing out loud this time, though it was absolutely not true. His sister Mia was the nicest person on the planet, with a smile that could charm angels and devils alike. "She home yet from the big city?"

"Tomorrow for two weeks," said Dad. "Though I'm not sure if she's still bi or if it's boys this summer."

"She's *always* bi, Dad," said Finn, kindly but firmly. "But I think she's seeing a guy named Toby."

"You know," said Dad, conversationally, "I don't care who she loves, to be honest, as long as they're nice."

"Can you imagine Mia putting up with someone who's not nice?" asked Finn, arching his brow even though his Dad couldn't possibly see the sarcasm on his face.

"No," said Dad. "At any rate, your Mom packed you some lavender honey and she says to be sure and have a spoonful every day."

"Thank you," said Finn. Lavender honey was the most sought-after flavor of honey that his Dad's farm, Finnwood Farms, produced. "Tell her thank you for me, will you?"

"I sure will. And listen—" Dad paused, and Finn knew what was coming. "I sure as heckfire hope you get this audition thing with the ghost folks—"

"The Ghost Force," said Finn, being helpful.

"The Ghost Force will love you and your ghost hunting skills, but you know you can always come home to Finnwood and work on the farm with me and your mother. There's plenty to be done here. You could write about ghosts, too."

"I know, Dad." Finn couldn't think of more words to say than that. Finnwood Farms was a family business. Dad and Mom had bought the property north of Harlin years ago from an elderly widow whose husband had died. They'd renamed the farm after him when he'd been born and replenished the soil and planted a small assortment of crops that they sold at local farmer's markets, but their big sell was honey, local honey, drawn from bees who danced in the air above the lush rows of lavender and the green swaths of alfalfa.

There was no better smell in the world than those fields, no better sight than the green and purple against a blue sky, no better thing than to lie awake in bed on a warm night in August and hear the rain pattering on the plants.

There was nothing better than the farm, but it wasn't the whole world. It couldn't be everything. At least it had started feeling that way, when Finn had been halfway through college. Now that he was done, having just graduated in May, he wanted to test that theory. Hence the audition tape to Ghost Force, who could hire him on to be the local man in the field, so to speak.

The applicant who was chosen would cover hauntings and spirit activity in Colorado, New Mexico, Wyoming, and Utah. Ghost Force would cover half the cost of setting up a van that he could live in, a van that Finn intended getting painted up to look spooky and evocative. Dad had joked he should get it painted to look like the Scooby-Doo van, which would be fun, of *course*, but it would be too noticeable and not suitable for a serious-minded ghost hunter like himself.

"You need to spread your wings, and I get it, son, I do."

"I know you do, Dad," said Finn. There was nobody more supportive than his Dad, unless it was his Mom or Mia. "And I love the farm, but I just feel I need to do this. It's all so perfect there, but I need to know if there's more."

"There's always more, Finn," said Dad, perfectly serious. "The question to answer is whether it's worth it."

"I know." Finn put down the EVP recorder and checked his phone for the time. "All right, I'm off. Dinner's at seven, and then the tour starts at eleven."

5

"Whooooooo," said Dad, making his best fake ghost sound. "I'm a ghooooost!" Then he laughed. "Try the chicken, I'll be here all week."

"Love you, Dad."

"Love you, too, kiddo."

Tapping the phone off with his thumb, Finn got up to put the EVP recorder back on the bed. He evaluated the equipment, all lined up in a row, and knew that while he might want an SLS camera, he didn't need more stuff. What he needed was a chance, a chance to prove that his life could be interesting, that he wasn't just a farm boy born to cut alfalfa and tend to bees. Sure, it had been fun when he was a kid, but it felt dull, now, compared to the dream of hunting ghosts.

The ghost bug had hit him hard two years before when his Nana had died. Nana Agnes Richter had lived in Denver in a retirement community, playing bridge with her gal pals, and going to dances, living her best life. It had been after a New Year's Eve dance that she'd gone home and died peacefully in her bed with a smile on her face. At least that's what Nana's friends told him, and he'd believed it, wanted to believe it. Then he found out it was true.

He'd been staying in his old bedroom at the farmhouse before going back to the college dorms. The funeral was an oddly cheerful and well-attended event with many people devoted to Nana in attendance—more people than he realized had been her friends. That night he had gone to bed missing her so much that he felt like he'd been whacked up one side of his body and down the other with a very large broom handle.

Sleep had been restless and evasive, and he'd sat up at one point, thinking that his Mom had come in to comfort him. That was like her, except the person standing at the foot of his bed had not been Mom. Mom didn't have goofy, curly hair like that, nor retro cat-eye shaped glasses, nor a house dress that had been artfully altered to look stylish. Nana did.

As Nana stood there, the shape of her was vague, like she'd been outlined in a soft grey crayon. Finn had looked at her with his mouth open, arms shaking beneath him. His heart raced, not with fear but with the joy of seeing her again.

He'd been a little remiss in visiting her since he'd started college, but when he had taken the time to drive to Denver, she'd always greeted him with the same warmth, with the same offer of chocolate covered graham crackers and milk, as though he was a small boy of seven or twelve instead of a fully grown man in his early twenties.

That kind of love was hard to come by and he'd treasured it, always. And then she'd been there, at the foot of his bed, looking at him like she had a secret to tell.

"Nana?" he'd asked, keeping his voice low so as not to disturb anybody in the house, as they had all been a little worn out by the funeral and needed their rest.

She had seemed to move toward him—to float, really— until she was close by his side. His brain had fired off questions, alight with amazement, but he could hardly find the words to speak as she reached out and seemed to touch his face. She didn't really touch him; he didn't feel any physical sensation, but he had sensed it. The hairs on his neck rose up and all of him tingled.

"I'm all right, Nana," he'd said, not really understanding why he felt he needed to soothe her in any way. "Are you all right? Are you happy?"

He had sensed that she was. He'd sensed that she nodded at him, tipping her head to the side, in that way that she had, as if she was appraising him to see if there was anything he needed or wanted.

"I got the cookie jar you left me," he'd said, wanting to cry at the thought of the five dollar cookie jar Nana bought from Target years and years ago. The thing was old and a little rusty around the edges, the plastic lid had a chip in it, but it was Nana's cookie jar. Even empty of cookies, it had been full of memories when he'd held it in his hands. "But I gave it to Mia. She's the one who's going to have kids, not me. You know that, right?"

Nana had seemed to shake her head. She knew all about him being gay, though they'd never really talked about it. She didn't seem to care about that, only that he was lonely, only that he needed someone in his life to love him.

That he was practically a virgin had seemed to be an easier topic of conversation between them. She'd been forever getting phone numbers off waiters and busboys in restaurants they'd dined in when he visited her. Most of those dates had gone well, and he'd had some fun, but nothing had ever come of them.

"Are you going to visit Mom, too?" he'd asked. "She misses you. I heard her crying."

The question had seemed to move through Nana's form and the energy shifted in the room, as though she was already walking to the door to open it, even as she stayed where she was.

"You can go, Nana," he'd said. "I'm going to be okay, but she needs you now."

As her form had drifted into nothingness, her energy had shifted, moving around in a little circle before going out the door, leaving him with more feelings in his heart than he'd known what to do with. He'd gotten up in the dark, not turning on the light as he paced the room, until he came to a stop in the place where Nana's ghost had stood. He'd stood there for a good, long minute before he crawled back into bed.

The tears that had waited and waited came in a small storm, then. He buried the sounds in his pillow, and in the morning, was as cheerful as could be expected, though he looked at his Mom, waiting to see if she would say anything about Nana visiting her in the night. But she didn't.

Nana had come to him two more times, looking fainter each time. She left traces of herself in his heart as well as the very strong feeling that she would always be looking out for him. Finally, when Nana wasn't coming to his room anymore, having said her final goodbyes, it seemed, he brought it up to Mom. She'd cautiously admitted that yes, she'd felt something, but she had not known what it was, only that she wasn't scared.

Dad had been asleep in the bed beside her, but when he found out about Nana's ghost he'd pretended to be annoyed that he was the only one who had not seen a ghost—he, who adored Stephen King more than any of the author's other readers.

This was, of course, to distract Mom from her grief and give her something else to focus on as she joined the playful teasing about the letter to King that Dad had written. But later, when she'd pulled Finn aside and wanted to know more, he told her everything, every detail, from the warmth of Nana's presence to the love he'd felt filling the darkness of his room.

After that, after everything had settled down from the funeral, he'd started researching ghosts and hauntings and everything he could think of for an explanation. Right away he'd found that those who passed on typically wanted to be sure their loved ones were okay, so they would come back and visit for a few nights before floating off to the afterlife, or whatever it was that awaited them. Some ghosts came back for revenge and carried dark feelings and energies with them, wanting only to do harm.

Nobody knew, of course, what was really there after a person died, be it a heaven or a hell or a limbo of some kind. There was was tons of evidence to indicate that *something* was going on, and that spirits and ghostly energy hung around for a while—or even forever—depending on how they died. Nana had died happy, by all accounts, so he figured she was in some Big Bopper Heaven where dances were held every day and her dance card was never empty.

But what about other ghosts? Did he have a gift, or had he just been close with his Nana, who loved him, and was therefore able to see her after she passed away?

He'd wanted to know so he started watching YouTube vids about ghost hunting, and read all the books. Finally, he'd bought an EMF meter on Amazon for around twenty-five bucks. There were more expensive ones of course, but he was a college student on a budget and needed to be sensible. He'd also made sure to get his homework done and to show up at his work-study job in the library on time before allowing himself to play with the EMF meter.

He'd gone into old buildings on campus first, figuring they'd have energy—and yes, they did. Of course, the EMF could pick up electrical signals from wires, too, but he made sure to do readings in dark corners, and at different times of the day.

If the signals came from wires, they'd be the same readings each time. If the signals didn't come from wires, but from paranormal energy, the readings would shift and move, and then—yeah, baby—he had a ghost on his hands. Or at least the revenants of a ghost, as some weren't as potent and tended to move on more quickly than others.

He'd felt he could sense them talking to him, their voices coming across like faint whispers that he couldn't understand. That was when he bought an EVP recorder so he could listen to their voices.

Not sure what to do with the results of his solitary ghost hunts, he'd joined several local ghost hunting groups, most of which were silly excuses to go drinking in graveyards and to brag about their encounters to anyone who would listen.

The group he liked was a small group of guys and gals in south Boulder who, when they'd found out he wasn't the drinking-and-bragging type of ghost hunter, welcomed him cautiously and taught him what they knew. They called themselves the Boulder Paranormal Society and it was they who had shown him the possibility of being a ghost hunter for a living.

Of course, there were those who hunted ghosts to be Instagram or Youtube famous or whatever, but then there were those who truly wanted to know about the unknown, who wanted to help people. Then there was the Ghost Force, a group on Youtube who had it all: a great rep, cool gadgets, and were making money.

By the time Finn had been involved with the Boulder group for a year, auditions for Ghost Force had opened up for additional members. Finn was determined to be the one picked. You had to turn in an audition package that consisted of three EVPs with analysis, ten pictures of ghostly apparitions (only three of which could consist of just orbs), a night time infrared recording with temperature readings from the night of the recording, motion sensor data, and a writeup of the whole thing.

For extra oomph, you could document any personal experiences from your own life, so Finn intended to tell them about Nana. Finn also sensed that the Ghost Force was looking for authenticity rather than anything showy, so he fully intended to admit any data, even if it didn't support proof that there was life after death.

Which was why he was staying at a fancy hotel only half an hour from home, looking for ghosts and feeling a little lonely. But then, he was always alone. Why? Because he was the kind of guy who lived in his own head and was currently the type of guy who holed up in an old hotel just so he could chase after ghosts. Nobody wanted to be with a guy like that. Right?

CHAPTER TWO

The Harlin Hotel was a grand old lady of a building: three stories of sturdy red brick, a new slate roof, and just enough coyly painted stick work and gingerbread trim to let you know she'd kept up with the latest fashion as far as she could. That she sat on Main Street with rush hour traffic going by did not deter from the old-fashioned charm within, did not distract from the way the building had been refurbished to the last detail, retro but not overly so.

The building had good vibes, at least to Finn. This hotel was where his Nana had stayed whenever she'd ventured this far north, and it was where his parents liked to go for a romantic getaway that wouldn't take them too far from their beloved bees and lavender.

All in all, it was a good place. That was why, at 11 o'clock in the evening, he was standing in the lobby with a small group of like-minded folks, doing his best not to bother the ghost tour guide with too many questions. It was also why he'd left all of his gear in his room. He wanted to honor what the ghost tour guide and the hotel were doing, which was promoting their three ghosts as a reason to stay.

The ghosts were represented by portraits of each, all in a row along the wall, their Victorian-fussy wooden frames gleaming in the low spotlights aimed at each of them. Below the portraits was a long, polished wooden table with feet the shape of lion's paws for feet and little roses carved along the sides.

On the table were three notebooks, each filled with articles about its ghost, including the local obituary, letters from people who'd had sightings, and general information about the weather and other happenings on the day that they died. Each one of them had been associated with the hotel in some way, and all three ghosts purportedly had died under mysterious or violent circumstances.

The lobby where the twenty or so people in their tour group gathered felt a little crowded as people lingered in front of the lion-legged table, but then, the lobby was only meant to be passed through. The tour guide, a nice young lady, was dressed in an old-fashioned dress from the early part of the previous century, with her hair done up in a sensible bun.

"Now, we're going to spend some time here in the lobby. Then we're going to go up to the room where Daisy McKee stayed while she mourned her fiancé, who went down with the *Titanic* on that fateful night in April, 1912."

Finn grinned to himself. His room was right above Daisy's and he fully expected to get some great readings after the tour when he went into it by himself later, with the hotel's permission, to take photographs and readings. There was nobody staying in the room because it was *haunted*. It was perfect.

"Later we'll go down to the river. It's only a ten minute walk to the place where she drowned herself out of grief."

The group nodded appreciatively and made appropriate small sounds, as if to express sympathy for the drowned girl. Which might be true, though Finn suspected that some were on the tour out of boredom, or were there only because their boyfriend or girlfriend made them come. Others were there out of macabre interest, with no real love for or curiosity about the idea of life after death. Some, though, like himself, had a genuine interest, and he felt he could see it

14

on their faces as they listened to the tour guide this really meant something to them.

"Before we head up, be sure and take a moment to look at the portraits of our ghosts and memorize their faces," said the guide. "You might meet up with one of these ghosts and you will want to know who you're dealing with, right?"

This was greeted by a small group laugh.

"Also, let's take a moment to look at the notebooks, as you might find information about the ghosts that can help you reach out to them, to communicate with them. Now, does everybody have their divining rods? Be sure to hold them out straight as you stand in the hall upstairs and wait your turn to go into the room. Be sure to stay quiet, so as not to disturb the other hotel guests, alive or otherwise."

There was another laugh from the group, which told Finn, in no uncertain terms, that the whole point of having the tableau was to draw customers who wanted a special haunted experience—but not too special. Nobody really wanted to stay in Stephen King's Overlook Hotel. Nobody really wanted to encounter a terrifying ghost pointing to the gash in its neck, its mouth moving with silent screams as it asked for help to solve its own murder. That happened on *Ghost Whisperer* and in scary movies, but in real life? People wanted the cute version; they wanted Casper, not *The Sixth Sense*.

As the group milled about the lobby, mostly talking to each other, messing with their divining rods, all borrowed from the hotel, Finn went up to the tableau to study the images and flip through the notebooks.

The portrait of Daisy McKee showed a photograph of a young blonde woman in a blue evening dress that had a square neckline. She wore a long single string of pearls that dropped as low as her waist. She was looking up, as though seeing wisdom from the angels, her teeth barely showing behind her small smile.

The photograph had been touched up, painted to look realistic, but all it had done, as far as Finn could see, was made her look like a haunted mannequin.

He opened the notebook about her. A printed newspaper obituary, now yellow with age and currently sealed in a plastic sleeve, stated that she had drowned by her own hand in St. Vrain Creek during the spring thaw, June 5, 1912. The sad tale included the tragic death of her fiancé and her fiancé's sister on the famous *Titanic* sinking, making her the hotel's biggest connection to that event.

Letters from guests in the notebook told of how Daisy would come into the room late at night, when the occupants were in bed. She would race around as though trying to pack her things to leave for New York so she could identify the body. How people scared out of their minds could have gleaned all that from the single visit of a harried ghost, Finn had no idea. He suspected the hotel had dressed up the story so folks would know what they were getting into.

Witnesses to Daisy's distress wrote how they wanted to help her find her suitcase and her silk stockings but had no idea how to do this. All were moved by Daisy's plight, and wrote that they thoroughly enjoyed their encounter with her.

The portrait of little Ruby Hopkins, ghost number two, was actually a painting of a girl of about seven years old in a blue sailor dress. Her hair was all flyaway squiggles and curls, pulled to the side and topped with an enormous, truly enormous, blue bow.

She looked like she was reaching down for something, her body leaning to one side, and Finn got the impression that the portrait had been painted from a photograph and that some detail had been left out in order to concentrate on the little girl. Looking at her made him feel a little sad that her life, just getting started, had been cut short.

As he waited for the lobby to clear out so he could be at the back of the tour and watch people's reactions, he flipped through the notebook about Ruby. The little girl's obituary, printed in the *Harlin Advocate*, was dated June 6, 1912, which was odd, because that was the day after Daisy McKee had died.

Ruby's obituary was also twice as long as Daisy's, as she'd been an only child, best beloved of her parents, the golden light of their eyes, and on it went, quite effusively. There were even more letters from guests who often encountered Ruby, they said, in the lobby of the hotel, dancing and playing with a little dog. The ghostly child and dog would dash between things, leaving behind them flickers of light and energy that astonished guests and left them with a feeling of melancholy.

Evidently the dog had been named Leo. There was black and white photograph of a rather large grave statuary, a crying angel that stood over her grave in the Pioneer Cemetery, one of the dog, alone, at his young mistress's graveside.

As to how the poor kid had died, she'd been out on the sidewalk in front of the hotel, walking just ahead of her parents. Evidently, Leo had rushed into the lobby, and Ruby had tossed her red rubber ball to entice him out.

In trying to get Leo's red rubber ball out of the gutter so she could toss it for him again, Ruby had stumbled into the street and been run over by a Model T Ford. With so few cars on the road at the time, it had been a fluke accident in the middle of the day, made all the more tragic by Ruby's tender age.

As Finn flipped to the end of the notebook, there, in a plastic sleeve, was a sepia-toned photograph that showed all of Ruby, from her curly, bow-topped head, to her white middy dress and black stockings. At her side was the detail the painted portrait had left out: her faithful Jack Russell terrier, Leo, whose energy practically vibrated off the photo as he looked up with adoration at his young mistress.

It was odd that both ghosts had died within a day of each other. Perhaps there'd been a particular vortex of energy that had kept both ghosts around after their deaths? Or perhaps the hotel wanted to only display information about ghosts who died in 1912, on account of the date was strongly associated with the sinking of the *Titanic*—always a big draw for seekers of the morbid and bizarre.

Finn was actually surprised that there wasn't more about the *Titanic*, but the hotel made only subtle references to it, mentioning it here or there, like an added bonus rather than the main attraction, because they were too cool to be more obvious about it.

The last glossy wooden frame on the wall held a rather faded copy of a copy of a newspaper photograph of a young man. The edges of the portrait were almost invisible; the black and white contrasts were so badly rendered that it ruined the effect of the image, and made it hard to make out the features as they had been in life.

But there were traces that Finn could see: the curve of a cheek, the tender glint of the young man's eyes, the curl of fair hair over one eyebrow. The young man might have been cute in real life, but then again Finn's impression of sweetness might be amplified by the distance of years. Young men in 1912 were hearty and industrious—not interested in other fellas, alas.

Also woven into the portrait was a sense of longing, though maybe that was Finn's own loneliness echoing back. What would have been like to live back then, not knowing that your life was about to end?

The pages of the notebook revealed that the young man was named Arturo Larkin. He'd lived a simple life, staying at the boarding house on the other side of the alley from the hotel. He'd distributed newspapers for a local man and had been a familiar figure on Main Street as he went up and down with his handcart. All indications pointed to him being happy with his little life.

The original photograph had been taken on a day in May, when the local newspaper, the *Harlin Advocate*, had been doing a piece about the growth of the relationship between newspapers and trains. The notebook contained only a description of that article, and not a facsimile or anything.

Another article at the back of the notebook, this one an actual clipping from June 7, 1912, stated that Arturo had been found dead in the alley. It was thought that he'd, perhaps, jumped to his death from the top of the boarding house out of grief over the sinking of the *Titanic*. That didn't make much sense, as the *Titanic* sinking had been in April 1912, and, as far as Finn could tell, the young man had no connection to the doomed vessel.

Perhaps Arturo had been distressed over the fact that he'd broken up with his girlfriend, or that he was merely selling newspapers for a living. Arturo's obituary, also an actual brown-stained and faded clipping, was quite short; it stated his age, the same as Finn's, as 24 years old, and it described a sad end to a short life that was unremarkable except to note its passing.

There weren't many letters from guests about encounters with Arturo, but all of them were short and terse. People described how they'd been scared to see him on the back stairs that led to the alley.

They wrote about the darkness they felt when they opened the door to the alley, how sad they felt, how grief-stricken, how some kind of black energy tried to suck them into it. All in all, it seemed that encounters with Arturo were of the scary, not-fun variety, rather than the jolly, tell-your-friends-at-cocktail-parties kind.

Something inside Finn twinged sadly at the fact that Arturo's life was now merely an added benefit to a fairly pedestrian ghost tour: *You might get scared but he can't hurt you, ha ha.*

With a snap, Finn closed the notebook and trotted across the lobby, trailing after the last person in the ghost tour. He rolled his shoulders to relax himself as he climbed the stairs. He wanted to find out whether the energy in Daisy McKee's room was real ghost energy or just the ordinary drummed-up kind produced by the expectations set by the hotel and the guests on the various ghost tours.

It turned out that the experience was a little of both. Certainly, as everyone waited in the hall for their turn in Daisy's room, giggling and chatting as they played with their divining rods, there was good energy in the hallway, though not the contemplative kind.

Once Finn got his chance to go in the room, along with four other guests—two couples who mostly had eyes for each other—he was able to feel Daisy's energy. He had to focus, though, to block out the sound of the tour guide's voice and the shifting, lovey-dovey behavior of the couples as they clanged their copper divining rods together just for fun. Ducking his head, he half-closed his eyes and did his best to listen to her, to see what she might say to him.

Ghosts rarely spoke to him in words. He always figured that was because most of them had lost the true use of their vocal cords. Instead, ghosts made a kind of humming sound that seemed to morph into one kind of emotion or another that he felt he could recognize.

It was from that sensation that he would interpret what they were saying to him and, really, all most ghosts wanted was for someone to listen to their tale of woe. They wanted someone to know how they died. Whether it had been scary. Who they missed. Why they thought they were stuck in the afterlife instead of moving on to wherever it was that souls went.

Finn's only regret was that other than listening, he couldn't do a damn thing to help them move on. But listening to them seemed to calm them, and maybe, just maybe, they would be able to move onwards on their own.

Dad had mentioned a time or two that writing down the stories might be a good way for the ghosts to feel that they'd not been forgotten. Typically, Finn always dismissed these ideas because writing down a ghost story wasn't as exciting as posting a ghostly video on YouTube. In the meantime, he turned his attention to Daisy.

He didn't see her shape or anything, as there were too many lights in the room and too much activity. He thought he felt her by the dresser, so he moved in that direction. When he stood next to the dresser he looked at the far wall, letting his eyes go unfocused and his peripheral vision take over. There she was, but she was faint, so faint, mostly only an outline, as though her energy was nearly gone.

The feelings that ebbed from her were of distress and panic, but it felt as though she'd been through the motions of trying to pack so many times she was exhausted of it. Which then begged the question: if she'd been packing to go to New York to identify the body of her late fiancé, why on earth had she gone to the river to commit suicide? It made for a good story, of course—the frantic packing combined with the watery death—but face to face with it, it made no sense.

Opening his mouth to ask, he immediately snapped it shut. The ghost tour was for fun, and anybody on it was just looking for a good time.

Nobody wanted to get dragged into the details of it. Nobody wanted the spell of a possible ghost encounter dimmed by anything as boring as facts. Between packing and getting on the next train going east, Daisy had stopped in her tracks and committed suicide as though her whole life was falling apart.

After everybody had a chance to hold their divining rods out straight and pretend that the rods had crossed, indicating the presence of ghostly energy, the tour guide led them down to the lobby—mostly for the atmosphere, as the stairway was a little dark.

As the group went down the stairs, which were mostly used for emergencies, Finn glanced up the stairs to the landing of the floor his room was on. He could hear the sound of someone shouting the same phrase over and over, as well as the sound of something banging—which might have been trash can lids, or it might have been a wrench on a steam pipe, he had no idea.

Nobody else on the tour seemed to hear it. They were all having such a good time and not concentrating the least bit. The whole thing must have been his imagination anyway, so he followed the tour guide up the main hallway to the lobby.

The lobby was warm and bright and very welcoming. It was hard to focus as the group chattered excitedly around him, even though the tour guide raised her hand for silence.

"This lobby was the last place little Ruby was seen alive," said the tour guide. "She wasn't a guest here, but she didn't live far. This was a street corner that she knew. It seems her dog, Leo, ran into the hotel when a guest opened the door, and there was much to-doing as Ruby came in to get her dog. Then she threw her red rubber ball out the door to coax Leo to go outside, but the ball went into the gutter. The rest, you know. Poor Ruby went to get the ball and was run over by a Model T Ford."

The tour group made sad noises, but small ones, as though they were having a hard time feeling anything but remotely interested about a little girl who'd died over 100 years ago. Besides, it was plain to see, Daisy was the ghost star of the show, the one everyone in the group had come to hear about.

Finn felt he saw Ruby out of the corner of his eyes, but she was a fleeting trace of white and shadow. He thought he heard a dog barking, but he couldn't be sure that it wasn't a real live dog somewhere in the neighborhood. And, with a low thud, like a small red rubber ball hitting a wall, she was gone.

Maybe he'd go down to the lobby in the middle of the night and see if he could find her, find her energy. Maybe even capture a photograph of her. Ruby deserved to be seen, to be listened to, just as much as Daisy and Arturo.

The tour guide led them out and onto the sidewalk. The June evening, just before midnight, was a bit chilly, but the sky was clear and the wind was soft. There was a smell of rain in the air and, from far away, the scent of lavender.

Secretly, Finn figured it was the smell of lavender growing on Finnwood Farms. The wind was from the north and softly, tenderly, moved around them in delightful ways, seeming to ease the ghost tour group into a semblance of quiet as they walked down the slope toward the river.

On the left side of the street rose the new condos where the packing plant had once been. On the right, just on the near side of the train tracks, stood the old power plant, now converted into an internationally famous cheese importer.

The old train depot sat boarded up and unused, though Finn figured the city might want to do something with it, as they'd not demolished it yet. On the far side of it was the Grange, where dances and community events were held. The whole area, once very work-a-day and industrial, was now quite up and coming for young married couples and single folks just starting out in their careers.

After a brisk walk beneath the streetlights, the tour guide gestured that they should gather on the bridge, which was probably much wider and more sturdy than the bridge that had existed in 1912. There the tour guide held up her hand for everyone to listen.

"Records indicate that poor Daisy leaped from the bridge," said the tour guide in a clear voice. "But I have it on good authority that she waded in from the bank below us, into the foamy rush of snowmelt that was the St. Vrain Creek at springtime. They found her body half a mile down, cold and lifeless and battered by rocks."

Finn wanted to ask who had found the body and how long it had taken them to find her, and on whom she had it on good authority? He supposed he could research all of that online later and not disturb the storytelling vibe the tour guide had going on.

"Daisy McKee was mourning the death of her fiancé, Gerald Cren-shaw. Tragically, she decided her life had no meaning and she killed herself rather than go on. Now, why don't you all hold up your divining rods and tell me if you can determine which side of the bridge she entered the water on."

Like obedient and obliging guests, everyone in the tour group held up their divining rods and stood on one side of the bridge. That is except for Finn, who cocked his eyebrow at the tour guide.

She knew who he was, and though it probably would have been easier for him to fit in if he had brought along his divining rods or picked up a pair when she was handing them out. It was too late for that, so he just stayed quiet and watched as everyone in the tour group, one by one, determined that poor Daisy had gone in on the west side of the bridge. Finn knew they were wrong, and the tour guide probably did too, but she nodded and smiled.

"Congratulations everyone, you are right! Poor Daisy went into the water on the west side of the bridge, and probably was dragged under by the force of the water moving under the bridge."

Finn felt the energy from the other side of the bridge, the east side, and wanted to go over to it. He could feel Daisy humming at him, and got the sense she was tired of hanging around her own watery grave, that she longed to move on and join Gerald in the afterlife.

As to what Gerald had been doing on the *Titanic* with his sister, rather than being with his fiancé, the tour guide never said. There must have been some important reason for him to go that far away from his young lady love just to take a trip on the biggest, most osten-tatious ship the world had ever seen.

Wondering idly how many ghosts haunted the middle of the Atlantic Ocean, Finn turned his attention to the east side of the bridge, and pretended he didn't hear Daisy's humming, didn't feel her energy. Another night, it might be nice to come back on his own and listen to her, but that stood a good chance of calming her to the point where she moved on and then—voila! The hotel would be down by one ghost and they wouldn't thank him for it. It was probably better to not come back, though he still didn't know whether or not it was his assistance that helped the Sterling school ghost into the afterlife.

"Did anybody feel Daisy's spirit?" asked the tour guide. "Did anyone have their divining rods cross?"

She waited until everyone nodded and some giggled as their divining rods crossed over each other, as though they'd been affected by Daisy's energy.

"We'll head back to the hotel now," said the tour guide, nodding as she saw all the half-hearted raised hands. "If you are brave, we can go up the sidewalk to the alley where poor Arturo plunged to his death. Everybody ready? Let's go!"

The tour guide was chipper, as though she was trying to bolster their spirits and energy against a truly horrible encounter. But by the time they'd gotten to the entryway to the alley, a less than ten minute walk, it felt to Finn as though the group had seen enough and just wanted to go home. It was after midnight, after all.

When they arrived at the alley, it was immediately evident that the alley was less salubrious than the hotel bar, and less enticing than a nice warm bed. The whole length of it smelled of old garbage and there was a whiff of pee and cheap beer near the dumpsters.

Half the group turned in their divining rods to the tour guide and sloped off. The other half huddled together attentively.

"Everybody hold up their divining rods," said the tour guide. "Hold 'em straight and in the stillness, see what you can feel happening."

The stillness was interrupted almost immediately by a police siren blasting down Third Avenue, the blue and white lights casting sharp-edged brightness on the brick wall of the hotel and the greasy surfaces of the alley. Everybody laughed, but the laughs were short-lived. The divining rods, Finn noticed, were all over the place.

The back of his neck was itching, and he heard, once again, the rhythmic shouting, as though someone was calling for attention in a bustling crowd. He didn't know what to make of it, didn't ask the questions he wanted to ask, even though he knew there was a story, a deeper knowledge to be found about Arturo's death.

"This place in the alley, right here," said the tour guide. She pointed to a spot at her feet as though she was directing their attention to something remarkable, when really, it was really only a greasy splotch that might or might not have been the actual place where Arturo Larkin had breathed his last. "This is where he died after throwing himself off the roof. Nobody knew his body was here until, at dawn, when the milkman came by and found him."

Finn, wondering why a milkman would be in an alley when surely deliveries of milk were made to front doors in 1912, kept his mouth shut. At the same time, he felt wave after wave of something dark and sad that ribboned around him in low, anxious layers, as though Arturo had come to tell him a secret.

Ghosts had lots of secrets. Some wanted to harbor those secrets in their fog-covered hearts. Others, as in this instance, wanted to tell what they knew, wanted it so badly only they didn't know how.

Arturo had a secret, a big one—something heavy and despondent. As the energy came at Finn, over and over, he had to use the heel of his hand to wipe away tears that felt chilly on his face. What on earth had Arturo felt as he climbed the stairs to the roof of the building? What thoughts had he scattered as he fell, and cast into the unknown darkness beyond death as he died?

With a gasp, Finn was brought back to attention by the tour guide going around to each person to collect the copper divining rods. He hadn't borrowed a set, so he waved his hand at her, and nodded, acknowledging that this was her tour, that she was in charge. But he was shaken by the energy in the alley, and longed for something sweet to chase away the swamp of sadness that still lingered inside of him.

He heaved a grateful sigh when the tour guide led them through the back door, past the emergency stairs, and into the lobby. There, Finn felt the gentle presence of small Ruby, but it was again gone in a flicker, as she headed off, probably looking for her beloved Leo.

"Does anybody have any questions?" asked the tour guide. When nobody did, she nodded. "Now, you all have coupons in your hands—

that's on the back of your printed tickets—for a discount for our summertime ghost tours where we explore Main Street and all of its ghosts, including the infamous Barber Shop ghost who is said to haunt customers to this very day!"

The group applauded and, without much ceremony, dropped their divining rods in the bucket the tour guide held for them, then left the hotel to go to their cars or wherever they were headed. Someone snagged the tour guide for a question, and Finn heard them talking about a ghost-themed birthday party, but he wasn't up for waiting around to ask the tour guide about the three ghosts. She probably thought he was competition anyway. Besides, he needed to set up his equipment, take a shower, and settle into a quiet state where he might hear Daisy talking to him.

Ghosts tours were fun and all but they were loud, often upbeat affairs, and who could listen to a ghost amidst all of that? Not him, that's for sure, so, with a nod to the night clerk, he headed up the stairs, taking them two at a time all the way up to his room on the top floor. The carpet muffled his tread, but there was real wood beneath the carpet, though in his own room, the wood was bare, a special treat in a hotel, he knew.

Taking off his coat, he put his old-fashioned hotel key on top of the dresser and looked once more at his gear. He set the alarm for three a.m. which was when he intended to go down and stand in Daisy's room to feel what he could feel.

He busied himself setting up the digital camera, took a few energy readings, and made sure the EMF recorder was on and the batteries were in place. Then he took a hot shower and enjoyed a pre-ghost hunt pleasure, his hand on his cock with the warm water spilling over him, the faint smell of the summer evening air, the tang of the river as it quickly evaporated with an application of soap and a good lather with the washcloth.

By the time he got out of the shower, dried off, and dressed in comfortable sweatpants and a t-shirt, he was ready to settle in for a good night of hunting. This would be a fun job, if he could get it, and then it would be his whole focus, his whole life. Now, if he had someone to share it with, that would be very well and good, but he had to start, he had to work towards something, otherwise he'd be getting nowhere fast. The farm felt like it was nowhere and the Ghost Force felt like it was somewhere. In the back of his mind, though, he sometimes wondered if Dad wouldn't turn out to be right in the end.

CHAPTER THREE

S hrugging on his jacket, Artie looked at the stack of papers in his handcart. He had all the major papers from that morning's train: *The Denver Post*, the *Rocky Mountain News*, and the *Daily Camera*. He also had most of the local papers, even if they didn't sell terribly well all the time, because people liked hearing about themselves and their own communities as much as they liked reading about the doings and goings on in the big city, where fantastical things happened to faraway people.

The *Erie Echo* and *Brighton Banner* were two local favorites, as was the *Harlin Advocate*, which had the biggest circulation out of all the smaller, local papers. He had a few copies of the *Trinidad Times*, which had a reputation for describing the most scandalous events in a way that invited speculation that they could one day be turned into a moving picture show.

All in all, the stack was quite heavy as he hauled the old-fashioned two-wheeled cart his boss, Joe Moody, had bought off a Mormon. Joe should get a Model T or some such to haul papers, or *papes*, as they were called, up the hill from the train depot to the corner of Third and Main, where the young newsies waited every day to get their papes so they could start selling.

At least it wasn't winter, at least it was already getting light out and the chill of the evening was vanishing beneath the warmth of the rising sun. But the blocks were long and, as he trudged past the noisy packing plant and the squat, almost elegant power plant, the route truly was uphill all the way. By the time Artie got to the top of the hill, he was sweating and starving, his stomach growling and his throat dry.

"Hello, Artie," called one of the newsboys as Artie arrived at the intersection and stood with his hands on the handles of the cart.

"Hello, Stanley," said Artie as he smiled down at the boy. Stanley was one of his newest recruits, old enough but not too old at fourteen years of age. Plus, with his whiskey-brown eyes, the sweet sprinkle of freckles across both cheeks, and that wide, engaging smile, he was a favorite among the bankers and farmers and ladies and their maids and pretty much anyone who had business in downtown Harlin in the mornings. "How many will you have today?"

"I'll have twenty of everything, and extra of the *Trinidad Times*, if you got 'em."

Stanley was smart, but not greedy. He knew that, sure, most folks wanted the bigger papers, as they had more value for money. But he also knew that if he ran out of those, the smaller papers would then sell. This was in direct contrast to Artie's other paperboy, Bobby Foss, who only wanted to sell the *Denver Post* and the *Rocky Mountain News*, all the other papers being beneath his dignity to deal with.

Stanley had only been on the corner selling papes for about a week now, but already he was doing better business than Bobby. But then, Stanley had a charming way of selling. He'd hold up the pape and shout so earnestly about the most recent headlines that folks couldn't help themselves and wound up stopping.

Bobby, on the other hand, shouted in a hard voice and almost seemed to be demanding that people buy from him, rather than Stanley. The two sold while standing across the street from each other on either side of Main Street and, all in all, in spite of the rivalry between them, business was good.

"Here you go, kid," said Artie. He counted out the papers and handed them in a neat stack to Stanley. "That's going to be ninety-three cents, rounded up. I'll write it in the book. Good luck!"

"Thank you, Artie," said Stanley. He crossed the street to the west side to stand in front of the Harlin Hotel, which, while it wasn't the bank, was pleasant in the early morning sunlight and had a nice stream of pedestrian traffic.

"Why does he get to go first?" demanded Bobby. "I was your first newsie, right? Huh?"

"Because he's more polite than you, Bobby," said Artie. He counted out thirty of each of the big papes, and handed them to Bobby. "There you go, your usual. Ninety cents. I'll write it in the book and good luck."

It was a little hard not to favor Stanley over Bobby, though Artie should be proud to have two newsies to manage and look after. Harlin wasn't as big as all that, after all, with less than ten thousand residents. Many were shop owners and farmers and grocery store clerks; some of them were even considered in the elite rank, with such lofty professions as bankers and doctors.

Downtown Harlin was showing signs of growing, though, and the population seemed prosperous and full of energy. It was a good place to live after the seemingly darker streets of Denver.

Sure, Denver had a lot going for it; there were more people who wanted to buy newspapers, there was the trolley system to get around town, and some of the buildings were over three stories high. The problem with Denver, of course, hadn't been with the city itself, but with Artie.

In his loneliness, he'd made the mistake—the very *bad* mistake—of being honest with one of his fellow newsies at the lodging house. After which, Cecil had tramped Artie's name all over the lodging house, the newspaper offices, the local diner, everywhere that Artie called home.

The disowning had followed—the cold shoulders, the chuffs upside the head—all of which seemed to spiral his life down into one big bruise. The worst had been when Artie found himself cornered in a dead-end alley by three thugs from the newspaper. He'd been quickly subjected to a beating that had started off hard and was just about to move to brass knuckles when the cops showed up.

They weren't there to save Artie, but to put a stop to the noise, as Artie had picked up an old length of wood and had used it as a baseball bat against the trash cans lined against the brick. The noise had shot straight up the brick walls, clanging like the brass of heaven's trumpets, and his shame had followed him as he'd ducked the arms of the cops and ran back to the lodging house as fast as he could.

Cecil and some others had seemed surprised to see him coming through the door of the common lodging room, where they all slept in wooden bunks. All the lodgers, newsies and grocery boys alike, had moved to the side as Artie came into the room that they all shared, perfectly silent as he went into the communal bathroom and washed up at the long metal sink.

Nobody offered to get him a chunk of ice for a penny to put against the side of his face. Nobody asked him what had happened, which must have been because they already knew. He had to sleep half sitting up in the dark with the streetlight shining through the curtainless window near his upper bunk, waiting for the blood to drain from his nose down the back of his throat, his face throbbing, his ribs feeling twisted and cracked.

When Artie had arrived at the lodging house, straight off the train from Chicago, looking for work, Cecil had seemed nice, at least at first. Cecil had shared his best tips for selling lots of papes and given him directions—to good corners that were sure selling spots, to the best diners, to the cheapest coffee in the morning—like he was the king of the streets. He was very businesslike and organized, and had seemed eager to take Artie under his wing.

Cecil's companionship had eased the ache of loneliness in Artie's heart, and soothed the edges that had been torn when he'd uprooted himself and fled the Chicago streets where each act of trust, each honesty he'd shared, had only brought him more trouble. Telling Cecil about how it might be swell to get each other off, as fellows in Chicago sometimes did, had been a big mistake. Cecil had drawn back, shocked. Even though Artie had done his best to backpedal and pawn it off as a joke, in the end the knife had gone deep and it had all gone bad.

It wasn't a week after the beating by the three thugs that Artie had hopped aboard the *Shoshone Zephyr* and made his way to Harlin. In a new town, a new place, he'd have a chance to keep his big mouth shut. Keep his heart closed off and never, ever, tell anyone the truth again.

So far so good. He'd found a cheap room on the third floor of the Clarkson Boarding House, which he had all to himself, and only had to share the single bathroom with other boarders. He'd gotten a job working for Joe Moody, the newspaper and mail distribution agent at the depot, handing out papers to newsies and selling the rest from the handcart.

Joe Moody didn't give two figs to know anything about Artie except that he showed up on time, was scrupulously honest about the day's takings, and kept his nose clean. So Artie slept in a decent boarding house just off Third Street. Didn't drink much. Never got arrested.

At least not yet. There was always a chance, of course, that someone would suss out his true nature and turn him over, even though there was no reward money. Artie meant to keep his mouth shut, to keep his distance from anyone who drew his eye or teased his heart that there might be a chance to get to know them. But with Harlin being the third city he'd tried, he knew that there was something about the way he was, some fey essence about him that signaled he was not like other fellows.

No, it wasn't that he wasn't courting a lady on each arm, as everywhere west of the Mississippi tended to have its share of bachelors. He didn't talk big, nor brag, nor spout off facts like some spectacle-wearing whiz kid, none of that. He was a regular guy, and he acted like a regular guy.

Well, except for the fact that when he looked in the mirror, he saw what everyone else must be seeing: a sweet-faced young man with cornsilk blonde hair, a dimple in his cheek when he smiled, and the sugar-pink lips of a girl on her first communion.

That he was on the thin side didn't help with any of this either, and most folks figured him to be a pushover. That and the fact that he had eyes only for the males of the species—and the fact that he liked nothing better than to suck cock and to get his cock sucked—all of this added together to make him into what seemed like a mistake of nature. He was a freak of sorts, one who didn't love who he was supposed to love.

He'd left Chicago the year before because the streets were choked with filth and he'd seen a poster about how clean it was out west. He'd left Denver three months ago because the streets were thick with people who hated him, and Harlin had seemed a very easy-going, small town option. So far, so good.

Taking the papers left in the hand cart up Main Street, he slowly sold as he went, a penny a pape. Doing it this way outsold the newsies standing on the corner, as he had a route of regulars, like he was a kind of delivery boy.

Shopkeepers came out to get a stack of papers to sell in their stores. The shoeshine boy bought some of yesterday's papers at a quarter the price to place beneath newly shined shoes that had been left with him, both to protect the shoes and to show off what he could do. It was the same at the butcher, though he bought both: today's papers to sell in his shop and yesterday's papers to wrap around chunks of beef, since it was cheaper than buying brown paper fresh off the roll.

All in all, Artie sold out in about an hour or so, then trundled the cart back to Third and Main to help the newsies sell off the last of their papers. Well, mostly he stood on Stanley's corner, shouted *Extra, Extra*, and blasted off whatever headline was above the fold. Then he went to Bobby's corner and did a bit of the same.

In the end, all the papers were sold well before noon, and as he gathered the appropriate amounts from each boy for their sales that day, half of what they'd taken in. Then he handed them each a nickel as a tip. This nickel came out of his own pocket, but Joe usually paid him back half of that, so he wasn't out a whole ten cents. That way, as Joe surely knew, the newsies would come back the next day and be energized to sell even more papes. That was what kept business good.

"See you fellas tomorrow," said Artie. "You did good today."

"I can't come," said Bobby, his voice barely rising above a whine. "Ma says I gotta watch my baby sister while she and Dad go to the Chautauqua in Boulder for a big do."

"All day?" asked Artie, though what he really wanted to do was to fire Bobby and ask Stanley if he had any friends like him that he could round up to sell papers.

"Naw, it ain't all day," said Bobby. "I don't think she likes me selling newspapers on the corner, but I reckon if I show her this nickel she won't be so sore about it."

"So, the next day, then," said Artie, trying to pin Bobby down to a commitment. "The day after tomorrow."

"Maybe," said Bobby. "I'll ask."

Bobby had actually been selling papes for about a year. Every so often his Ma would get herself into a bit of a fit about it and make it so Bobby couldn't. That would last a few days, and then Bobby'd be so much trouble at home, evidently, that she'd let him sell again, just to get him out of the house.

"Looks like it's you and me tomorrow, Stanley," said Artie. "We'll sell plenty, you'll see."

"His real name's Wilifred," said Bobby as he shoved his money into his pocket.

"I'm Stanley now," said Stanley, sticking out his chin, his dark eyes fierce and bright. "Stanley is what my friends call me after the boxer, Stanley Ketchel. He won that fight with Jack Johnson in 1909, you know."

"You can be anything you want to be," said Artie. He placed his hand on Stanley's shoulder, feeling glad he would have a break from Bobby for at least one day, maybe even a few. "Never you mind him. And Bobby, let me know when you can sell papes again, okay?"

"Sure thing," said Bobby, but the polite tip of his cap was surly and he loped off without a backwards glance.

"You need any help with that cart, Artie?" asked Stanley in that way he had, sort of sweet and just glad to be of use. Had Stanley been five years older, Artie might have feelings for him, but Stanley, while cute, was too young, and too green, and he probably liked the ladies anyhow.

"No thanks, Stanley," said Artie. He hefted the handles of the cart, and shrugged his shoulders to balance the empty cart. "But you're good to ask. See you tomorrow at seven, sharp, right?"

"Yes, sir," said Stanley. "And thank you for the nickel!"

With that Stanley headed up Main Street to wherever it was he lived. Artie didn't rightfully know more about Stanley than what he'd seen: that Stanley was a good kid, a hard worker, and he always seemed to be in a good mood, chipper and upbeat. Which was a far cry from Bobby, whose mother lived in a large house on Emery Street and seemed to like to lord it over people.

Artie trundled the cart down Main Street, over the bumps where the flagstone sidewalk ended, and just across the tracks to the distribution shack where Joe Moody's business was. There, he upended the cart to let the wooden wheels dry, and swept the floor of fragments of paper and dirt.

When Joe came in, he handed over the money from that day, the bank's receipt from the day before, and the little scrap of paper where he wrote down the figures from the morning: how many sold, profit turned, papers ripped and sold at a discount.

"Looks like a good day," said Joe, in his laconic way, the words clipped and to the point. "Here's your two dollars from the papes, and fifty cents for hauling and cleaning."

"Thank you, Joe," said Artie. Then he waited for the favor Joe would ask, as he usually did because while Joe hated banks, he knew that the money was better off being stored in one. "Anything else?"

"Here's the cash," said Joe, handing Artie a small canvas bag full of coins. "Bring me the receipt tomorrow, eh?"

"Sure thing, Joe."

Artie hefted the canvas bag in his hand, tipped his cap at Joe, and headed back up the hill.

Oddly, nobody ever bothered him on this kind of errand, even though he was carrying at least twenty dollars in that canvas sack. There was word on the street that Joe kept a shotgun in his desk and if you messed with him, his boys, or his profit, he would bang a hole in you quicker than anything. Artie was under a cape of protection as he walked past the power plant and the packing plant, both of which seemed to tower over him.

When he'd first arrived in town, he'd gone to both looking for work, but the power plant needed educated men and the packing plant wanted muscle, neither of which he had. Luckily, most after- noons he managed to earn fifty cents an hour working in the page setting room at the Harlin Advocate, or helping clean up or some such. By the time he finished, he was usually starving and looking forward to the simple boarding house meal with a great deal of antic- ipation.

Today, he couldn't wait for it that long so he took Joe Moody's money to the bank, got the receipt, and headed to Ziegfeld's Diner for a cup of coffee and a pastrami on rye. He could afford it, at least now, while the money rolled in.

He did the math in his head. With the distribution job and the newspaper work, he brought in around twenty-seven dollars and fifty cents a week. The boarding house was ten dollars, since he got a discount for renting weekly, and had his own room, to boot. That left him with seventeen dollars and fifty cents to put beneath the floor- boards each week, at two dollars and fifty cents a day. Except for today, as lunch was going to cost him that fifty cents, but it would be worth it, and his stomach wouldn't be hollering at him all afternoon. Besides, Ziegfeld's did a great pastrami sandwich.

The best week he'd ever had since arriving in Harlin had been the day the *Titanic* had gone down. He and Bobby had sold out all of the papers within the hour, and the *Harlin Advocate* had rolled in the money printing newspapers all day. They'd sold each paper at double the going rate at two cents each, but nobody cared. Everybody had wanted to read about the famous ship that couldn't be sunk and the *Harlin Advocate* had the only print shop for miles that could keep up with the demand.

Artie had taken home ten dollars in coins that day. As he'd put the money beneath the loose floorboard in his room, not knowing what else to do with so much money all at once, he'd gotten the idea that making more money was better than making less. The way to make money was to be the guy who distributed the papers from the train deliveries, not the guy who dealt with the newsies.

In short, Artie wanted to be like Joe Moody, who answered to nobody, had a shotgun in his desk, and called the shots. He wanted to buy Joe's distribution business, to take over for him and make money for himself. He'd hire only the best newsboys, and contract with the newspapers, big and small, for a better rate than Joe, if that was even possible.

Thus he was saving for that day. Thus he didn't get a slice of rhubarb pie to fill the corners of his stomach and to finish the last slug of coffee with, no matter how much he wanted it. Besides, Hannah Clarkson, the blousy and frazzled owner of the Clarkson Boarding House, did a pretty good supper.

CHAPTER FOUR

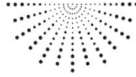

The noise in the print shop had risen to the point where it started stabbing at Artie's ears. He wasn't a delicate flower normally, but sometimes the ruckus and the pounding of the presses made him feel like he was back in Chicago, choking on smoke.

The tension in the room reminded him of living in the lodging house in Denver, skulking around so nobody would notice him and decide he needed to be taught a lesson about loving other men. Never again would he tell his secret to another living soul. Never again. He'd go to his grave unloved and unwept before he ever opened his heart, or admitted that sometimes he liked to be on his knees while he unbuttoned a gentleman's trousers for the purpose of pleasuring another man with his mouth.

"I'm going to head out, Norm," said Artie, pretending very hard that he didn't have a difficult headache.

"Did you get the case boxes all cleaned out?" Norm Ector owned the *Harlin Advocate* and, being a very busy man, barely raised his head from the chart he and the floor supervisor were bent over, perusing the final list of articles for the next day's paper.

"Yes," said Artie.

He waited patiently while Norm chewed his lower lip and wondered, yet again, if he was attracted to Norm's brains or his tall stature. Not that he'd have approached Norm because Norm needed about fifty more pounds on his skinny frame for Artie to be interested. Not that he'd be going up to his boss for sex. Not that he'd be approaching anyone in Harlin for anything remotely resembling sex.

Besides, Norm did not have the kind of mouth that invited frenching, so he was so far off base it was hard to understand why Artie was staring. He could stare forever, but wanting a thing didn't make it so. He'd just have to ignore the urgings of his own body to find someone and do something about the way he wanted to hold Norm's hand and ask him if he'd like to step into a back alley, just this once.

"Here's your pay." Norm reached into his pocket and plonked two quarters on the edge of the table, carefully not looking as Artie came up and swooped the money into his pocket.

Artie'd already spent money that day, but business was good so if he wanted a beer after supper, he could have one. As for now, he was going to take a walk down by the river and watch the spring snowmelt make interesting patterns in the twilight of evening.

"Thanks," said Artie. "See you tomorrow?" That was his casual way of asking if there was work.

"You might check," said Norm. "Nothing's for certain."

Since that was pretty much what Norm said almost every day, this didn't worry Artie. He nodded and headed out, his hands in his pockets, his cap on the back of his head as he strolled down Main Street to the river. Taking a walk in the early evening was a damn sight better than sitting in his room at Clarkson's Boarding House.

Sure, in the winter, when he'd first arrived, he'd been too sore and emotionally bruised to do much more than sit on his bed, leaning against the wall with the blankets around his shoulders, waiting for the dinner bell. But that had gotten boring fast, especially since at the time he couldn't be bothered to make friends with any of the other residents of the boarding house. He still couldn't, and now he didn't have anyone to talk to. Hence the walk to the river so he could watch the sun set.

40

In Chicago, the sun went down behind the buildings and that was it. In Colorado, when the sun set, it shifted below the edges of the mountains, casting long jagged shadows as though someone had taken a knife to them. Here, a little bit of poetry happened in the sky, where angled ribbons of sky-blue pink and orange shifted into dusky purples as the clouds were backlit with an unseen light. It was often beautiful in a way he'd not expected when he'd first moved west, but now anticipated as though it was his own moving picture show.

The flagstone sidewalk ended at the railroad tracks, so he picked his way across the iron rails and headed down the slope, past the tall packing plant and the squat, brick power plant. As he walked, he listened idly to the clangs of machinery, smelled the dust of carbon and smoke, and wished that the river was further away from the plant. Of course, both industries needed to be near the railroad tracks, for parts and shipping, but the plant was noisy and its smell tainted the air.

Down by the river, he loosened his shoulders as the sounds drifted away behind him. The narrow wooden bridge across the water seemed too spindly to cross the wide expanse of the river, so he ducked down along the bluffs.

Moving along the grassy bank, he went all the way to the river's edge, where the normally calm green and brown river wended its way to the east. As his boots tipped into the mud, the water rushed like an angry thing—all sharp edges and movement, bouncing and slashing in the air with the weight of the spring runoff.

Back home, rivers were wide and important, almost majestic, even. But here, out west, the rivers made their own statements, sang their own songs, and blasted their way to anywhere they wanted to go. Or at least it seemed that way to Artie.

Rivers never had to worry about who they loved or what they wanted in return for that love. Rivers kept their own secrets, told their own tales. Were their own masters. Which Artie was, too, in a way.

He had determined to come out west, and so he had. He had determined not to trust another human being, and so here he stood: on the banks of a bratty, self-important, self-directing river, watching the sun go down, watching the farmlands shade with purple as the sun sank lower behind the clouds and the mountains.

When the sun went down, the air got chilly fast, so although he'd gone without his jacket all day, he now wished he'd brought it. It was back at the boarding house with his meager collection of things: spare shoelaces, extra socks, a book or two, and the brass compass he'd owned forever and now truly forgot the origin of. Underwear for winter. A straight razor and shaving kit. Spare shirt. That was it. He was dirt poor and there was no arguing about that, although his life was looking up at present.

Without any streetlights, in the gloomy dusk the river soon turned into a dark ribbon of black and blue and grey. The water splashed beneath the pylons of the wooden bridge, slapping against the rocks and the mud between the tall spring grasses. He needed to turn back or he'd miss dinner, and have to spend more of his own coin to eat, and he would because he was again starving.

Cecil had often asked how he managed to put away so much food at a single sitting without having a little belly to show for it. Artie had shrugged and grinned, thinking that maybe Cecil, who patted Artie's stomach while he was saying it, was flirting. Turned out he wasn't. Turned out Artie had been desperate for company and, apparently, none too picky about it. Which, yes, had been his mistake. He wasn't going to make it again, so why was he still thinking about it?

Shrugging off his worries, Artie turned to go up the gravel path along Main Street, going once again past the packing plant and the power plant. The packing plant was lively most hours of the day. As it was, the twelve-hour shift horn rang and the yard flooded with men, grimy from their work and headed home, dinner pails in hand.

He was doing his best to hurry along and stay out of the way, focused on getting to the boarding house, when he ran into Horace and Ricky, who also lived at the boarding house. They shared a room just down the hall from Artie's room, and walked hard in their boots on the floorboards, and hogged the bathroom at the end of the hall. While they didn't dare make trouble for Hannah Clarkson, they tended to be the first ones to take their share, and then some, from the platters of food as they went around the table.

They also acted like Artie was some kind of pet to them, but their play was hard. It had only taken Artie around half a minute to know they were no friends to him, but they kept at it. Rough punches to the arm, sly shoulder bumps, their raw, beer-soaked breaths in his face on a Saturday night, the taunting growing and then fading. All of this made him feel as though he was on some kind of weird fairground ride: *Let us abuse you for a penny, only a penny a turn! Step right up!*

He avoided them as much as he could, always careful when he did encounter them, to make sure they didn't know he didn't like them. It was preferable that they had no idea how he felt about them so he could stay beneath their notice as much as possible. Otherwise, it would come to a fight. While he had a good chance at holding his own, at least one-on-one, a fight would draw attention from the local cops, which was exactly the last thing he wanted.

When he heard the low cat whistle, it was obvious that the pair had spotted him.

"There's our little bit of fruit," said Horace, singing it out loud and clear for all to hear.

"Our little fruit," said Ricky, being, as always, Horace's echo.

Artie rolled his shoulders back, slapped on a smile, and didn't cringe as they came up to him. Horace slung a heavy, sweaty, begrimed arm around Artie's neck and gave him a rough hug, his greasy hair hanging over one eye.

"How's the papes today, boy-o?" asked Horace, grinning. He slung his tin lunch pail high in the air, just missing Artie's face. Artie didn't duck.

"Sold lots," said Artie.

"What were you doing down here?" asked Horace as they walked along, the crowd of men growing and thinning like a live snake going up the flagstone sidewalk. "Still trying to get a job at the plant? You'll need to put on weight to do that, you slip of a thing, you."

"Naw," said Artie, pretending like the teasing was all in good fun, which, at this point it was.

The funny thing about it, the *queer* thing about it, was that the way Horace and Ricky went on. You could easily think that they half meant the odd compliments they flung his way, as though they were homosexuals, too, only they didn't know it. That, being completely confused about their attraction to Artie, they'd buried it deep. Which was why it came up like a festering splinter through the skin.

Of course, these were his own highly-charged thoughts about the subject and not even close to the truth, for if either Horace or Ricky discovered they liked men, they would both tie heavy stones to their necks and throw themselves in the St. Vrain Creek at springtime. Or maybe that was just a dream in Artie's own head, since everything in Harlin was nearly perfect except for the ever-near presence for Horace Crane and Ricky Beasley.

"Hope that old bitch doesn't serve that lamb stew again," said Horace tossing his lunch pail in the air and catching it. The edge of the metal whistled in the air.

Artie stopped himself from jerking his head back but he didn't say anything to defend Mrs. Clarkson's cooking. Her food, while not fancy, was decent and filling. There was always butter and honey on the table, and something sweet for dessert, even if it was only stewed prunes with cream.

His one meal of the day came with the lodging fees he paid her, so he always made the most of it, eating all he could. Then he'd stumble to his room, wash up, and go to bed early so he could get up with the sun and do it all again the next day. It was a good life, all in all. Now, if only they'd leave him alone.

"I'll give you my dessert if you'll sing a little ditty for me," said Horace.

"He's a canary," laughed Ricky, though it all made no sense that he did.

"Don't know any songs," said Artie, though he did know a few, since the boarding house was just across the street from a saloon. The saloon had a player piano, and the rousting rhythms of ragtime came and went on the evening's breezes. He just wasn't about to tell them that.

"You should learn some," said Horace. "I'll make you sing for me one day, you can bet on that."

"No bet," said Artie, forcing a smile, even though the tone in Horace's voice and the look in his eye promised that the threat would come true if Horace wanted it to.

Artie could already picture himself backed into a dead-end alley singing his heart out like a newly-baptized choir boy in the hope that Horace wouldn't bury his head in the nearest rain barrel till he pissed himself with fear of drowning and begged Horace to let him up. It would come down to that or fighting Horace till the cops came and arrested them both, which would almost be worse.

They went up Main Street and turned on Third to go up the alley behind the boarding house. This way, they could go in through the kitchen and get a hasty wash before they sat down at the table with the other boarders. Mrs. Clarkson was mighty strict about cleanliness, and didn't hesitate to throw someone out and refund their money if she discovered they'd brought lice into her place.

The kitchen was awash with cabbage steam, the smell of boiled potatoes, and yes, thrice-reheated lamb stew, which, thankfully, was almost gone. Tomorrow, Mrs. Clarkson would sear some meat she'd gotten on sale from the butcher and make a different stew that would last about three days.

On the counter, Artie saw the newly baked cherry pies. Of course, the cherries were preserved ones left over from winter, but it was better than stewed prunes. Maybe Artie would pretend not to want all of his pie and he'd push it over to Horace like a gentle bribe. Horace was rather a pushover for bribes. If Artie was still hungry, he'd sacrifice a dime and head to the automat and get his own pie and eat it in peace.

"Oh, look," said Horace as they trundled into the dining room and found their places at the long table. "Did you see? She's got cherry pie."

"You can have mine," said Artie, sacrificing his dessert all in one go. "I'd rather have rhubarb."

"That you saying rhubarb, Artie?" called Mrs. Clarkson from the end of the long wooden table where she and the hired girl were placing platters and bowls. "Turns out I have it for them who don't care for cherry."

"Thank you, Mrs. Clarkson," said Artie as he put his cloth napkin in his lap.

Internally, he shook his head. Horace didn't mind Mrs. Clarkson playing favorites, as long as that favorite was him and, sometimes, if it was Ricky. Artie figured he'd eat his dinner and the dessert as soon as he could, faster than Horace, at any rate, and then make himself scarce.

There'd be nothing to do in his room so it would be boring. There was no movie palace in town, and he'd never signed up for a library card. Maybe he'd make do with the pleasures of his own right hand, or maybe he'd hold his compass and turn it this way and that, dreaming of all the places he'd never visit. Or maybe he'd just have a quick shave with whatever hot water was available and go to bed.

Shaving at night had the benefit of not needing to do it in the morning, when Horace and Ricky were surely up and at it, hogging the sinks and the black coffee that Mrs. Clarkson set out for boarders. He could move to another boarding house, but he liked this one just fine, and usually he was smarter about staying out of Horace and Ricky's way.

Tomorrow, he'd do better, and if he went down to the river, he'd make sure to head back up the hill before the end-of-shift horn rang at the packing plant. There was always something to watch out for, but as far as that went, Harlin was a fairly easy place to watch out for them. He hardly had to stay on the alert as much as he had in Denver or Chicago, so he was content where he was. Content to stay, even if it was lonely sometimes.

CHAPTER FIVE

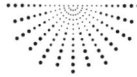

The batteries had died in the EMF meter, but Finn had spares, so that was lucky. Everything else was in working order. He set up the video camera in his room with the motion sensor on, set up the thermometer, and laid out the velvet cloth with salt on it. Above that, he set up the brass pendulum so that if a ghost moved the pendulum, it would trace a path in the salt. It was old school for sure, but he'd heard the Ghost Force team talking about such tried and true tools and decided to use it.

In the morning, he would photograph the cloth and salt to see if there were any paths. He wasn't sure there'd be any useful readings, at least not for his audition package, but it was worth a try.

He could taste the garlic on his breath from the wonderful meal he'd had earlier that evening at a local Italian eatery down the street, and thought about taking a shower and brushing his teeth before he went down to Daisy's room to take some photographs. Nobody would care at this hour and hotels had all the hot water in the world at their disposal, so he hopped in the shower, brushed his teeth, and came out feeling like a new man, ready to take on any number of ghosts.

Getting dressed in a grey t-shirt and jeans and sneakers, he checked the power cords on the video camera, clicked the EMF meter on and off to test the batteries, and walked around the room with the infrared thermometer to see what the base temperature was before he started stirring up energies in the spirit world.

Checking the time on his phone, he saw that it was just after midnight, which was the perfect time to begin. He recorded the temperature and time in his ghost notebook, which was just a cheap pocket one from Target, and checked over his recording equipment one more time.

Everything was working smoothly, though he didn't imagine he'd get much, not with him in the room and the lights on. Besides, he wasn't feeling anything ghostly, nothing was stirring the hairs on the back of his neck, nothing was drawing his attention. Maybe the energy of Daisy, from the room below, was at peace for the moment, for certainly nothing was coming up through the floorboards. It was time, then, to go down to her room.

He picked up the old-fashioned room key, slung his camera strap over his shoulders, and double checked that the flash was on and he'd adjusted the camera for low-light conditions. Then he headed down the back stairs, tiptoeing on the bare wooden steps as quietly as he could, and headed to Daisy's room.

Letting himself in silently, he waited for his eyes to adjust to the half-darkness. There was some light coming in through the gap in the curtains and, of course, the night light in the bathroom, but it wasn't enough to make much of a difference, and it was perfect for the camera.

"Hello, Daisy," he said to the air as he lifted the camera and turned it on. The camera was a comfortable weight in his hands, the plastic and metal cool to the touch, giving him the sensation that he had the right tool for the right job. "I've come to take your picture, if that's okay with you."

There was a low shift of energy near the dresser, where he'd felt Daisy before, on his last visit to the room with the tour group. This time, the energy was lower, and whether that was because it was after midnight, or Daisy was just that exhausted and sad, he didn't know.

Figuring it was better to be sympathetic, especially with a ghost like Daisy, who had died a sad death rather than a violent one, he made his way, walking quite gently and slowly, over to the dresser.

"The flash can't hurt you," he said. "I'd like to tell your story, if I could."

While he waited, he took a few pictures, aiming the camera lens at the dresser and the wall near the dresser. He also took some pictures of the area near the door, as doorways tended to also be places of transition—especially if someone had left the room in a hurry to commit suicide. Then he considered the idea of collecting the stories of ghosts he'd encountered, and wondered whether publishing a book would help with his application to the Ghost Force team.

"Do you miss your fiancé, Gerald?" asked Finn, though he knew the answer would have to be yes. Every single person who'd written about their experiences with Daisy when staying in her room talked about feeling Daisy's grief over the loss of her fiancé. He took a few more photographs while the energy swam about the room in the way of a lost thing.

He pulled out the EVP recorder from his pocket and clicked it on.

"Daisy, sweet Daisy McKee," he said to the air. "Do you miss Gerald?" It was often easier to ask yes or no questions, as overly complicated or open-ended questions sometimes seemed to confuse the spirit world, and Daisy had it hard enough. "It's okay if you do. I miss my Nana, though I didn't lose her on the Titanic. She went dancing New Year's Eve—"

The voice-activated EVP recorder vibrated when he spoke, but when he stopped talking the recorder kept going, like it was hearing something only it could hear. There was a sharp click when the recorder went off, then it oddly turned on again and hissed as it picked up silent sounds.

Finn shivered as the room grew cold, making him wish he'd brought his pen thermometer with him so he could record how far the dip in temperatures went.

"Everything's okay, Daisy," he said to the air while the room slowly warmed up. He took a few photographs of the entire room, especially of the center, where the room was staying cold. "You can be sad if you want. I'd be sad, too, if I lost a good looking hunk like Gerald."

The truth of the matter was, Finn didn't know whether Gerald was good looking or not. If he could afford to take the *Titanic*, though, and not be in steerage, he was probably dressed pretty dapper, and could afford the best antimacassar oil money could buy.

Maybe Finn ought to do a little research on the backstory between this tragic couple, and write it up for his audition package for the Ghost Force. They'd probably think well of him for being so diligent. He could do that in the morning, after sleeping in and having a good breakfast.

After another half an hour of pictures in the semi-darkness and no more EVP evidence, Finn yawned. It was after two o'clock in the morning, and he wouldn't last much longer unless he started moving around. It'd be a good idea to check the camera in his room, maybe take some readings in the hallway, but all in all the evening had developed into something fairly non-ghostly, so maybe he'd just go to bed.

He packed up his equipment, then he shut and locked the door to Daisy's room, carefully. As quietly as he could, he carried everything up the back stairs to his room. As he put everything on the table, stacking it to keep it out of the way, he thought he heard something in the hallway.

He poked his head out, then stepped out and started down the hallway to the back stairs. By the time he got there, he could hear the same noises he'd thought he'd heard before. Someone was shouting something, over and over in a rhythmic way, as though trying to get someone's attention amidst a huge crowd of people, all of whom were intent on their own pursuits. There were, oddly, car horns that sounded like they came out of an old cartoon, where the Model T's seemed to have personality, as though they were alive.

As he stood at the top of the wooden steps to the second floor landing, something came at him. A dark energy, howling as it rose, made the hairs on the back of his neck stand up. No ghost had ever hurt him, but there was always a first time, right?

Not moving from that spot, he let the blackness rise and surround him. It almost took his breath away and now he knew what everyone had been talking about in their letters about Arturo. Arturo was mad and scared—a whirling energy that didn't quite know what to do with itself. Well, maybe Finn could help.

"Arturo," he said, gently. "How can I help you? Are you lost?"

A sound came at him, a low moan, rising up the stairs and shifting as it came, making the hair on Finn's temples move.

"Arturo," he said. "Do you know what happened to you? Please tell me. How can I help if you won't talk to me?"

The energy shifted once more and stopped right in front of Finn, drawing itself up into a slender figure, sweet-faced for all it was grey and shimmery. Arturo was here with him now, looking just as he had when he'd died in 1912.

"Arturo?" asked Finn. "Did you really throw yourself off the roof of that building?"

Arturo opened his mouth—his eyes were dark holes, and the line of his shoulder was transparent, as though it had been drawn with pure fog. He was looking directly at Finn, as though he was really there at the top of the stairs, and his expression was desperate, searching.

"How did you die, Arturo?" Finn asked again.

Arturo's mouth was moving over words that Finn couldn't quite hear. First, there was a soft sound, like a whispering wind—a low hiss that rushed at him, forming words that turned into a roar.

"Save me. Saaaaaave meeeee."

With an abrupt flicker, all of Arturo shifted in an unseen breeze—then he was gone. Leaving Finn alone, his knees shaking as his heart pounded in his chest. That kind of encounter had never happened before, not so directly, and never with a ghost talking to him like that. But Arturo had. It was as if he knew that Finn was the only person who could help him.

From the darkness of the stairs, he heard more noises, and so he went down, following them. As he went, he felt he was falling more than walking, as if he'd been in an elevator that had dropped out beneath him.

At the bottom of the last flight of wooden stairs, it was odd that he could see daylight coming through beneath the bottom of the door to the alley. It might be streetlights, sure, but the light was too bright and warm for a streetlight someone had plonked in an alley to give a semblance of safety.

He also heard shouting, coming from close by, and scuffled feet and finally—oddly—the thump of a body being shoved against the door. It was really late for that kind of activity to be going on in an alley. Maybe the cops were already on their way, but maybe they weren't and somebody needed help.

He kept looking at the light coming from the bottom of the door. Then he pushed and stepped out into the soft glowing light of an early evening in June. Which was odd, because it was well after midnight.

He barely had enough time to register the daylight and the disparity of time when someone was shoved against him and he had to brace to keep from getting banged into the brick wall. Two grunt-looking guys, greasy haired and sweaty, held their fists up as if they were going to have another go at the poor fellow Finn now held in his arms.

He didn't know what the fight was about, though it looked more like the two guys were ganging up on the other one. They showed evidence of cut lips and bruised faces and looked strong and tough and very pissed off.

"Hey," said Finn, shoving through his own confusion with some force. This might be a dream—or everybody in the alley was a ghost—he didn't know. He was still dizzy from his encounter with Arturo. "That's enough. You two back off or I'll call 9-1-1."

"Nine-what?" asked the taller of the two. "An' who the fuck're you?"

"Get lost," said the other one, a weedy looking guy who stood half a step behind the taller one. "This ain't none of your business."

"I'm making it my business, asshole," said Finn, gently pushing the guy in his arms to the side. He didn't like fighting but he'd never backed away when it needed to be done. "You want to come at me? Then come at me."

The alleyway was wide enough to have dumpsters and loading bays and a car or two parked along it, as Finn remembered from the ghost tour. Only, oddly, none of that was in evidence; there were only a few wooden crates and tin trash cans, the kind he'd not seen in years.

There was the same lingering odor of grease and dirt, and a whiff of something that might have been tucked away, unseen and rotting. All of this flickered through his awareness in the odd evening light as he watched the two bullies shuffle a bit, like they had no idea what to do with this new situation.

"This ain't over, Artie," said the taller of the two to their victim, his face smudged with grease and sweat.

"Ain't over, Artie," said the other one, just as grimy, his voice a creepy echo.

"I know it ain't," said Artie. He wiped his upper lip with the back of his hand, but this just left an inelegant smear from the blood pouring from his nose. "You fellows don't know what you're talking about, anyhow. I'm just like you. I'm just a regular guy."

"That ain't what Cecil said," said the taller one. "I got a brother who works in a restaurant near the lodging where you stayed. Word's getting around, faggot. Word's gettin' around."

"Cecil's a liar," said Artie, his face flushed red as he raised his voice. "You believe someone you never met, Horace? Huh? Or someone you shared meals with, all these months?"

This seemed to throw Horace, the kind of guy Finn recognized as having more muscle than brains. Obviously he'd been looking for excitement of some kind and Cecil, whoever that was, had lit the fuse.

"I don't know, Horace," said Finn, adding his opinion to the mix. "With a name like Cecil, you know he's got to be some kind of wuss." Finn didn't know this for a fact, but sometimes a distraction was as good as a clenched fist. He shrugged, as though Horace was kind of crazy for believing Cecil. "Go with what you know, buddy, huh?"

"Aw, go to hell," said Horace.

"Yeah," said the other one. "Go to hell."

At the end of the alley, a figure appeared, a cop of some sort, wearing a thick, blue uniform, a tall rounded cap. In his hand he carried a billy club, and Finn couldn't see evidence of a gun anywhere.

All at once, the air across Finn's skin felt cold, and the smells of the alley made him sick to his stomach. The two hoodlums, as Finn noticed now, were oddly dressed in suspenders and thick trousers as they clattered across the alley and went into the building across the alley from the hotel. The cop swung his billy club once or twice, as if in warning, and ambled down the street.

Meanwhile, Artie was still trying to clean the blood from his nose, his hands shaking. He was shorter than Finn, and slight all the way through, his collarbones sharp beneath his skin. When he looked up at Finn, his blue eyes swirled in a way that lingered between anger and confusion and Finn recognized him from his portrait in the hotel lobby. It was Arturo; he'd saved him, just like he'd wanted to, just liked Arturo had asked him to. Finn had come back in time to 1912 to stop this man from dying by falling off a roof.

Arturo—*Artie*—was dressed the way Horace and the other guy had been, in a collarless shirt with suspenders, thick trousers, and lace-up boots. His hair was cut in an odd, retro way that Finn had seen on Instagram, short on the sides, and with a long forelock.

All of this felt surreal, for some reason, as though he'd fallen asleep in Daisy's hotel room and was now dreaming that he was standing in the alley behind the hotel in the soft light of a spring evening. But Artie was real, the faint scent of his sweat was real. The alley was real. All of it was just as real as real could be. There was something about it that he couldn't put his finger on, was like he'd stepped into a picture that had suddenly and inexplicably come to life.

"You okay?" Finn asked. "I don't have any tissue on me for that nose, but maybe you should get some ice for that eye. You hurt anywhere else?"

"Naw," said Artie. His whole chest lifted as he sighed and turned to look at the door the two bullies had disappeared through. "I just thought it would be different this time if I kept to myself. No luck."

"Pardon?" asked Finn. "Different how?"

"Never mind." Artie turned back around to face Finn, lifting his chin as if dismissing the fact that there'd been a fight at all. "You're a good guy, I take it, rescuing poor schmucks like me."

"Looked like you had 'em on the ropes, I'd say," said Finn, smiling at the feisty tone of Artie's words, the set of his shoulders. "What's their problem anyway? What were they doing?"

"They wanted me to go up to the roof with them for some reason," said Artie. "I told them I didn't want to go, but they insisted."

"What?" asked Finn, and every hair on his body felt electrified. "They were taking you up to the *roof*?"

"Just bored like a couple of brainless meatheads," said Artie. "When I said no, that's when they brought up—never mind. Thank you for stopping them."

"Glad to help," said Finn, all kinds of mixed feelings rushing around inside of him.

The article about Artie's death had been wrong. It hadn't been death by suicide, where Artie had flung himself off the roof, no. The truth was, two homophobic assholes had decided to bring down their holier-than-thou wrath and rid the world of another gay man. It wasn't right, had never been right, but he'd never encountered that kind of rage before.

He looked up and down the alley, mentally taking notes of the details, like a woman dumping a bucket of water from the window or the laundry hanging from fire escapes. There were tin cans arranged outside of a doorway and a runnel of water floating down the middle of the alley.

He was sure that the alley last night had parking spaces and dumpsters, and definitely no dumping of water or thin, soap-greyed laundry fluttering in the light breeze. Maybe it had been too dark to see all of this, or maybe it had always been like this only he had never slowed down to look.

The last thing he wanted to do was to leave Artie behind, but he could feel the pull of the stairway, as if the announcement had been made that the train home would soon be pulling out of the station. It was an erratic tug by unseen hands, filling him with a strong urge to get going.

"You going to be okay getting home?" asked Finn. He wanted to reach out and give Artie's shoulder a pat in commiseration, but Artie seemed as wound up as a stray cat at the moment and probably would shove Finn's hand away and growl at him—or spit.

"I live here." Artie jerked a thumb over his shoulder to indicate the building that Horace and company had just gone into.

"In there, with them?"

"Mrs. Clarkson'll make sure they don't cause any trouble," said Artie with a shrug.

In that little moment of silence that fell after his words, he looked down the alley to where the setting sun was casting long yellow and blue shadows. His profile was etched in gold, his lips pink, those long eyelashes somehow making him look even more vulnerable than a young man normally was.

"She doesn't like trouble in her boarding house, you know," Artie added. "And if she can't, I'll just move on. Like always."

"Like always?" Finn didn't realize he'd asked the question aloud until he heard his own voice. "I'm sorry, dude. That sounds rough."

"It'll get better," said Artie. He straightened his shoulders and lifted his chin and looked at Finn, square on, as though Finn was the enemy, only he wasn't afraid at all. Wouldn't let himself be. "It always does."

"Well, hang in there," said Finn, oddly despondent at the thought of saying goodbye so quickly. At the same time, Artie had gumption and pluck and a whole host of other strengths that made him a survivor.

"I will," said Artie. "Gotta go. That's the dinner bell."

"Bye," said Finn. He raised his hand to wave an awkward goodbye as Artie ran across the alley and slipped inside. He wanted to follow, but knew that he couldn't.

The light from the end of the alleyway was sinking into darker colors of rose and deep blue as a little wind whipped the paper trash around his feet. There was almost no other sound, just a faraway dog, a tinny beep from a car's horn, a woman shouting at her children. Finn never saw a car go past, and when he looked up, the sky was the cleanest blue he'd ever seen, darkening into nighttime twilight.

He needed to go home right *now*.

He opened the back door to the hotel, and started up the stairs, going two flights at top speed.

Oddly, when he got back to his room, the windows showed only pure darkness tempered only by the street lights blaring into the room. Off on the horizon were sheets of faraway lightning, almost too faint to be seen through the light pollution, too far away to hear the thunder. But he had a feeling it was getting closer, had a feeling he'd be hearing it soon.

He checked over his equipment, a habit that soothed him, enjoying the click sounds from readjusting the camera stand, letting himself be calmed by the silky feel of the plastic beneath his fingers. The only strange thing was the fact that his watch and the timer on the camera seemed to be separated by fifteen minutes. The timer had half an hour to go. His wristwatch, on the other hand, said it was fifteen minutes later than even the clock on the nightstand next to the bed.

Absently, he adjusted the time on his watch, checked the time on his phone to be sure, and shook his head to dismiss the weirdness of it. It was an old watch, after all, with two hands, one for the minutes, one for the hours. It used to belong to Nana's husband, ages ago, and he'd been grateful to get this small token from her when he died. Watches were funny things, and old ones tended to keep their own time.

Dismissing all of this, he got ready for bed and turned off the lights, letting the camera whir down and finish, letting the silky feel of the clean sheets soothe him. In the morning he'd have breakfast, check his readings, do some research, type up his findings. He'd be ready to submit to the Ghost Force by the end of the week, well ahead of their submission deadline. All he had to do was believe that he could make it, that ghost hunting could be a real career for him.

Though, just as he was falling asleep, he remembered his ghost, Artie, who looked slight and sweet with his sugar pink lips, but in whose eyes Finn had seen something else altogether. Something tougher, more resilient than Finn had imagined when he'd looked at Artie's portrait. He was brave to go up against two bullies by himself, and the fact that he didn't protest what they'd called him told Finn all he needed to know about Artie's backbone. Even in 1912, Artie knew who he was, and there wasn't anything Finn admired more than a guy with guts.

A wave of sadness swept over him. He'd probably never see Artie again, never see those eyes, so blue, looking at him as though he was an unexpected but very much welcomed pleasure.

Artie had been so resigned as he went into the boarding house he called home. The only trouble was, the building Artie had gone into was an Elks Lodge, not a boarding house. It was the Brotherhood of the Something Something, Finn couldn't remember.

It was too late at night, or rather, too early in the morning to be trying to think things through like this. He had a few days to make his dream come true and he was going to make the most of it. But as he slept, his dreams, rather than becoming famous on a Youtube channel, were of a young man in suspenders who looked at Finn with his eyes full of blue and grey storms, his whole being flickering like sheet lighting, all full of energy with nowhere to go.

CHAPTER SIX

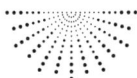

A rtie slunk in through the back door of the boarding house, stopped to wash his hands and face in the kitchen, then slid into the dining room where every single head turned to look at him for being so late. Of course he was late, of course he was. The last thing he wanted was attention and here he was getting it as he sat down and pretended to be calm, so calm, even though he was still shaking from his encounter in the alley.

Horace and Ricky were at the far end of the wooden table, already grabbing the platters and bowls from Mrs. Clarkson, taking what they wanted, as usual, without thinking about anyone else. There was enough to go around, anyway, and Mrs. Clarkson started another bowl and platter at Artie's end of the table so there was plenty of fresh beef stew and scoops of succotash and biscuits for him to take. He ignored Horace and Ricky and, really, everybody at the table. He spoke only when spoken to, or passed the salt or the butter, going on as he always did, trying to get by, as always.

The only thing that made the evening meal any different, besides his throbbing nose and the blood that stained his shirt collar, was the memory of the young man in the alley. He'd stood a head taller than Artie, and had matched Horace in the breadth of his shoulders, with so much muscle and power in that chest—a chest that Artie had, yes, banged right into when he'd been thrown.

That body had force and power held in check, but instead of joining in the fun of beating Artie into a pulp, the stranger had saved him, had stepped in front and taken the force of whatever Horace had been handing out. Without a blink or a pause, the stranger had stood up for Artie.

Horace and Ricky had wanted to take him up to the roof. He'd no idea why, but obviously they'd figured out it was his special place. When he'd refused, they'd started with the name calling and had meant to slam him against the wall of the hotel again—but the young man had caught him, held him still and safe for the briefest of moments, and then let him go.

Artie didn't know whether his arms were tingling from the strength of that grip or the feel of the warmth of the young man's body; it was all the same now, flickering through him like an energy he'd never felt before. And the smell of him, all too brief, had been like a faraway spring that Artie kept racing toward but never fully expected to reach.

Not only that, but the stranger had been so cool, so confident. Horace and Ricky had called Artie a faggot, but the stranger hadn't even blinked an eye at this. Instead, he'd stood his ground, had warned Horace and Ricky off and then stayed around to make sure Artie was all right. His clothes had been quite strange, fitting close all over his body, the cloth a little more refined than Artie was used to seeing in a country town. His dark hair had tumbled around his temples and his eyes had been the most brilliant dark blue, the curve of his mouth wide as he'd smiled at Artie.

Artie's first instinct had been to back off from the draw of that smile, the kindness in those eyes. He knew, well and good, beyond any shadow of a doubt, that he could not trust anyone. Especially not a stranger who, once he found out what kind of man Artie was, would be all a-lather to join forces with Horace and Ricky to make sure that anyone of Artie's ilk would not walk the street unafraid. Instead, much to Artie's surprise, the stranger heard he was a faggot and didn't care.

Before Cecil, Artie had been cautious about his own true nature, careful that he did not show too much or reveal his feelings. But he had. And, after Cecil, he was always afraid—too afraid to enjoy the pleasures of his own body and too afraid to reach out, though he knew there were others like him.

He knew there were men who congregated at special below-street bars along East Colfax in Denver to meet in secret. He'd heard about the special codes that they knew, and had read the secret, cleverly worded personal ads in the *Rocky Mountain News* so they could know each other and meet up.

Artie had never had any money to place one of those ads, never had a clear idea of exactly which bars on East Colfax were the right bars. He'd lived a lifetime, it felt like, knowing there was a world of people he could connect to but not knowing exactly how to go about it.

The struggle, a fearful dance between being alone forever and being arrested when he reached out, was never-ending. And now, now that Horace and Ricky knew, or thought they knew, now that Cecil had set the local dogs on him, he knew he had to figure out what to do.

As he ate his beef stew and biscuits, he pretended to listen to the old guy sitting next to him. The old guy went on and on about how the new automobiles were going the devil's speed and there ought to be a law, and all the while, Artie thought about taking the *Shoshone Zephyr* headed north. He could check out the towns along the way, from Casper to Cody, Wyoming and maybe even beyond, though he had no real desire to live in such windy, barren country.

Wyoming might be pretty enough, but it was sparsely populated and he would stand out even more than he did now. For what young man would spend his days in a boarding house unless he was nearing the end of his life or was a lunkhead with no ambition?

He was neither. Yet, here he was with no idea what to do next, though he imagined he'd stay where he was for a bit and see which way the wind blew. Rumors were just rumors after all. If he could avoid Horace and Ricky, like he usually did, then he'd be fine. They'd get bored and move on to some other distraction and leave Artie to his own business of working hard and saving money.

Which begged the other question, should he take his meager savings to the bank in town and start an account? The money he was stashing every day beneath the loose floorboard was growing all the time, and the paper dollars would be a temptation for mice and such.

The money might be safer in the vault at the bank. It could also mark him as a man of prosperity if he was seen going into such a building, not for Joe Moody, but for himself. He could get to know the tellers, the bank manager, too, which might make him seem a better prospect come the day he needed an extra signature to get a news-paper distribution business of his own. That was, unless he left for Wyoming.

"More biscuits, Artie?" asked Mrs. Clarkson.

She was standing at his elbow, holding the platter of biscuits in front of his face. There were two left, so Artie took one and the old guy he was sitting next to took the other one. There wasn't any butter left, but there was plenty of gravy in his bowl to sop the biscuit in. There was a slice of rhubarb pie after that, to fill any empty corners in his belly.

By the time he was finished, Horace and Ricky had already gotten up from the table and sauntered out, hands in pockets. They were probably on their way to the saloon across the street. There, they would spend their money on drink, leaving their heads even more muddled come the morning when, hopefully, they would have forgotten all about Cecil and his rumors.

"Thank you, Mrs. Clarkson," said Artie as he got up from the table. "That was mighty fine."

"You're welcome, Artie," said Mrs. Clarkson.

Climbing the rickety stairs to his room, Artie contemplated taking a quick bath, even though it wasn't Saturday, just to check the state of his ribs and the low throb along his middle. The beating he'd gotten had been quick, but it could have turned ugly so fast.

It was important to assess the damage. If it was bad enough, he could head out to the drug store for some aspirin powder to keep the aches down. He needed to keep working, to save money so he could get his own business, keeping himself ready for that was of utmost importance.

The hallway on the third floor was empty, so he took his thin towel and washcloth and what was left of his bar of Castile soap, and headed to the communal bathroom. There, he filled the tub halfway with as much warm water as there was to be had, stripped down to the skin, and slipped in.

A fine mist rose from the surface of the water, enveloping him in a small but determined cloud that fogged the small window and left droplets along the rim of the tub. It was nice to soak, nice to close his eyes and press his neck gently against the cool curve of the tub. Nice to just be for a minute. The door was locked, and everybody was busy with their early evening business. Nobody would bother him.

It was also nice to let his mind wander to the young man in the alley—his thick, dark hair, his broad shoulders, the way he'd stood up to Horace and Ricky. He'd paused to look Artie up and down as though he was seeing something nice. He'd also smiled at him, a warm, comforting smile that drew Artie to it as powerfully as a faraway blue sky, where dreams not only lingered but lived.

Artie wasn't used to being looked at that way, as though he was pleasant to the eye rather than being a mistake of a man with not enough muscle and too much of an air of sweetness and softness about him. He ate as much as he could, and worked hard, and though his muscles were steel-hard and corded beneath his skin, his clothes still hung loose on him and he still looked weak.

It'd be nice to meet the young man in a regular way and not during a fight. Where had he come from so quickly? The hotel, maybe, or from around the corner? He'd certainly gone into the hotel when he left. Either way, Artie vowed to keep his eyes out so he could at least ding out the young man's name, shake his hand, and say thank you. As to what might follow after such a meeting, he could hardly dream about.

Tending to business, Artie sat up in the tub and washed himself all over with the soap, taking time to check his ribs and the tenderness of his belly as he lathered with the washcloth and gently scrubbed. Then he washed his hair, after which he slid down in the tub and floated there for a minute, letting the water rinse away the soap.

He'd be fine come morning, but maybe he should get dressed and head out for that aspirin powder. Thus decided, he got out of the tub, dried off, and pulled the drain in the tub, watching the water swirl away for a long minute. Then, quietly, almost shyly, he propped his elbow against the door, buried his head in the crook of his elbow, and took himself in hand.

His cock was still slick from the bath, and the relaxation of the warm water, the stillness around him, the bit of privacy, all of this made it easy to pleasure himself in a hasty, fugitive way—a way that, when he was finished and cleaning himself off with a damp wash-cloth, only served to emphasize his continued loneliness.

If only he knew how to find others like him. If only he had the guts to reach out to those like-minded fellows when he did find them. If only he didn't have to be looking over his shoulder his entire life, every waking minute. If only, if only.

There was no sense in dwelling on what could never be. It was just a waste of energy, so he got dressed, gathered his towel, washcloth, and soap so he could dry them in his room, and headed back up the hall.

Once in his room, he put on his socks and laced up his boots. He put his things away, grabbed a dime from beneath the floorboards, then grabbed another one and headed down the stairs, scurried along the alley, and went around the Harlin Hotel to Main Street.

There, everybody in town seemed to be out and about, enjoying the deepening twilight as it turned into night, and the sweet breeze that came from the north, seeming to carry the scent of lavender. He joined the enjoyment, in a way, allowing himself to partake in the communal sense of pleasure as he hustled to the drug store over on the next block. There he bought himself a bottle of aspirin powder for a full dime, rather than just a packet for a penny. The bottle would last him a lot longer and he had a feeling he'd need it again, and sooner rather than later.

Instead of a beer, he stopped in at the ice cream parlor. They'd had a brisk bit of business on such a nice evening and were all out of ice cream. He got a root beer and sat at the end of the marble-topped bar to enjoy the tang and sweetness of his drink. All the while, he watched the young couples coming and going, dressed in fine clothes. The ladies wore those broad hats they seemed to favor, though some had trimmed hair and those close-fitting hats that must have been measured to their heads to fit so nicely.

The young men were sporting flat straw hats and pencil-thin mustaches, dandies all with their chosen lady on their arms. They were handsome, of course, and normally he would have liked to have met one of them. But after the sturdy handsomeness of the young man in the alley, the dandies seemed slick and over polished.

Overhead, the ceiling fan swirled slowly, and though it was really too cool to need such movement of air, it added to the sense of energy in the little ice cream parlor. Artie was glad he'd chosen root beer instead of real beer, which only would have made him feel sad and muddle-headed when he went back to his room.

After his root beer, he sauntered back to the boarding house. With the weight of the bottle of aspirin powder in his pocket, he looked around and realized it had grown fully dark.

As he passed the Harlin Hotel, he bumped into a young woman dressed city-nice. She was also in a hurry, as though she was late to a fancy dinner party she had been invited to. Her eyes, as they flicked over him, weren't unkind, but she was clearly in a hurry, as though she imagined there was dreadful news waiting inside the hotel for her.

Murmuring his apologies, Artie stepped back to let her go into the hotel, then made his way along the sidewalk and up the dank alley to the back door of the boarding house. It was funny how the boarding house and the hotel were of such different levels of prosperity and yet were so close to each other, separated by only an alley. That's how it was, rich and poor living so close together, yet not connected at all.

Shrugging off these odd, contemplative thoughts and the memory of the young woman, Artie let himself dwell on the dark-haired man who had rescued him. From whence had he come, and where had he gone? Was he staying at the hotel, or did he have a place in town? How could he find out when he had to work all the time?

It would be rude not to thank the young man the next time they met, should fate allow such a pleasant encounter. It had been nice to be looked at in that way, with the expression in those kind blue eyes telling Artie something quite different than any had told him before, from his time in the orphanage to the newsies lodging house in Denver. The expression that said he was pleasant to look upon, that he was worthy of being smiled at. That he was something good and decent. That he was fine, just the way he was.

All of these ideas were too odd to be thinking and it was almost too new to hold onto. So he shrugged them off as he climbed the stairs to his room. He nodded as he saw Mrs. Clarkson go into the front parlor, and sighed as he thought how differently his life might be going if he wasn't the way he was. If he didn't like men. But he did.

When he got to the third floor, he went into the bathroom and quickly mixed a bit of the aspirin powder in the communal glass with water from the tap, then drank it down in one bitter swallow. Rinsing the glass, he took the bottle of power, went into the room, and locked the door behind him.

He stored the bottle in the small dresser, next to his extra socks and his brass compass. Then, shoving the drawer closed, he went to the window to look out as he did his best to put away all the thoughts that were distracting him. The swiftness of oncoming summer. His plans for a distribution business. Horace and Ricky and their intermittent bullying. Mrs. Clarkson's good cooking.

All that left him with was the ribbon of thoughts about the young man in the alley. The sweet way he'd smelled. The gentle strength of his hands. The nature of his confidence in the face of those two meatheads. The laconic smile as he looked at Artie, and how his mouth had opened as though he'd wanted to tell Artie something, like a secret.

Through the dusty windowpane, he could see the dark line of the horizon between the brick buildings in town. Beyond the railroad tracks, above the river, sheet lighting flickered in a diamond-brilliant and energetic but entirely silent dance, like stars streaking back and forth along the night sky, lighting up the clouds behind them.

If they were stars, he could have made a wish on them, a wish for everything to go as planned. He didn't need for his life to be one where he was a rich man, didn't need to own an automobile or live in one of those fancy houses, didn't need to wear a raccoon-skin coat or anything. He just wanted to be happy. Wanted someone to be happy with. Wanted something good, measured in very simple ways. To be safe. To be loved.

Was that too much? He didn't think it was, so he looked out the window, with its somewhat brick-narrowed view, and thought about the star-bright lightning, and wishes, if they could come true, what happiness that would bring.

CHAPTER SEVEN

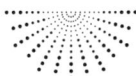

Finn checked the camera again. Next, he checked his watch, now set to the right time, and huffed out a breath. Technology was easy. Well, it *should* have been easy, but what the video on the camera was showing him didn't make sense. With a click of his thumb, he set the video back to the beginning, and watched as he viewed it at high speed.

It showed the corner of the room, his room, above the sad and tragic room where Daisy had once stayed. The first part of the video was brilliant, with white orbs floating all around.

While some people would have dismissed the images as dust motes, dust motes did not go in one direction, stop, and then go in another direction. Dust motes floated gently around without any direction, drifting as the wind would take them. These orbs had purpose, and zoomed about as if they had someplace to be. They marked the air with their traces of energy and though they couldn't be seen with the naked eye, to Finn they were proof that something was going on.

The weird part was what the camera showed as it rotated around, taking in the full circle of the room. It showed him getting up at just after midnight and going out of the room. At the fifteen minute mark, he was back, then got into bed, seemingly content with what he'd found in the night. The only problem was that he'd been out of the room at least half an hour, maybe more.

He'd first gone to Daisy's room, took some readings there, talked to Daisy for a bit, then thought about his life. The usual.

Then he'd met Artie's ghost on the stairs, and upon hearing sounds and thumps, had gone down the backstairs of the hotel and into the alley. There, it had been daylight, an early evening in June. The alley had been different than it had been the night before, seemingly wider and less packed with cars and dumpsters, though it had been just as insalubrious as before.

There, he'd rescued that guy from a sound beating at the hands of two greasy-haired bullies—that beautiful guy full of piss and vinegar who only wanted Finn to go away. And so he had, getting back in his room to discover that his wristwatch had been fifteen minutes off from the clock on the nightstand.

He'd fixed his wristwatch, and set it to the right time, but now the footage on the camera, all timestamped, was reminding him that there was a discrepancy of fifteen minutes or so that he could not account for.

The difference between what his camera had recorded and what his wristwatch had indicated could have been a glitch, a jump in electricity, or maybe the watch was just old and couldn't keep time very well. Not that he'd trade it in; it was from his Nana and had a nice, hefty weight on his wrist. Besides, he was starving, so he turned the camera off, finished getting dressed and headed down to the hotel restaurant, where he ordered pancakes with extra butter. Drank a ton of coffee, and enjoyed the best bacon he'd ever had.

After he ate, he paid the bill and strode into the hotel lobby. There, as though he'd summoned her, he saw little Ruby out of the corner of his eye. Nobody in the lobby paid any attention to her and he felt a little lonely, as he always did, being the only one he knew who could see ghosts. Maybe someone in the Ghost Force could, which might explain their rise to fame. He'd find out—if he got accepted, that is.

Ruby chased after her dog, shouting ghostly encouragement to him to come outside, to be a good boy. He most assuredly was, and some echo of the pup actually came up to Finn and sniffed at his feet, giving a small, ghostly bark before racing after his beloved mistress.

Ghosts of kids always made him feel sad, but in this instance, Ruby had her dog with her and didn't seem lonely or even very forlorn. Still, she was too young to have died, especially in a freak accident as she had.

Finn went over to the little tableau, where the portraits of the three ghost guests hung on the wall and the tidy notebooks, full of details of their lives, sat patiently waiting on the lion-legged table. He looked at the pictures on the wall again, absorbing the creepy stillness of them.

The colorization of the photograph of Daisy McGee still made her look extra dead. The portrait of Ruby made him feel a little sad to think of her and her little dog, Leo, and how both of their lives would have gone to their natural end if she'd only been more careful about chasing her red rubber ball. And then there, at the end, was Artie's portrait, making him feel even worse because he'd not saved Artie from his untimely end.

But, oddly, the picture of Artie looked different than it had the night before. Finn had been unable to make out Artie's features before, as the portrait had resembled a badly-done woodcut more than a reproduction of a newspaper photograph. Now, though, the edges were more clear, as though someone had taken more care with the reproduction, gotten a better photograph, and had more time to set the ink properly.

The odd thing was that in the light of day, with the early morning sun streaming through the sparkling windows, Artie looked like he could step out from the picture and say hello. The hairs on the back of Finn's neck stood up as though he'd been shot through with electricity. With his fingers on the edge of the notebook about Artie, he leaned forward and squinted, trying to make out the curve of the jaw, the sweet set of that mouth.

"Anything I can help you with?" asked a voice from behind him.

Half-jumping out of his skin, Finn whirled around to see the hotel manager, Mrs. Brice, a short, bespectacled, slender woman of middle years, who had an air of experience around her, and no patience for fools. She wore her double breasted thin wool suit like she'd come straight from New York and didn't see any need to change her style just because she was currently working in flyover country.

"Didn't mean to startle you there, young Finn," she said with a now-gentle hand on his arm.

"Hey there," he said with a smile. "I was wondering if I could take these notebooks up to my room and study them."

"Is this for your application to Ghost Force?" she asked, smiling back at him, looking up through her stylish wire-framed glasses.

"Yes, ma'am," he said.

"Well, I don't know," she said. "Suppose someone wants to look at them? They'd be missing. So here's what I think."

She turned to look at the room, waving her forefinger as if directing a band. A few people went past them on the way from the hotel registration desk, a fine, polished wooden structure that spoke of days gone by when everything was made to last lifetimes. Finn ignored Ruby racing around the room, ignored the faint bark from the ghost dog, and concentrated on Mrs. Brice.

"Why don't you bring your laptop or whatever down here, and we'll supply you with coffee and some sweet rolls." She looked at him, nodding. "That way, we can tell folks when they ask, oh, there's our resident ghost hunter, researching our ghosts. You won't be a huge draw, but I tell you what, you'll validate our three spooky guests here."

"That sounds like a good plan," he said, a little overwhelmed at her generosity. Though, if he were to look at it from her perspective, him coming to the hotel specifically to stamp his ghost hunting card gave the hotel an air of mystique and gave the idea of having three ghosts more weight. The bottomless carafe of coffee, and maybe some nice pastries to go with it, didn't sound too bad, either. "Let me just go grab my stuff, okay?"

At her nod, he raced up to his room, grabbed his laptop, then put it down and changed into a button down shirt and the light suit jacket he'd brought, just in case someone wanted to interview him about what he was doing. Then he picked up his laptop, a small notebook, and a pen, locked the door behind him, and hurried down to the lobby.

There he found a table had already been set up for him. It was out of the way of traffic, but right next to the tableau, so he could be seen from all angles, and especially when people came in the door. They'd even moved the potted plant out of the way for him, and a nice wait-ress from the restaurant was bringing his carafe of coffee, a supply of cream and sugar, and two cheese danishes on a small, paper-lined plate for him.

"Are these okay?" she asked as she set everything down, moving them from her tray to the table. "Just let me know if you prefer a different pastry, or run out of cream."

"I sure will," he said, giving her a smile. It was such a nicely-run hotel, from the management to the staff, and surely the reason his Nana favored it when she came to town. "Thank you so much."

He watched her walk off, then poured himself some coffee, prepped it, bit into the danish, and then brushed his hands and got up to grab Daisy's notebook. Flipping through it, he skimmed the news-paper article and the letters from hotel guests who had encountered her, noticing something odd.

The *RMS Titanic* had gone down in April, yet she'd not killed herself until early June. Why on earth had she hung around the hotel that long? Had she been waiting for word of her fiancé—and, if so, why wouldn't she just go to where she normally lived to do that?

He did some quick research on his laptop about the tragic sinking, how long it had taken for the death rolls to be published, how the investigation of the sinking had gone. Then he searched a Titanic-based website specifically on Daisy McKee, and then on Gerald Slater, her fiancé.

Evidently, Daisy, her health destroyed by the *Titanic* tragedy, had been advised not to travel, and so she had stayed at the hotel, waiting for word. It turned out that Gerald had a sister, Maude, and that she'd been on a business trip with him through Europe in the month before they embarked on the *Titanic*. As to why Gerald was traveling with his sister, when he had a fiancé at home and an August wedding planned, that took a little more digging.

Google threw up all kinds of links, and a rabbit hole of research loomed before him. Was it worth it to click on just a few more entries to try and unravel the mystery? That might be a yes, especially if Ghost Force appreciated his attention to detail and besides, the human interest factor was always a strong hand to play in ghost hunting. People were always interested in the back-stories of ghosts and how they'd lived before they died.

He clicked around the internet for a while before stumbling on a website that seemed to be a collection of odd bits of information all loosely related by the fact that the subject matter dealt, in some way, with the LGBT community, with facts both historical and new.

He entered Daisy McKee's name in the search box and was surprised to get a hit right away. Daisy McKee was listed as a victim of suicide, not because her fiancé had perished on the Titanic, but because Gerald's sister Maude had also perished, or so it had been assumed at the time. Daisy had not killed herself because of losing Gerald, the theory went, but because she'd lost *Maude*.

Love letters between Maude and Daisy had been discovered, unearthed during the refurbishment of a farmhouse outside of Chicago. The tragedy of the doomed relationship between the two women was added to by the fact that Gerald had poisoned Maude and left her for dead on an English moor after he discovered that it was not *him* that Daisy loved, but his sister. Then he'd boarded the *Titanic* and sailed to his death.

Daisy had been despondent over Maude's death. It was only after her suicide that Maude had made a full recovery and discovered, in a terrible real-life version of Romeo and Juliet—only in this case Juliet and Juliet—that Daisy had died by her own hand thinking that Maude was dead.

Maude had never gotten on the doomed ship. After sending a telegram to Daisy, and never getting a response, she'd lived out her days in England in a sort of dreary half-slumber, dying in her bed, still heartbroken over Daisy.

All of this had come to light in the decades that followed, when lesbian relationships were no longer a secret to be kept. Had Daisy waited even a few days in June, the telegram from Maude would have arrived, and the two women could have built their lives together.

Finn's fingers paused on the scroll pad as his throat grew thick. The entire tragedy could have been avoided had Gerald not lashed out at his sister, had communication lines been quicker, had Daisy waited.

Had everything worked out, the hotel would have had one less ghost, but it would have been better, all the way around. It was just a case of bad timing, that's what it was, and he brushed the corner of his eyes with his thumb and wished there was something he could do about it.

"Another pastry, young Finn?"

Finn looked up at the bespectacled face of Mrs. Brice, ever attentive to her guests' needs.

"I'm good," he said. "This coffee is terrific."

He wanted to be polite, but he also wanted her to go away. He could hear Leo barking, as if in a panic, and he could feel Daisy moving about in the floors above.

Somewhere, in the alley behind the hotel, Artie had died. Finn's head was starting to ache with keeping the facts straight in his head, and his heart was hurting over the loss of life, the loss of potential happiness, and he wondered at himself and his desire to make a living exploiting that.

"I'm glad to hear it," she said. "How's the research?" she asked. "I've had several hotel guests inquire as to what you were working on so studiously, and it was a pleasure to tell them that you were researching our lovely ghosts."

"That I am," he said, doing his very best not to look down at his laptop reread the last paragraph posted about Daisy and how she'd been waiting for Maude, but it was hard, and he felt the strain on his neck. "I'm just about finished with this one—"

He stopped, wondering if it would be helpful if he added what he'd discovered to the notebook and wrote about how if only Daisy had waited, she'd still be alive. But that felt too much like he'd be trading on her sadness for the entertainment of tourists, when what Daisy deserved was to rest in peace. That or have ended her days happily in a relationship with Maude rather than as a victim of the machinations of the villainous Gerald.

"I'm just about finished for the day," he said. "Maybe I'll go for a stroll and get some lunch."

"You should try Ziggy's Diner," she said in response to this. "They have great chili, great Polish food."

"I know all about them," he said, feeling his spirits rise at the thought of taking a break. "Maybe I'll call my folks, too."

"Your folks?" she asked, being the polite hotel manager that she was.

"They live north of town," he said. "They own Finnwood Farms? Bees and lavender," he explained, seeing her puzzlement.

"Oh, Finnwood Farms." Her eyebrows rose. "I've bought their honey in the past at the farmer's market at the fairgrounds. It's wonderful."

"That it is." He smiled at her, always pleased to meet a fan of Mom and Dad's honey. Mom had packed him some of her special lavender honey, so maybe later he'd take a spoonful of that and feel better as the sweetness and the sense of home spread through him.

"And they know you want to be a ghost hunter?" she asked, and it was easy to see that she thought he was foolish for picking spirits over flowers.

"They do," he said. "They're very supportive, and I'm going to give this my all, and if it doesn't work out, the farm awaits me."

"That might be for the best," she said. "People always love honey." With that, she gestured that he should continue with his work, waving one slender, elegant hand, and went over to the front desk, all business in her sharp city suit.

Unspoken, of course, was the idea that ghost hunting faded in and out of popularity; it became the rage, and then became silly. Honey, on the other hand, was a long-loved staple.

He might be foolish to want to make a career of ghost hunting. Then again, he could sense three ghosts in the hotel, well, two inside and one in the alley, and if he walked down the street to the haunted barber shop, he would, no doubt, encounter Shorty, a former barber who was said to walk back and forth in ghostly silence after the barber shop had closed for the day.

He had a connection with ghosts and what would be foolish was to not make something of that. Right? To help ghosts in some way, to listen to their stories? Maybe what he should do was to focus on writing down what he learned about them and selling the stories as books online.

That felt like a whole other life direction, and too much to think about right now, so he swallowed the rest of his coffee, licked his finger to dab a bit of frosting still left on the plate, and shut down his laptop. He needed fresh air, and then he needed to write up his notes in preparation for sending them to the Ghost Force folks. The result of his application to join the famous team would tell him, soon enough, whether this whole experiment was folly—or not.

Getting up, he left a huge tip for the waitress since it didn't look like the hotel was going to charge him for the eats and treats. He tucked his laptop and notebook beneath his arm, and went over to the row of portraits on the wall, carrying Daisy's notebook with him to put it back in its proper place.

As he looked over the portraits, he again had the feeling that Artie's portrait had, just the day before, been indistinct and vague to the point where most of the features were a blur. He'd focused on the curve of Arturo's cheek, the glint of his eyes, but he'd had to squint the whole while.

Now, in the light of day, the portrait was more clear, more sharply rendered, and was in fact, a completely different photograph than it had been yesterday. He could see, in the sad curve of Arturo's eyes, that the young man had sought a dream, only to have the promise of that dream cruelly snatched away. Which of course was the effect a young, sudden death had brought about, though Arturo could hardly have known his end was coming so suddenly. Finn had not saved Artie and, in fact, had probably not gone back in time at all.

On impulse, he flipped open Artie's notebook. There, to his shock, was a copy of the article about how Artie had died—only this time, instead of the article describing how he'd jumped to his death on the day *before* Daisy's suicide in the roaring waters of St. Vrain Creek, his body had been found in the alley the day *after* Daisy had died. He'd been left for dead after a severe beating.

His heart racing, Finn flipped through his mental notes, sure that the date of Arturo's death had preceded Daisy's.

The police had been unable to discover the identity of the perpetrators. Had they had access to modern DNA testing, Finn knew they would have found out who killed Artie in a heartbeat; the young man had died with blood on his knuckles, which meant that he'd fought back and gotten in some blows of his own. He'd fought back against Horace and Ricky and lost.

Finn flipped through the notebook, eyeing the now-familiar handwritten letters. There were only a few, all of them about the scary encounters hotel guests had experienced when they dared slink down the back stairs and open the door to the alley. There, they'd heard screaming and shouting and felt the dark, sucking energy that was, most likely, Artie experiencing his death throes, over and over.

Past that, at the end of the notebook, in a plastic sleeve, was another newspaper article dated June 6th with an upbeat title: *Local Boy Saves Sad Damsel From Raging River*. So which was it? Had Artie died the day before or had he saved Daisy from her suicide attempt? Both could not be true, but it was as if a little tiny time slip had occurred where both were possible.

As he read the article, his jaw dropped, shock coursing through him. There, in ebullient, 1912 style, the article described how young Arturo Larkin, Artie to his friends, along with another young man who he only knew as *Finn*, had come up behind young Miss Daisy McKee. Upon seeing her despondent and sad, they followed her to the river, there to stop her from throwing herself into the foamy, spring melt-enraged waters to her death.

The article went on at length in the same fashion, over-describing everything. The article also harped on the fact that Daisy's fiancé had drowned on the *RMS Titanic* in April of that year, milking the fact for all that it was worth. But it was the names of the two young men that drew Finn back to the beginning of the article.

The article from June 6th stated very clearly that Artie's companion in rescuing Miss Daisy McKee had been a young man only identified by his first name: *Finn*. Of course they couldn't find the real Finn, as he'd not yet been born, and was only now reading the article where he'd been able to make a difference.

Somehow, fate was sending him a message, as if inviting him to override the constraints of any time paradox. To take a chance, step back in time, and make a difference— even though, in the current time, in the *now*, Daisy McKee was reported to have drowned in that river.

How had this one article, one simple copy of an article written way back when, been able to retain the evidence of another timeline? Had he gone back in time and saved Artie and Daisy? Or had he gone back in time because the article said he'd done those things?

Gingerly, Finn slipped the newspaper clipping out of its plastic sleeve, and squinted at it close up, reading every word. It read the same: together, Finn and Artie had saved Daisy McKee. He'd been there; he knew that was how it happened.

On impulse, Finn flipped the article over and found a tidbit about an electrical storm that had swept the area, coming in from the south and wiping out lightning rods while wreaking havoc on the glass insulators on telegraph poles, cracking them and turning them to black.

Finn remembered the sheet lightning that he'd seen from his third story hotel window, how unseasonal it had seemed, how eerie and strange. August was usually the season for thunderstorms and violent weather like that, not June.

Had the weather had anything to do with his ability to seemingly go back in time? The whole thing was crazy, just crazy. Electricity in sheet lightning that far away and distant did not cause a portal in time to open up, even in the back stairs of a very old and elegant hotel. Things like that just didn't happen.

But somehow it had. Here was proof, typed up years ago on a thin and sepia-faded scrap of newsprint. If he were to open the notebook tomorrow, would the article read the same? Or would it tell a different story?

Trying to figure all of this out was making his head ache. Hunting for ghosts, for evidence of the afterlife, was one thing. Trying to figure out how time travel might work, and what would cause a paradox like the article he held in his hand, that was another entirely.

Taking great care, his hands shaking, Finn slipped the article back into its plastic sleeve and closed the notebook. Looking up at Artie's portrait once more, Finn could see the encounter in the alley with new eyes. He'd gone back, and somehow interrupted Artie being taken up to that roof. Then the both of them had gone on to save Daisy.

What did it all mean? When had he gone back? Should he try again? Would he be able to open that door and find himself once again experiencing a June evening instead of it being what it really was, the middle of the night? Or was he so jacked up on an entire pot of coffee that his mind was racing double—no, triple time—and making up all kinds of things?

This was what he was going to do. He was going to go upstairs, put away his laptop and notebook, rinse his face with cold water, and have a spoonful of Mom's lavender-flavored honey. Then he was going for a walk so he could clear his head.

He was going to walk up Main Street and check out the haunted barber shop. He was going to stroll to the diner and maybe get himself something sweet to eat. He was not—was *not*—going to imagine that he could affect time in any way, especially not in the way that the newspaper article seemed to suggest that he had.

He couldn't control time. He couldn't make the stairway become a time portal once more to save a sweet-faced young man once more so the two of them could save Daisy. Could he?

CHAPTER EIGHT

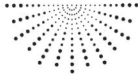

aggot.

F   The word trailed after Artie like a silent, deadly hound as he went out the back door of the boarding house and stepped into the warm evening, boots splashing in the water that pooled in the bricks. It had rained that afternoon, and it might rain some more later, but for now the clouds in the sky overhead were dancing away, all purple and rose, as though they were the skirts of an actress taking a bow before her next act.

Pushing away these fanciful thoughts, Artie looked behind him to see if Horace and Ricky were following him for more of their usual treatment. Since they somehow found out Artie's true nature from Cecil, they'd upped the ante with their bullying; fortunately they'd been at work all day at the packing plant.

Once he was back at the boarding house, Mrs. Clarkson, with uncanny timing, seemed to be around at the right moment, and Artie had done his best to avoid them at dinner. They must have gotten distracted by something inside, since they weren't right on his heels, so that was good. As to how long his luck would last, he had no idea.

Just then, across the alley, the back door to the Harlin Hotel opened, and out stepped the young man from the night before. He was wearing those too-tight-to-the-body clothes again, and his dark blue eyes were smiling as he strode across the alley to where Artie was still deciding whether to go left or right.

His head was full of thoughts of hauling stakes and moving to Wyoming where surely, *surely*, nobody knew Cecil; and now here was this young man, this handsome fellow, looking at Artie as though he was a treat to the eyes.

"Arturo, right?" asked the young man, a smile curving his lips. "I mean, Artie." He held out his hand for Artie to shake, and Artie took it, questions flying through his head. Nobody knew his real name, not even Mrs. Clarkson. It had been given to him by the orphanage when he'd been born, but everyone had just called him Artie.

"I'm Finn," said Finn. "Didn't mean to startle you, but I heard the shouting again. Thought I'd come down, though I guess I'm not really surprised to see you again. It's midnight where I am, but it's a beautiful summer's evening here."

"What?" asked Artie, totally confused.

Now that he knew the young man's name, the shape of him, the defined and dark angle of his eyebrows, that tumble of dark hair, those strong shoulders, all of it drew together, sharpened to a point that caught in his throat and made it hard to ask all the questions he wanted. He was just trying to make himself spit them out when Horace and Ricky came out of the back door to the boarding house and stopped short when they saw that Artie had someone with him. Someone strong. Someone who wasn't afraid to stand beside him as he stood up to his own personal bullies.

"What day is it?" asked Finn. He was almost ignoring Horace and Ricky coming at them, like he was bored with them already, but in a perfectly lovely way. "What year is it?"

"June 6th," said Artie, wondering how Finn wouldn't already know this. "Thursday. 1912."

"Then we have time," said Finn. "C'mon, follow me."

Artie cast a brief look over his shoulder at Horace and Ricky, who seemed frozen in their tracks by the fact that Finn slung his arm over Artie's shoulder and the two of them were about to simply walk away.

Artie figured this was a better way. Better than trying to duke it out in a two-against-one alleyway brawl. Besides, he rather liked the feel of Finn's arm around him.

It didn't solve his overall problem forever, as his energy in avoiding them would only last so long. It also didn't make the choice for him whether he should go to Wyoming or not, but he was safe for the moment.

On the other hand, it was no hardship to be held so close to Finn's side as they walked down the alley to Third Street. There, the traffic passed slowly by as the neighborhood cop swung his billy club while walking his beat, and children raced with their nickels to the ice cream parlor. Harlin was a nice town, and had it not been for Horace and Ricky, it would have been the perfect place.

"Where are we going?" asked Artie, as Finn's arm slipped from his shoulder and he scrambled to keep up with Finn's long legs.

"Here."

Finn drew to a stop on the corner of Third and Main in front of the Harlin Hotel and stood there, scanning the street up and down as though looking for someone he knew.

"Can I help?" asked Artie.

Artie scanned the street, too, but without knowing who or what he was looking for, it was hard to be of use.

The evening was a typical one for the season with folks hurrying home for their dinners or, having already finished, were now out for a stroll in the sweet and wholesome early summer air. Children amused themselves by jumping over the narrow ditch between the sidewalk and the dirt street, or clonked on the planks that had been laid over them to help people traverse the short distance without getting mud on their shoes.

"There she is," said Finn, pointing down Main Street where it sloped toward the railroad tracks. "Jeeze, is she wearing the same dress from the picture and everything?"

"Who?" Artie had no idea what was going on, but he knew he wanted to help Finn in any way that he could.

"Her." Finn pointed to the retreating back of a woman who was headed down the slope of the sidewalk that ran in front of the squat, brick power plant. "That's her. Daisy McKee. Let's go."

"Okay."

Artie hurried at Finn's side, glad to be out of harm's way, glad to have another moment to spend with the astonishingly beautiful Finn, who had the confidence and grace of a fellow who knew where he was and where he was going. Unlike Artie, who now that he'd been found out, was flooded with doubt.

They hurried down the flagstone sidewalk, racing over the steel rails of the train tracks to catch up with the young woman just as she reached the rickety wooden bridge that went over the river. There, she paused, her diaphanous skirts floating about her ankles in creamy, blue swirls.

Looking upstream and down, the pink twilight made her cheeks rosy and soft, her eyes glittering and dark. It was obvious that she was in some distress, even though she'd spoken to nobody on her way.

It was then that Artie recognized her as the young woman he'd bumped into the night before after he'd bought his aspirin powder. When Daisy McKee saw the two of them, she peered around the edges of her hat and clutched her gloved hands to her bosom, as though she feared they meant her harm.

"Daisy," said Finn, with the familiarity of a gentleman who has already been introduced to a lady. "Daisy McKee, right?"

"Yes," she said, her voice faint. "What do you want? I'm only taking a walk by the river, so there's no need for anybody to bother with me."

With sad eyes, she turned away, looking at the river as though she meant to find answers to questions only her heart knew. The hairs on the back of Artie's neck stood up; there was something very wrong here.

"But there is someone to bother with you. Bother *about* you. Won't you come away from the bridge, Daisy McKee?"

Finn held out his hands to her as though he meant to catch her when she fell. As though he knew she would fall and had shown up at that very moment to prevent her from something awful happening to her. Below the pylons of the rickety bridge, St. Vrain

Creek roared and snapped, as though with its mouth open, waiting for a meal.

All of this sifted through Artie's thoughts as he stepped a bit back. If Daisy made a dash for it, he would be able to sense her springing into action and might be able to stop her. Why he should want to prevent a young woman from taking an early evening's stroll was beyond him. He only knew that Finn—his own protector from the day before—had shown up again, and seemed in earnest desire to save her from something.

"You don't have to jump in the river, you know," said Finn, his voice soft as he inched closer to her. "It's running pretty high with the spring thaw, right? But you don't need to go like that and let me tell you why."

"What business is it of yours?" Daisy's words, the haughtiness of her tone, made Artie want to start making excuses for troubling her. By her clothes, her broad-brimmed hat, the string of pearls around her neck, the softness of her skin, she was a well-to-do young lady who was used to getting her own way. Used to getting what she wanted merely by gesturing for it. "It isn't, not any of it."

"What about Maude?" asked Finn, startling Artie with the specific nature of the question.

Artie had never seen Finn around the town—and it was a pretty small town—yet he seemed to know Artie and Daisy, and knew how to handle Horace and Ricky. Now he seemed to know someone named Maude. Who, by Daisy's reaction, was also known to Daisy.

"Maude has passed on," said Daisy, her voice cracking on the words. "She died when the *Titanic* went down."

"Only she didn't," said Finn, taking two steps closer till his strange canvas shoes touched the edge of the wooden bridge where Daisy stood. "She's not in any of the death rolls. I checked. I double checked."

"Those reports are faulty," said Daisy, lifting her chin in defiance. "Even the White Star Line says they are. Gerald said both of them were taking the *RMS Titanic* back to America, so they must have done. He would never lie to me."

"But he did," said Finn. "Daisy, I swear to you, Maude's alive. I know she is."

A brisk wind skittered across the surface of the spring-churned river, the dark sky settling overhead, turning the waters inky black and blue. Daisy's face, half limned, half in darkness, went pale. She seemed to stumble and reached out for the wooden railing to support herself.

"That's cruel," she said, her chin tucked down, tears streaking down her face. "So many cruel things and this just the last."

"But she is," said Finn. He didn't step any closer, but he leaned toward her just a little bit. Artie kept his mouth shut, eyes wide, not understanding any of this. "I wondered why your fiancé would travel abroad with his sister, so close to your wedding. That was scheduled in August, right?"

"Yes," she said, the word slow and soft. Which told Artie that the fiancé and the sister somehow had equal footing in Daisy's mind. "But what's it to matter anymore? They're both dead and I'm all alone."

This admission seemed to make her feel faint, for she swayed to the side, trying to grab hold of the railing and failing. In another moment she would tumble into the water despite Finn and Artie being right there. The water would sweep her under the bridge, taking her down in a white, foamy grip. Which seemed to be what Finn was determined to protect her from; he leaped into action and grabbed Daisy around the waist, holding her close to him, totally ignoring all propriety.

"Listen to me," he said, his mouth close to her ear, arms around her waist in the fashion of a lover, his words hurried. "I know about you and Maude, how you feel about each other. I know about the letters you wrote. I know that you'd been engaged to Gerald but that you'd fallen in love with Maude. And she's alive. He poisoned her and left her for dead on the English moors, but she survived and is recovering even now. If you wait, just a few days, then I promise you a telegram will come from her saying, as clearly as she can, that she loves you and is coming home."

Her eyes wide, she looked up at him. Her mouth fell open as she held up her gloved hands as though she didn't quite know where to put them.

"Maude?" she asked, her eyes glinting as they pooled with more tears. "She's alive?"

"Yes," he said, his voice firm. "The records don't exactly say where she is, but she's been ill, fighting off the poison since before the *Titanic* sailed. But she never got on board. That was Gerald's plan, to cast confusion of her whereabouts, so he said she was on the *Titanic* with him. Maybe he'd planned on reporting later that she'd fallen over-board, but, oddly, his plans got shot to hell. You just need to wait for her telegram and then you'll see."

"Are—are you lying to me?" she whispered to him, eyes wide as tears streaked again down her pale face. "Please tell me you're not."

"I'm not," he said, setting her on her own two feet, wiping her tears away with his thumbs. "Maude Slater is alive and getting stronger every day."

"How do you know all of this?" she asked. She patted her face with her gloved hands and smoothed her skirts, just a a moment away, as Artie sensed, from all out disbelieving Finn and throwing herself into the river as she'd planned.

"Doesn't matter how I know," said Finn. "I know about the letters between the two of you, I know about your relationship. I know that love is love, and I know this: if you wait a few more days, you'll get that telegram and your life will become what you always dreamed it would be. Can you wait? Wait for Maude to reach out to you?"

"I—I'm not sure," she said. She swayed on her feet, and some resolve must have come upon her, for she looked at Finn. "A telegram, you say? Within a few days? From Maude?"

"No more than a few days," he said. "I'm not sure of the exact date, you see." He smiled. "Let us walk you back to the hotel so you can wait for that telegram in comfort."

"Please, miss," said Artie, adding his desire to help to the conversation. "You have hope now."

"Yes, all right," said Daisy. It was easy to see she was quite shaken by the whole encounter and how quickly her desire to kill herself had turned into a desire to live, and all because of the promise of a stranger.

"I'm Finn, and this is Artie," said Finn, pointing. "We're going to walk you straight to that hotel and put you in the care of the manager. It's a good hotel. It's always been a good hotel. You'll be well looked after there until Maude comes home to you."

Finn took her arm in his and nodded at Artie to follow as they walked slowly and carefully up the street, crossing the tracks to where the flagstone sidewalk started. It was getting dark, and normally a young woman of means and breeding such as Miss Daisy McKee would not allow herself to be in the company of men who were strangers to her. But for some reason she was trusting Finn, just as Artie had trusted him. Together, in a short while, they arrived at the hotel, where the hotel manager hurried out, a square piece of paper in his hands.

"Miss McKee," said the manager, the fussiness of his attire and his greased-down hair easily erased by the kind look in his eye and his attentive concern. "This telegram came for you. It's from England."

"England," she said, her voice faint as she took the telegram. She turned to Finn. "You already know what's in this, I think."

"I do," said Finn with an easy smile. "But tell me this, if you would. If you were going to throw yourself in the river, why did you pack all your things?"

"So nobody would have to bother with them when I was gone." The statement came out flat as some shock must be coursing through her at what she'd almost done, and she ripped open the telegraph envelope, her gloved fingers making her clumsy. A moment of still-ness fell as she read the contents of the telegram. "It is from Maude. She's *alive*."

Miss Daisy McKee lifted her eyes to Finn, and glanced at Artie, who'd played only a small part in her rescue.

"How can I ever thank you, young Finn?" she asked.

"Answer the telegram and then unpack," he said simply, though he seemed to twitch when she called him *young Finn*. "Have a drink. Settle your nerves. Rest up. Wait for Maude to come home."

"I will," she said. "I'll wait right here for her. Right here. Forever if I need to."

"She'll come home to you," said Finn. "You have the world ahead of you, now."

"I do," she said. "And thank you."

With a small, regal nod of her head, she went into the hotel, where the manager was kindly waiting for her. That left Finn and Artie standing on the flagstone sidewalk outside of the hotel amidst the dwindling number of passers by who were soaking up the evening's air as the night drew to coolness and the promise of rain was made real. Artie's knees were shaking, so he tightened his legs and pretended he wasn't as astonished as he was by what had just happened.

"Buy me a drink?" asked Finn. "I could sure use one."

"Sure," said Artie, feeling in his pocket for change, trying to hide his pleasure at the thought that his brave and handsome boy wanted to have a drink with him. "I've got two bits for that, but the saloon is a ratty joint. Sure you wouldn't rather have a piece of pie and some coffee at Ziegfeld's Diner?"

"*Ziegfeld's* Diner?" asked Finn, as though Artie had suggested they walk through fire. "Sure. They've got good food, and I guess that reputation's been building for years."

Artie opened his mouth to argue that the diner had opened in 1910, and had barely had time to get going, so how could it have a reputation. On the other hand, he wanted to get to know someone who talked so easily about a young woman having another young woman as her love interest without even batting an eye, so he snapped his mouth shut.

"This way, mister," he said, pointing down the street. "I mean, Finn."

"Sure," said Finn, who tried to smile as he wiped at his eyes with trembling fingers. "It's good to meet you again, by the way, Arturo—I mean, Artie."

"How do you know my real name?" asked Artie as they started

walking the few blocks to the diner. "Nobody calls me that. Nobody really ever has."

"It's a very long story," said Finn, his grin good natured—and frankly, all of him very good looking as he walked at Artie's side. "Remind me to tell you about it one day."

The evening's darkness, the slight patter of rain, created a cloak of privacy around them as they walked along the sidewalk, hiding them from the fading traffic as they crossed the street to the diner. When Artie opened the door, the diner gleamed all black and white floors and shiny red stools. Though there weren't many people at this hour, everybody turned to look at Finn, which Artie could hardly blame them for.

Finn was as handsome as a devil and confident as a prince and maybe the answer to the questions he'd been having, for surely Finn knew the answers. He'd not batted an eye when telling Daisy about how Maude loved her. He'd said the words, *Love is love,* like he believed it was true.

If that was so then he must know where Artie could find his own kind. And not in some sleazy rat trap of a bar on East Colfax, or a personal ad in the wanted section of the *Rocky Mountain News,* so coyly written as to seem to be in a code: *a man wants another man.* Artie wanted another man and the fire that had been for so long dimmed now sparked to life inside of him.

CHAPTER NINE

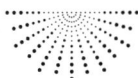

Ziegfeld's Diner, when Finn opened the door, was much as he remembered it in his own time, which was a relief, as he thought he might have messed up everything he'd ever known by messing with time.

The odd sensation of dropping down an elevator shaft that Finn had gotten when he'd walked down the back stairs washed over him once more. For anyone else, anyone not connected with the spiritual world, this might have been cause for alarm, but not him. He knew what was possible, knew that things weren't always what they seemed. Besides, he could write this up for his application and knock it out of the park for the Ghost Force audition. He'd tape himself talking about it. He'd show them that he could do good things in the spiritual realm. That maybe he could help with more than just entertaining people with stories about ghosts.

Rescuing Daisy had just been the start, and while it probably wasn't good to mess with time too much, certainly going back and helping Daisy and Maude live a happy life, well, who knew what good things could come from it? Too many people had perished on the *Titanic* already, and, after Daisy's death, Maude had merely wasted away in a bed somewhere in England. Pulling her back into time, giving them both their lives back, surely that was the better choice.

Well, there was no going back from it now and he didn't want to. Daisy had her telegram and was hopefully answering it even now. He didn't know what it would all look like in the morning, after he'd gone back up those stairs, but for now he was glad he'd done it. Glad he'd messed with fate. Glad he was at the diner with Artie.

Since it was after the supper hour, the diner was relatively empty, so Artie led the way to a booth in the back next to the last bank of windows. The black and white checkered floor beneath his feet was the same as from his own time, and while the swirly seats in front of the long counter were now leather instead of vinyl, as in his own time, they were the deep, satisfyingly deep, blood red color.

The paint on the walls was a starker white, and there were crisp-looking black and white photographs of dancing girls with close-cropped hair and bee-stung lips in all sorts of what must have been considered quite lascivious poses, but which looked, to his eyes, contorted and frozen. Also in evidence was a large display about Mr. Florenz Ziegfeld himself, a dapper looking man of his time. In his portrait, he confidently wore a bespoke suit, smiling a very small smile, as if he knew he was a hit even before the diner chose to name itself after him and honor his legacy.

In Finn's own time, the diner was called Ziggy's Diner. He'd always assumed it had been because the future- current owner had a thing for David Bowie and loved Ziggy Stardust with all of his heart. Both of which could be equally true, as the future diner was decorated with photographs of Bowie, some autographed, and the vinyl record album cover, all nicely framed.

The atmosphere, here, in 1912, was much the same as Finn recognized, low key and friendly, though there was the slight funk of old food, and the windows were fogged up with the heat from the kitchen as the evening cooled down outside. All in all, he felt pretty calm about where he was and when he was. As he sat down in the booth and watched Artie slide into the other seat, he knew he could get back to his own time, and that no time would have passed when he got there.

He could enjoy himself a bit, and leave behind the worry about whether his saving Daisy would change the past and future time continuum—resulting in a new alternate reality, as Doc Brown had put it in one of his favorite movies. None of this would amount to much and maybe it was all a dream anyway.

"Pie and coffee sound good?" asked Artie, reaching into his pocket as if to check how much money he had.

"Sure," said Finn. It was 1912 so life was still good, people had money to spend, and all the pictures Finn had ever seen of Harlin in the early days made it look like a nice, safe place to live.

A black-skirted waitress came over to them. Her hair was pulled back into a puffy bun, and she wore a white apron that covered her from neck to ankle, looking like a much dowdier version of the ghost tour guide. She looked tired after a long day's work, but she politely pointed to the chalkboard menu.

"We're all out of cherry pie, but we got apple, if that'll do you."

"Yes, please, miss," said Artie, the words sounding overly polite to Finn, but then, that was probably the style of the day.

"For both of you?" asked the waitress.

"Yes, please, miss," said Finn, copying Artie's words exactly.

He put his hands on the old-fashioned wooden table that gleamed from its many cleanings. In his day, the tables were all retro-styled formica, but there was something homey and gentle about the wooden tables now.

As they waited for their pie and coffee, they looked at each other. Artie seemed to look a little dubious about their encounter, now that they had stopped moving—now that they had sat down and had nobody but each other to contend with.

It occurred to Finn that their previous meeting, where he'd rescued Artie, had already changed the time continuum and was the reason that his portrait in the hotel lobby had changed as it had. Had this evening's encounter also changed time? It was making his head whirl a bit, but he was distracted from that line of thinking when Artie nodded at him.

"I didn't have a chance to thank you properly for yesterday, as well as today," Artie said. "So thank you."

"They been at you for a while?" asked Finn, and was a little startled when Artie tightened his jaw and looked away, telling Finn in no uncertain terms that the answer was yes.

"They beat you up before?" asked Finn.

He paused as the waitress came by and plunked thick white china plates down, both with huge slices of apple pie that looked very fresh, and which had been heated up in an oven, and still had little bits of steam rising from the pastry flakes.

The coffee was served from a large, tin pot, which must have been heavy; the waitress had to make a second trip for the white china mugs, and poured the coffee with both hands. She brought them a little pitcher of cream, and pointed to the sugar bowl with a flick of her finger as she walked off, skirts flicking around her booted ankles.

"It's a long story," said Artie.

"I'm sure it is," said Finn. Then with a laugh, he added. "I've got time."

"Who are you?" Artie's eyes narrowed as he asked the question, as though Finn was, in his consideration, quite possibly the enemy.

"I'm a stranger in these here parts," said Finn, but then he stifled his snort, as he didn't think that kind of sarcastic, movie-quoting humor had been invented yet. "Just passing through."

"On your way to where?" asked Artie as if he was truly interested in the destination and not just making conversation.

"That is also a long story," said Finn as he scooped up a forkful of what turned out to be delicious, buttery and sweet, just-rightly-spiced apple pie. "But what about you? What about those guys? Is this just the next in a long line of bullying or what?"

Artie looked out the window at the darkness in the street, with the window reflecting the half of his face that Finn couldn't see. Artie's profile was softened by the glass, though in his eyes Finn could see that he seemed to be carrying a huge weight on his shoulders, had been for a while, and that the weight had just been added to.

The feelings that he had for this ghost he'd met were moving quickly into more, lacing through his heart in a way he'd not thought it would. If only Artie belonged in Finn's own time, then they could take their time and really get to know each other.

"You know, Artie," said Finn, quite gently, as though he was talking to a ghost, which in a way he was—a very sweet-faced ghost whose repeated brushes with death were causing Finn's heart to ache. "You can tell me. Maybe I can help?" Though how, he didn't know.

"You can't." Artie picked up his fork and dug into his slice of pie and shoved some into his mouth as though it was the last bit of food he'd ever eat.

Overhead, the electric lights dimmed, and then stayed steady at that level of light, as if the energy source had been tamped down for the night. That they had electricity in 1912 wasn't a surprise, but the fact that there were streetlights on the edge of every block, did.

The lightning fixtures in the diner seemed a little old fashioned, but Finn supposed that in time they'd be updated, until finally, in his time, they'd be made more retro to fit people's ideas of what a diner should look like in the good old days.

As for Artie, he looked as real as he could possibly be, and in 1912 he was not a ghost. He had not yet died by being thrown off a building or getting beaten up by thugs. The question wasn't why those bullies were after Artie, but how they could be stopped.

Finn needed, *wanted*, to find out—because now that he'd met Artie, met him before he'd become a ghost, what he was looking for seemed to be morphing into something more than a position on the Ghost Force team and its resulting fame on YouTube.

He and Artie had saved Daisy McKee—so could they, somehow, some way, also save Artie from his own fate? Finn had never met a ghost before, and now he'd met two; this one, the lovely-to-look-at ghost named Artie, was drawing him in hard, making him want a different outcome for Artie—and maybe a different one for himself.

"Those are the kind of guys who would hassle kids on the playground, if they thought they were weak or different." Finn paused, and took a long sip of his coffee, which, even with cream and sugar, was quite bitter and not to his liking. Maybe that's how they made coffee back in 1912, or maybe it was from the brew getting acidy while sitting in a cast iron coffee pot all day. "I was a little different, especially in high school, and there were always those types of guys, you know. Guys who wanted to shove you into a locker, or put Nair on your head."

"Nair?" asked Artie. His mouth was full of pie and he seemed distracted by eating.

"Makes your hair fall out," said Finn, smiling at the memory of how he'd dodged that particular torture.

"Oh," said Artie, swallowing. "That would be a pretty mean thing to do, just for being different."

"It was," said Finn. "I lucked out that day, taking a different route."

"Sometimes that's what you need to do," said Artie. He sipped at his coffee and didn't seem to mind the bitter taste. His shirt cuff fell back from his wrist as he lifted the white china mug and then dropped back down again.

Finn liked wrists; they were the most delicate part of a man, and they led into forearms, all corded and muscled. But as he reflected on Artie's words, he reined in his thoughts and considered those words and the tone in Artie's voice.

"Sounds like you know all about taking that different route," Finn said. Then he asked, though he already knew. "It's because you're different from them, right?"

His shoulders stiffening, Artie sat straight up. With his face locked in stone, those blue eyes blazing, he looked at Finn, and Finn knew right away that he'd said the wrong thing and pushed too hard. Not usually a mistake he made, so he regretted it instantly.

"I'm not going to tell anyone," Finn said, his voice low. He bent forward so his words wouldn't have to travel very far. "I would never tell anyone."

"I don't even know you to tell you anything," said Artie, fiercely, then he shrugged and looked out the window, his hands in his lap.

"Even if I wanted to, I've learned the hard way that I can't. I can't trust anyone, not even you."

"I understand more than you think I do," said Finn, finishing off the last of his pie. "But look. I'll walk you back to your place, make sure you get there safe."

"That's fine for now," said Artie, and though the words came out harsh, he gave a shrug and a look of apology was on his face. "But what about tomorrow?"

"Don't know," said Finn. "But I'm going to think of something."

In the back of his mind, he considered what he'd done for Daisy, and whether it would work for Artie. The only trouble with that was, while he'd known exactly when and where Daisy would commit suicide, the information on Artie's death, like the exact time and date, were facts that he'd glossed over the first time. He needed to get back and do some research before he could figure out what he could do, if there was anything he could do.

The waitress came over and took Artie's money. The two of them left the diner to walk the few blocks down the nearly deserted Main Street until they were able to go around the alley, where the back door of both the hotel and the boarding house was. There, in the shadowed light from the single street light at the end of the alley, they stood looking at each other.

Beyond the city horizon, sheet lightning punched its way through the piling thunderclouds, but there was no sound of thunder, only the faraway smell of burnt ozone. On the back of the newspaper article about Artie there had been another article about the electrical storm. Finn could feel energy coming on the wind that whisked around their feet, and he felt the draw of the back stairs to the hotel as though someone was yanking on his skin.

"I'll be all right," said Artie.

"You sure?" asked Finn.

Something was swirling inside of him, telling him that this was important, that this guy wasn't just a ghost from the past but a living, breathing human being. He deserved happiness, and it wasn't just because he was pretty to look at either, with his soft, honey blonde

97

hair and those blue eyes that looked sweet as summer poetry. Artie was on the slight side, at risk from the bullies of the world, and Finn wanted nothing more than to protect him. But he needed to get back to his own time, he could feel it.

"I've dealt with them before, and I can keep doing it, long as I keep my head down." Artie ducked his head, his hands in his pockets. "But I sure do appreciate you looking out for me. I've never really had that before."

Finn's eyebrows rose in his forehead, and he reached out to gently touch Artie's arm.

"You take good care, you promise me?" Tugging at little on the sleeve of Artie's shirt, he got Artie to look at him. "Promise me. Just avoid those jerks, just avoid them."

"I will."

With that, Artie went into the back door of the boarding house as jauntily as though he wasn't walking into his own doom. Who knew whether those two bullies were hiding in wait, or whether they had a crafty plan to ambush Artie when he least expected it. But there wasn't anything Finn could do, that he felt he *could* do, not without, yet again, changing time into something completely different. The idea of that was filling his head so he couldn't hardly think.

He needed rest and he needed his laptop so he could research the whole timeline properly. There wasn't anyone he could talk to about this, not even his Dad, who was usually up for the most enlightened and far out conversations that Finn could come up with.

"Goodnight, Artie," said Finn to the evening air, then turned to open the back door to the hotel as the sheet lightning flickered in the distance and a mournful, long-away howl of a train whistle ribboned along the horizon as he went inside.

CHAPTER TEN

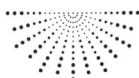

When Finn woke up, his mouth felt like it was filled with dryer lint, and his shoulders felt as though he'd tried to swim the English Channel. All at once, as he sat up, the flood of images from the night before tried to drown him. Scrambling out of bed, he looked out the window, at the soft early June rain, and thought about Artie. Artie had been real, very much alive, and the look on his face when Finn had said goodbye was tugging at his heart.

He needed to get some more research done. But first he needed energy, he needed a hot shower, and he needed breakfast. Pancakes would do it, both to lift his spirits and give him an excuse to get more butter into his system.

Within half an hour he was showered and shaved, wearing a fresh t-shirt, and clean socks and underwear, trotting down the stairs to the lobby, and in through the door to the small, cozy dining room. It was nice to eat his pancakes and butter and drink his coffee in the dining room while watching the rain fall in a delicate way past the windows.

In Colorado, it never rained for long, unless there was a storm; this morning, the clouds were already bumping themselves in an easterly direction, chasing each other away, which was good. Bees liked the rain, but they also liked sunshine, and Dad always said they made their best honey in June.

Leaving a substantial tip after paying his bill, Finn licked the maple syrup from his fingers as he stood up. Walking out into the lobby, he waved at the front desk clerk as he headed for the tableau about the hotel's ghosts. There, he was astonished to be faced with only two portraits on the wall, that of Ruby Hopkins and Arturo Larkin. The portrait of Ruby was exactly the same, with the same smiling little girl in her turn of the century middy dress, leaning down as though reaching for something. Which, as Finn now knew, was her faithful dog, Leo. When he flipped through the notebook, the details about her were exactly the same.

As for Artie's portrait, it was even sharper now, showing more of the features that Finn had seen, showing that blazing determination in his eyes, that set of his shoulders. It was as if the portrait had been taken with a very good camera, and then reproduced with some care. The notebook on the table was much thicker today.

But as for Daisy McKee, where in the hell was her portrait? Her notebook? Had what Finn and Artie done, their brave and kind deed, erased her from history somehow?

As he turned to go up to his room, Finn almost ran over Mrs. Brice, who had obviously come to greet him. As always, she was dressed for a New York City block, trim in her dark suit, and orderly from her severely tucked bun to her shiny black shoes.

"Hey, Mrs. Brice, good morning," he said to her, his heart thumping so loud he was sure she could hear it.

"Hello, young Finn," she said with a smile. "You look troubled. Anything I can help with?"

"What happened to—" Finn jerked his thumb over his shoulder. "What happened to Daisy McKee's portrait, did you decide to take it down?"

"I beg your pardon?" asked Mrs. Brice, looking over the top of her glasses at him. "Did you say Daisy McKee?"

Not knowing what to expect, whether she would tell him that they'd taken it down to clean it or that she'd never heard of the woman, Finn opened his mouth, struggling to figure out the best way to explain it.

"It's just that she's—she's missing." It was the best he could come up with. "Her portrait is missing."

"That's so odd," said Mrs. Brice.

"What's odd?" asked Finn, leaning forward, his whole body tuned to what she was going to tell him.

"Daisy McKee's portrait has never been in this lobby, though she once was a guest here." Mrs. Brice shrugged, for a moment wrinkling the fine lines of her suit. "She was my great aunt, you see, but I've never met anybody who knew about her. At least not these days."

"*Knew* about her?" asked Finn, his voice feeling faint in his throat, though he had an idea he was about to find out what effect his rescue had eventually had. He just hoped it was good. "Your great aunt?"

"She was a guest in the hotel, years ago." Mrs. Brice waved her hand as if to encompass all that had happened between now and then. "She'd been staying here waiting for word of her fiancé, Gerald, and she was so despondent over that, she went down to the river to kill herself by drowning. Can you imagine?"

"I can imagine a lot of people were affected by the disaster, for sure," said Finn, feeling the whirl in his stomach, which might have been a cold fear or a happy anticipation. "What happened to her?"

"She was rescued," said Mrs. Brice. "By two young men, one of whom she always referred to as young Finn, when she told the story, and then another fellow—" Mrs. Brice laughed and patted Finn's shoulder, winking at him. "You're one of the few people with that name, so that's why I always refer to you as young Finn, you see? You kind of look like her description of him, too, but maybe that's just the years playing tricks on my mind."

"I do?" asked Finn. Although his mouth was dry, sparks of joy leaped up through him, like stars shooting for the highest spot in the sky, for it was evident he had changed time, and for the better. "Did she ever marry?"

"Funny you should ask that," said Mrs. Brice. She smiled at him, as though touched by his interest in her family. "Long ago, they used to call it a Boston Marriage, but today they would just call her gay. She was a lesbian, you see, and she had actually been in love with Gerald's sister, Maude. They lived a long, long time together, even though for most of her life it was illegal. Isn't that sad?"

"Sadder to not have been with Maude at all, I think," said Finn, gently.

"But of course, young Finn," said Mrs. Brice. "We have two ghosts, and isn't that enough for one hotel?" She paused to gesture to the front desk clerk, as there were some bags sitting unattended by the front door. "There's sweet Ruby, and then there was the other fellow, Arturo Larkin, who was interviewed by the newspaper. See him there? Sadly, he died a terrible death the day after he rescued Great Aunt Daisy."

"Terrible death?" asked Finn, his heart beating even faster now. "What kind of terrible death?"

"He was stabbed to death with a knife right in the alley behind the hotel," said Mrs. Brice, shaking her head. "Such a sad thing to happen to such a brave man, and a cute one. Just look at the curve of his mouth, as if he's about to smile."

Artie didn't look like he was about to smile as his picture had been taken, not by a long shot, but Finn nodded his head in agreement. The thought of Artie being stabbed to death by a knife was overtaking every other thought, and he suspected the two thugs in the alley immediately.

The only thing that really mattered, though, was figuring out when exactly it had happened and going back in time to fix it, however crazy it made him feel to actually believe that he could do it.

How would he explain Artie's absence from the tableau to Mrs. Brice, who was so proud of her hotel's history? Then he realized, with a rush of shock, that he wouldn't *have* to explain it because it never would have happened. As for poor sweet Ruby, maybe he was on a roll and could save her, too; she and Leo deserved to stay together, a small girl and her beloved pet.

"Do you mind if I do some more research in the lobby today, Mrs. Brice?" asked Finn. He already knew by her smile that the answer was yes, but he wanted to make sure he wasn't going to be a bother. "With some more of those delicious pastries?"

"Certainly," she said. "I'll get a table set up for you now."

Going upstairs to get his laptop and notebook and coming downstairs to the sunny spot in the lobby was a kind of routine that made him feel better about things, made him feel calmer. He brought over the two notebooks from the lion-legged table and sat down with his coffee and his pastries and tried to concentrate.

He opened the notebook about Ruby and found that her story remained utterly unchanged: she'd been walking down the street with her parents and her dog. When she'd thrown her red rubber ball to coax Leo out of the hotel's lobby, the ball had gone into the street. She'd run to fetch it, and she'd been run over by a Model T Ford and died. All of this was as sad as ever, though his mind was racing with the idea that he could save her and wipe this sad story from the face of the earth.

As for Artie's notebook, the notebook was fatter now, chock-a-block with letters from hotel visitors who said that when they went down the back stairs, they could hear him screaming for help, over and over again until he went silent.

Finn felt a horrible sweat all over his skin, thinking of Artie dying like that. Thinking of him suffering when he was struggling already. Guests must be terrified to hear the screams and not know what to do about it, since the tragic death had happened so long ago. Their stories were much less about meeting some cute, harmless version of Casper the Friendly Ghost and getting a glimpse of the old days and more like one of the movies like *The Saw* and *The Cabin*, which Dad adored and that Mom secretly admitted to enjoy watching with him.

Finn had gone back in time twice now. Each time to the next, subsequent day, back in 1912. And each time, the newspaper article listed Artie's death a day later than it had before. Which meant that even though Finn had saved him two times, his death was still on the books. This time around, instead of falling from the roof or being beaten to death, he'd been slain with a knife, which was so horrible it left Finn with a cold, queasy feeling in his stomach.

The only saving grace was the newspaper article from the day after Artie and Finn had rescued Daisy from death by her own hand. Evidently, a reporter from the *Rocky Mountain News* had come by to interview Artie, after word had gotten around.

Maybe Daisy had told the hotel manager what had happened to her, and maybe the manager had contacted the paper. Miss Daisy McKee was staying at his hotel, and the article might bring in more guests who'd want to be associated with Daisy, who was associated with the sinking of the *Titanic*. It all seemed very glamorous and innocent from such a perspective as the present day.

Artie's picture in the cleaner copy of the article was even clearer than the current portrait of him in the frame, and it made him look noble and proud, but Finn knew different. Behind the pose that the photographer had, no doubt, asked him to strike, there was a shimmer of uncertainty and of doubt about his future. A future that, in retrospect, had been exactly one additional day.

The article spoke of his heroics, and his gentlemanly rescue of Miss Daisy McKee, and then went on at some length to discuss her connection to the ill-fated *Titanic*, finally bringing in, at the last, the names of her fiancé Gerald, and Maude, his sister. Who, the article noted with some old-fashioned relish, was headed back to America from England so the two women could mourn their loss of Gerald together for the rest of their lives. Daisy hadn't told the reporter everything true about her and Maude, but then, back in 1912, that was the sensible thing to do.

As for Finn himself, who had also been there, he was referenced by his first name only, and was mentioned by Artie as having played a large role in realizing that Miss Daisy meant to do herself harm. But since Finn hadn't been there for the interview, and his photograph not available, perhaps he'd been deemed as being less important. That was fine by him. Nothing could freak him out more than seeing his own picture in a newspaper article from 1912.

But overall, he was freaked out already, and his heart was pounding as he tried to figure out what he needed to do. His heart ached knowing that Artie had still died. The young man with the sweet face had trusted Finn enough to follow him to the river, and he had, just about, told Finn the truth about why he'd been bullied. It was too much. That sweet half smile he remembered when he'd sat across from Artie in the diner was just about doing him in. He needed to figure out what to do, but first he needed to calm the hell down so he could think.

He put the notebooks back on the lion-legged table, overtipped the waitress, packed up his notebook and laptop, and headed back to his room. There in the low gloom, with the curtains drawn, he heard the rain begin outside as he pulled out his cellphone and called his Dad.

"Hey, Dad," he said, sitting on the edge of the bed when he heard the click at the other end. "How they hanging?"

"Is that any way to talk to your *father*?" asked Dad, putting a serious tone in his voice that was completely erased when he laughed like water going down a drain. "But really, how is it going? Getting all the material you need for your application?"

"Got plenty," said Finn, though as he looked at his equipment, and thought about it, figured maybe he was lying. If the tableau was missing Daisy McKee, then maybe his camera and EVP recorder, and all his temperature readings in his Ghost Force application notebook would be gone too. It was giving him a headache trying to think about time travel paradoxes when all he wanted to do was change the fate of one sweet-faced ghost. Well, two, since he wanted to save Ruby, too. "But I had a question for you, if you have a minute."

"Sure," said Dad. "But is it a sister kind of question? Mia's here."

"No, just you, Dad," said Finn, lowering his voice so Dad would get the idea that he needed one of those father-son moments. "Just for a minute."

"Okay, Finn," said Dad, and Finn could imagine his face straightening into serious lines, the creases of ever-present laughter beside his blue eyes. "Shoot."

"So, you know how Jack Torrence, in the movie, ends up in that black and white photograph of the July 4th ball in 1921?"

"Sure," said Dad. "That's a great scene, a perfectly creepy scene, one of the most brilliant in cinematic history. But you do know, don't you, that he's not the reincarnation of the butler, he's supposed to be the reincarnation of Charles Grady, the previous caretaker who chopped his kids—"

"Yeah, Dad, right, but reincarnation isn't time travel—" Finn paused, trying to think of how to phrase it. "You think it's possible to go back in time like that?"

"That's not going back in time, kiddo," said Dad, answering the question in a perfectly serious way. "Jack Torrence is the reincarnation of the previous caretaker, so he's coming *forward* in time."

This wasn't the answer Finn wanted at all. He needed help. His Dad was really the only person he could ask, but it meant that Finn needed to ask the right question in the right way. Otherwise, Dad would start on about how *The Dark Tower* was a dud and even the handsome and talented Idris Elba couldn't have saved it.

"What about that movie Mom and Mia love so much, the one where that Christopher Reeve guy goes back in time. Is *that* possible?"

"You planning a trip to the past, son?" asked Dad, unable to keep the laughter from his voice. "I'm sure your mother will bid you bring some honey with you, as it was used for all kinds of medicinal purposes, back in the day."

"Just a theory, Dad," said Finn, not at all reassured about anything, let alone going back to 1912 on purpose. "But is it possible? You've read all those books, all the horror and paranormal books. Is it?"

"I would say," said Dad, with more consideration. "That yes, it is possible. All things are possible, you know. There are lots of theories, scientific ones, that I don't entirely understand. Plus, there's also lots of first hand stories. Are all those people making it up? I don't think so, because the stories are pretty specific and so varied. But then, I watch too many spooky time slip videos on YouTube. Just ask your mother."

"She watches them with you, I happen to know," said Finn, trying to be jocular about it.

His parents had minds that were flexible and interested in all kinds of ideas, which probably was what led them to starting a honey and lavender farm when all of their friends had been moving to big cities

106

to get big, important corporate jobs. Only now it meant that Dad wasn't saying no to what Finn was saying, wasn't denying that time travel was possible—just the opposite, he was agreeing that it was entirely possible. So unless Finn broke down and told him what happened on both occasions, Finn needed to make his own decisions on this one.

Why? Because Dad, and Mom when she found out, would surely forbid him from trying it. But he needed to try to save Artie from his terrible fate. And he needed to be careful because his heart would surely break if he went back and saved Artie again, only to find that Artie still died. All of this was a huge distraction from his Ghost Force application, but at the moment it certainly seemed more important.

"So think about it this way," said Dad, taking what sounded like a sip of his coffee. As always, Dad was treating the conversation with as much deference and consideration as he usually did, as though it meant something to him that Finn had asked the question. "A long time ago, we thought the earth was flat. Now, we've found out that the earth is not flat but is, indeed, quite round. Or nearly round, but that's a story for another day. The point is, just because we don't know a thing, doesn't mean that the thing isn't already true. You dig?"

"I dig," said Finn, using the retro-hippie word because his Dad loved to find old words and use them just for fun.

"So while you're trying to prove life after death," said Dad. "Maybe you're on the verge of proving that time travel is real, too? And wouldn't that be cool?"

"You can't be serious, Dad," said Finn, a little frustrated that Dad was so accepting of the idea. There was nothing to fight against. No-one to tell him it wasn't true, and that was the scary part. It meant that he'd really gone back in time twice, and once on purpose.

He was changing the time continuum, and creating paradoxes he had no idea what to do with. The only saving grace was that Dad, and hopefully the farm, and Mom and Mia, had remained untouched. In fact, most of the world seemed exactly the same to him.

"I'm perfectly serious," said Dad. "Listen, are you going to come home soon? Mia's here, and I need some help scything the early alfalfa and printing labels for the jars of honey."

"Another day or so, Dad," said Finn. He slouched forward, head hanging between his shoulders as he cupped the phone to his ear. "Just need a little more data and then I'll be home."

"Call before you leave the hotel," said Dad. "Mom wants to thaw one of the lasagnas in the freezer and we only have the large, and I mean *large*, ones left. We need to eat them before she can make more."

"Blame Mia for being on that low-carb diet last winter," said Finn, smiling a little, feeling better to hear so much *normal* in his Dad's voice. Too much had happened for him to be completely at ease, but at least Finnwood Farms was exactly the same as he remembered it.

"Yes, let's blame Mia for that," said Dad with a little laugh in his voice. "She might have asked Toby for a visit, but I don't know."

"Don't know what?" asked Finn, smiling even broader now, knowing what was coming.

"I don't know much, but I know I love you," said Dad, half singing it in his best Aaron Neville voice. "And that may be all I need to know."

"Love you," said Finn.

"Love you too, kiddo," said Dad in his normal voice. "Maybe go for a walk and get some sun. You sound glum."

"I will," said Finn, nodding. "Later."

"Later," said Dad.

Finn clicked the phone off with his thumb and sat on the edge of the bed for a good long time, wondering how a simple ghost hunt application had turned into a jumble of wanting to turn back time, like Superman turning the Earth backwards on its rotation to save Eve Teschmacher's mother in Hackensack. Only, this time, in the version Finn was living in, he was going to do his best to save one young man from becoming a ghost. He was going to save Artie Larkin from dying so that the cute old-fashioned guy could live out his life in peace and die a natural death, years and years later.

Finn's eyes grew hot and he had to scrub at them with the back of his hand. Maybe if he was getting this worked up about one ghost, he wasn't cut out for ghost hunting. Real ghost hunters never got this affected by thinking about how, if the ghost had never become a ghost, they would have lived a long and happy life. Ghosts were people whose spirits stuck around because they had unfinished business, unfinished lives. What could be sadder than that?

He might have saved Daisy McKee, but sweet little Ruby was still racing around the lobby, trying to coax her beloved pet outside just before getting run over. And as for Artie, he was constantly marching to his own death in that alley, over and over and over again.

It was horrible to think about. He had to do something. Only he didn't know what.

Could he truly expect to stay the rest of his life in the Harlin Hotel, going down those back stairs every night to save Artie? Unfortunately, the sheet lightning that seemed to be a partial cause of the stairs becoming a time portal only happened seasonally, in the summer—June at the earliest.

Come the fall, the sheet lightning would flicker away into nothingness, and the back stairs would become once more what they always were: a simple set of back stairs in an old-fashioned downtown hotel. So he couldn't mess around. He had to figure out what to do, had to save Artie, with his sweet face and that shy smile that came and went so fast it was like sheet lightning flickering in the sky, low on the horizon like a faraway promise.

CHAPTER ELEVEN

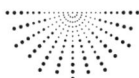

A fter sleeping on the floor rolled in a blanket, with the tall dresser pushed up against the door, Artie waited until the last possible minute to get up—long after he heard the horn at the packing plant and knew that Horace and Ricky were safely tucked away for the day. Then, after shoving the dresser back in place, he laced up his boots, splashed his face in the bathroom and, skipping the cup of almost-cold coffee that Mrs. Clarkson offered him, ran all the way to the depot, where Joe Moody was waiting for him with a frown.

"What're you playing at, boy?" asked Joe, already loading the papers dropped off from the first early morning train. "We got papes to sell and the news ain't getting any younger."

"I know it," said Artie as he hustled to load the rest of the papers into the hand cart.

"Good thing it's a slow news day," said Joe, letting him off the hook a little as he helped him load the cart. "Be sure to tip those newsies, or the one, if Bobby doesn't show up today."

"I will, Joe," said Artie, leaning into the handcart to get it going. "I surely will."

Using all his muscles, feeling himself warm up in the cool June air down by the river, Artie pushed the handcart across the dirt, across the tracks, and up the flagstone-covered sidewalk. There, on the corner in front of the Harlin Hotel, he found Stanley waiting for him. In spite of Artie's lateness, Stanley greeted him with a huge smile.

"Looks like it's just you and me today, Artie," said Stanley. He started helping sort through the newspapers, taking his usual to sell on the corner in front of the bank, then waiting while Artie wrote the amount down in his book. "You going to sell with me today?"

"That's a good idea," said Artie, feeling a little ashamed about wanting to hide in plain sight.

If Horace and Ricky happened to take a break from the packing plant, they couldn't do anything to him if he was right in public view, working with a young newsie to sell papers. No one deserved to be scared all the time, but he was finding it hard going. Maybe he should just pack up and head to Wyoming, take his daily pay from Joe and go, not even bother going to the newspaper office in the afternoon.

"I'll stay on this side for a bit, and be careful when you cross the street."

He watched Stanley cross the street, the large canvas sack over his shoulder loaded with rolled up newspapers banging against his thigh. Once there, he took out a paper, unrolled it and held it up for everyone to see.

"Extra, extra!" shouted the young Stanley earnestly. "Volcano in Anchorage, Parmelee dies in aircraft accident. Extra, extra!"

Artie joined in the chant, adding his deeper voice to Stanley's higher one, calling out the headlines, holding up the paper for all to see.

Because Stanley adorable, there were more men and women doing business with Stanley than with Artie, stopping to exchange a penny for a pape, and happily carrying them away. When Stanley's canvas bag was empty, Artie crossed the street to bring more papers over to fill it. He tousled Stanley's head as he arranged the papers so they'd be easier to pull out of the canvas sack.

"Good job, kid," said Artie, momentarily distracted by his own worries. "I'll tip you a dime today when I get back from my rounds."

"That's swell, Artie, and thank you." Stanley's smile was broad, his brown eyes dancing at the prospect. He picked up a paper and held it aloft, and chanted his newsboy chant, over and over. "Extra, extra!"

Artie headed up the street with his handcart, happy to be busy, distracted from his worries, happy to be selling papes to the butcher, and the shoeshine boy, the grocers, the diner, all his usual spots.

The air was filled with sweet sunshine, the puddles from the rain sparkling like mud-edged jewels in the street. The low ditches on either side of the street were flooded with rainwater, spilling out over their banks and making for slippery going. A few Model Ts sputtered past, flinging up arcs of water and mud, giving the morning a festive air as they honked their horns.

When Artie headed back down Main Street, his handcart empty, he found that Stanley's canvas sack was empty, as well. Artie tipped Stanley a dime, and hustled the handcart back to the depot, where Joe Moody paid him for the day's work.

"Here you go, the usual," said Joe in his gruff way. "Will you stop by the bank for me?" He handed over a roll of bills, stuffed in the red canvas sack. "Big one today. And also, there's a reporter here to see you."

"Here to see me?"

Artie stopped short, stuffing his pay in his pocket as he looked at the man who had obviously been waiting in the distribution shack. He vaguely recognized the reporter from the newspaper office who, as always, looked quite out of place in such a small town, dressing for the big city life he probably aspired to. He wore a brown city suit with an old-fashioned bowler hat, and had a large camera sitting on its box beside him. With a leather notebook in his hand, pencil poised, he looked ready to take on the world.

"Yes, indeed," said the reporter. "I'm Tom Dent of the *Harlin Advocate*. Seen you at the office; helping out, right? And I hear you have a tale to tell me, young man. About how you and your pal—where is he, by the way?—rescued poor Miss McKee from the raging torrent of the St. Vrain Creek and saved her from eternal damnation."

"That's true," said Artie, still not sure what to make of the fast surge of patter from the reporter. "We did, but it wasn't anything I did, really. Finn led the way."

Finn had led the way down to the river, after they'd saved Daisy. Then, after, they'd gone to the diner like two fellows on a date, should such a thing be allowed. Finn had been so kind and handsome, putting up with Artie sitting across from him like a dope with no manners. It was as though Finn thought Artie was worthy of being worried about. As though there was something wonderful to stay safe for. Like Finn was going to come back and check on Artie just to make sure.

And where did Finn live, anyway, when he wasn't rescuing Artie? Did he live in the hotel? Down the street? In another town? Artie needed to find out. He wanted to find Finn and thank him for giving him hope. Then, maybe, just maybe, they could take a walk together around the park in the center of town and go to the ice cream parlor afterwards and share a root beer float between them. It was such a sweet picture that he was startled when the reporter poked him in the shoulder to get his attention.

"Where's Finn? What's his last name?" asked Dent sharply, looking around, as if expecting Artie might produce Finn right then and there.

When Artie shrugged, having no idea how to answer either question, Dent scribbled in his notebook.

"We'll say that you led the way, and mention him a little. It'll make for a better story if we can put a face to the name. You in?"

"Could bring a lot of new customers," said Joe Moody quietly behind him. Since Joe had done so much for Artie, without really asking anything in return, Artie nodded even though he didn't want the visibility of having his picture in the paper.

"Sure," he said. "But make it quick, I got places to be."

He had lots of places to be that didn't include him being so close to the packing plant, where any moment Horace and Ricky might be taking a break and, suspecting he'd be in the shack, would come by. Not that anything could happen with Joe Moody so near.

Surely nothing could happen to him if there were other people around. He was such a coward, but he was tired of getting beaten up just for being who he was, just for having trusted a single, solitary human being for once in his life. Well, never again. Except maybe for Finn. He needed to find Finn.

The reporter asked questions in a barrage that felt like he was lobbing apples at Artie, one after another. Artie answered as best he could. Dent wanted to know how he and his friend just happened to be there as Miss McKee was walking toward the river. Then Dent determined how the pair had followed her and convinced her that her own tragic death would not bring back all the lives lost on the *RMS Titanic*—

"That's not really what we said to her," said Artie. "It was more about Maude. Finn said that Daisy should wait for Maude's telegram."

"Why should she wait for Maude, when surely her heart was grieving for her long, lost love?" asked Dent. "Her waiting for someone who's alive is not as good a story as her waiting for someone who's dead. It's only a good story if she pines away due to longing for a man she will never again see."

Scratching the back of his neck, Artie went over the conversation. He could see Finn in his mind's eye, clear as could be, with the dark, dusky twilight settling all around them on the banks of the river. Finn had such an easy-going manner, and confidence, and a sweet curl of hair over his temple.

He'd talked to Daisy as though he'd been acquainted with her a while. She, in turn, had responded to him immediately, as no woman he'd ever seen do, like he could charm the birds out of the trees.

Finn had said, specifically, *you fell in love with Maude* and *she loves you*, all without batting an eye, as if two ladies loving each other was very normal, even decent. Then he'd said, *love is love*, with such conviction.

As for Miss Daisy McKee, even being the very proper young woman that she was, she didn't even bat an eye. Most importantly, she'd not protested or claimed that it was not so.

By her silence on the matter, she had acknowledged that yes, indeed, Maude Slater was the love of her life. And now the notion of that entire encounter mixed with what Finn had said to him during their short meal at the diner. *I understand more than you think I do.*

As to what Finn understood, Artie had hopes, but he needed to be sure. He needed to find Finn.

Nobody, not even Dent, was stopping to ask how on Earth Finn had known Maude was alive, let alone the fact that there was a telegram coming from her. Artie'd had his suspicions but it took Dent getting it completely wrong to make it clear.

Finn knew things and had looked at Artie in such a way as to point Artie in the direction he never thought he'd go: Finn was like *him* and, somehow, he was connected to a whole world of people who were like him. As to where Finn had gone, Artie had no idea, but he needed to find him so he could ask him all the questions that were waiting inside him: *Where are there more like me and how can I find them?*

"Sure," said Artie, changing his tune, making up a story on the spot, a story that would sell papes. "It was all kind of mixed up, but it's clear to me now. We were hanging out, you know, how fellows do, and we saw her. We thought it was kind of strange that a pretty young miss was heading down to the tracks all by herself, dressed like she was."

"Dressed like she was?" asked Dent.

"Like she was going to a cotillion or something in her best dress and hat and gloves, like she had someone to meet." Artie figured it wouldn't hurt to put a spin on it, not if it sold more papers, not if Dent had it completely wrong from the start already.

"Was she in a hurry, her diaphanous skirts floating as though she was already a ghost, had already moved on?" asked Dent, scribbling madly, his bowler hat dipping askew.

"Sure," said Artie with a laugh. "Her wee feet seemed barely to touch the ground. It was all we could do to catch up with her, she moved so fast."

"Like she already had earned her angel wings," muttered Dent, writing in his notebook, trying to hold it steady as he wrote. "Brilliant, this is brilliant. I can finish this back at the newspaper office, but now, I need that picture. Here."

Dent put his notebook and pencil in his breast pocket and picked up the camera, fiddling with the levers and the huge flash bulb.

"Stand still," he said to Artie. "Give me a brave look. Chin up. There."

The interview had gotten irritating mighty quickly, but Artie stood there and thought of Finn, and thought of how he needed to find him, how he needed to stay out of Horace and Ricky's way. How he had a hundred problems that now all faded into the background because Finn was the guy he needed to talk to, the exact guy Artie had been looking for for so long. The guy who *knew*.

The flash exploded in his eyes and he winced, and blinked, trying to remove the ghosts and shadows in front of him that soon morphed into Dent and Joe Moody, standing there like they expected he was going to say something profound.

"When will that come out?" asked Joe Moody as he sucked on a toothpick, ever practical.

"Tomorrow's morning news," said Dent. He put his camera back in its big carrying case and adjusted his bowler hat on the back of his head, like he'd just spent a long, sweaty day in the fields, and was now pausing for a drink of cool buttermilk. Like he'd actually produced something of value rather than just spinning a tale of lies and half-truths. "If I can get this back, get it edited and typeset, it'll be a sensation, I tell you, a sensation."

"Print extra," said Joe Moody. "We'll need 'em."

"I certainly will," said Dent. "You'll be famous, young man, even if it's only for a day."

Artie didn't want to be famous, didn't want that much attention, which would surely bring a spotlight of derision and accusations his way. What he wanted was a quiet life selling papers, tipping newsboys, walking up the street selling from a handcart. And maybe someone to love, someone to be with, to come home to, there to share a quiet meal with by the light of an electric bulb. After which, they might go sit on the roof with a bucket of beer and two glasses and watch the stars come out, one by one, winking in a night sky of deep, mysterious blue. That wasn't too much to want, was it?

With these thoughts swirling in his head and with the change jingling in his pocket, Joe Moody's bank bag in his fist, he walked down by the river. He had to slink past the packing plant, huffing and churning at mid-day, but it didn't ruin his pleasure as he watched the clouds dance on the horizon and unnamable spring birds flicked across the surface of the foaming waters. The pylons of the bridge shuddered against the force of the current, but they held.

A stronger, wider bridge would surely be more useful, but Artie wasn't an engineer, only a lowly newspaper distributor with a limited dream that fate seemed destined to quell. Why was it that his little life was so fraught with one disaster after another?

Denver had been the perfect answer to Chicago, and Harlin the next stop after that. Now, here he was, contemplating going into the depot to pay the fare for a trip to Casper, maybe Thermopolis, where he thought he could find work on the railroad. It would be a tough life, but everybody would be too busy to ask nosey questions.

In the end, he didn't buy a ticket for the train but went to the bank for Joe Moody, and got a late lunch at the diner, sitting in the booth he and Finn had shared the night before. There, eating a simple meal of chicken fried steak with plenty of gravy, he thought about Finn and his beautiful hair, those dark blue eyes. How he'd listened so well, and spoke so gently that Artie had been on the verge of telling him the truth. All that, without any real reason to trust.

Finn was a near stranger to him. Yet he'd shown up in the alley twice, running interference between Horace and Ricky, coming in like he'd arrived on a whirlwind from some distant place as if he knew exactly where and when he needed to be to get Artie out of trouble.

That couldn't keep happening, so Artie's plan was to finish lunch, make his way back to the boarding house, wash up in the communal bathroom, and lock himself in his room until the bell rang for dinner. It was the coward's way out, but until he could get up the gumption to do something about it, like stand up to them again and again, or hop aboard the *Shoshone Zephyr* bound for parts north, he was stuck hiding.

The plan worked as well as it could, considering. After lingering as long as the waitress would let him at the diner, he'd made his way back to the boarding house. There, Mrs. Clarkson asked for his help in unpacking a new crate of water glasses that had just been delivered. He couldn't very well refuse her, and she'd been kind to him as well, so lingered in the kitchen, opening the crates, and handing each glass to her to rinse free of sawdust.

That was when Horace and Ricky, home early from the packing plant, found him in the kitchen. Without thinking he was safe as long as Mrs. Clarkson was near, he dropped a glass and ran out the back door, looking for a place to hide. This was ridiculous. His heart was going so fast, and the alley was near-silent, with the sweet June evening knowing nothing of his fear and his regret—that he wasn't someone else, someone braver, more able to stand up to the two of them.

Had it been one on one, sure, he could have managed to stand his own with either of them, but as it was Horace and Ricky both came out the back door. For some reason Horace was carrying a knife, hefted in his hand like a policeman's short billy club.

"You," said Horace, menace in his voice, pointing the knife at Artie. "C'mere."

"Hell no," said Artie, and he did the only prudent thing he could think of: he headed for the back door of the hotel across the alley. At least there would be people there—hotel staff, maybe a guest or two—rather than this empty, dank alley where the wind played a slow sad tune along the sides of the tin trash cans, shaking their lids. He was no match for the both of them, and he was surely no match for a knife.

Then the back door of the hotel swung open and Finn, of all people, stepped into his arms. Instantly, he saw Horace and Ricky striding toward them, and equally fast, he grabbed Artie and yanked him inside, locking the back door with one hand.

"Come with me," said Finn, his voice urgent, almost strident. "I need your help."

This was almost an exact repeat of the last time they'd met, and since that had turned out rather swell, Artie went where Finn was dragging him, all the way to the front lobby of the hotel and out the door.

Startled faces looked at them as they went up to the front door of the hotel, but Artie didn't care. He was safe, even if only for the moment, and he'd found Finn again. If they had a moment, Artie might ask him one of those questions he'd squirreled away in his heart, oh, so long ago: *Are you like me?*

CHAPTER TWELVE

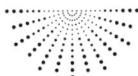

Finn had checked his camera, his EVP recorder, his notes. Everything about Daisy McKee was gone. The footage of his own hotel room, of him leaving and coming back was still there, but the photographs of her hotel room, the voice recording he'd captured, which might or might not have been her, was gone.

His notebook only referenced Ruby and Artie, and in much more detail, as obviously he had one less ghost to contend with. The only thing that saved him from full out panic upon considering that he'd completely changed history and the timeline, was the fact that he'd talked to his Dad. As far as Dad went, his references, his passion about horror movies, everything seemed the same. The way he talked about Mom and Mia was the same.

Finn had checked the website for Finnwood Farms, and it all looked as he remembered it, so maybe it was just the hotel's history that had changed, and the fact that they now only had two ghosts instead of the three had gone completely unremarked by anyone.

So, alternate universe? Alternate timeline? He had no idea, only that he was going to rescue Ruby and Artie and let the chips fall where they might. As long as he had the farm to go home to, he'd be fine.

The rest of the world might be even better for it, having three new, sweet souls, rather than leaving them for dead, for ghosts.

Going down the back stairs in the middle of the night was rather like taking an elevator ride to some black pit. His stomach sank as he went down, gripping the railing tightly so he wouldn't stumble and arrive too late to save Artie. Who, this time, was about to suffer a tragic death full of pain and fear, so sharp and unwarranted, that his cries for help—his cries of *pain*—could be heard by hotel guests over a century later.

For this young man, Arturo Larkin, surely the risk would be worth it. Finn had never really been needed in that way, the way Artie needed him. Sure, he helped out at the farm, had run errands for Nana when she'd been alive, but it was nothing like this. Nothing like the fact that Artie's very existence depended on Finn knowing when he would next die.

With his heart sharp in his chest, he reached the bottom of the stairs, and upon seeing the gentle daylight beneath the bottom of the door, took a deep breath and opened it. There, Artie looked up at him, just at the foot of the steps at the back door to the hotel, bathed in the purple light of an early summer's evening.

He'd been standing by the door as if he had expected Finn all along. Finn heard his gasp of surprise and quickly saw that Horace had a knife in his grimy fist. Ricky was standing close behind him, as if he didn't want to participate but just wanted a first row seat to the gore.

Wanting to pause to weep for the state of humanity, but knowing he needed to save Artie on this day, Finn grabbed Artie and yanked him inside, closing and locking the back door. Outside, he could hear the muttered swearing of the two bullies. Inside, the hotel became a refuge, a nicely decorated refuge that, to Finn's amazement, was still bathed in daylight. It wasn't nighttime, as in his own time, but was still late afternoon in June, 1912.

He thought that opening that door would take him back to his own time, but here he was, still in Artie's time. And he knew what day it was. It was the day that little Ruby had gotten run over by a car. He didn't need to panic because he had a job to do: to save Ruby, now that he'd saved Artie from that knife attack he should have died from.

The floor of the hallway leading from the back door of the hotel to the front lobby was tightly polished, the walls painted a soft white. The ceiling of the hallway leading to the lobby was covered in stamped tin. Low electric bulbs, their cloth wires exposed, trailing like swag beneath each light sconce, told him that the electricity had been put in after the fact, and that, back in the day, nobody knew how to do a good job rewiring. But to his knowledge, the hotel had never suffered any fires from electricity sparks, but had stood proud and strong through all of her refurbishments.

"Where are we going?" asked Artie, and if he sounded a bit breathless, he had good reason.

What he didn't know—couldn't know—was that he had been on the edge of a terrible death, one that would blast him into the history books, earning him pride of place in the presentation about the hotel's ghosts. That morning, he'd been famous; by afternoon, he should have been dead. And would have been, except for Finn.

"Errand of mercy, like before," said Finn, over his shoulder. The paper hadn't said what time Ruby would meet her tragic end, due to lazy reporting, but he knew it was today, in the early evening, when the little family had been passing by the front doors of the hotel. The open front doors, through which Leo would race, looking for excitement, something novel to sniff. "To catch a red rubber ball."

Artie stuck close to his side as they walked through the lobby. Maybe it was to avoid having to look at the mustachioed manager who eyed them suspiciously, even though it was obvious that they were just passing through.

Artie followed Finn's lead so they could save someone. He didn't ask any questions as Finn went to the front door and looked up and down the street.

"What are we looking for?" asked Artie.

Finn paused to look back at him. He knew what was going on and Artie didn't. Though it probably wasn't wise to tell him too much, he deserved to know a little, at least.

"There's a little girl by the name of Ruby," said Finn. "Her little dog, a Jack Russell terrier by the name of Leo, is going to run through this door. Ruby's going to toss her red rubber ball to coax him out. Only it goes in the street and when she chases after it, she's going to get hurt. We need to stop it."

Artie looked at him for a moment, his eyes so very blue and so very focused on him that Finn felt unsteady on his feet. He'd gotten used to being one of the go-along-to-get-along guys, not very exciting, not very noteworthy. Only now, the way Artie was looking at him, excitement rose within him at the thought of being on the verge of changing history again. He felt as though his whole being had been traced with a sharp hand, the outlines of him specific and clear, of who he was and what he might bring with him to contribute to something greater than himself.

All of this raced through him as they stood there, side by side on the polished marble steps of the Harlin Hotel, a grand brick building that had exuded grace and dignity from the first moment the dirt had been ceremoniously broken for the foundation. The gaze that Artie cast upon him was one of trust, as though he wanted to know more but was willing to wait because he knew that Finn would tell him. It made him straighten up, shoulders back.

"What if we just close the front door?" asked Artie simply.

"What?" asked Finn, feeling somewhat deflated, though he loved and adored the fact that Artie was taking him at his word.

The doors to the hotel stood open, probably to catch the early evening breezes. Maybe the manager, who usually stood at attendance most of the time, since they wouldn't have a proper doorman in a town this size, had stepped away, leaving the way open for a cute little dog to race through.

Finn remembered something about that in the article about Ruby's death, and he wished he'd paid more attention now. He'd been so set on the date that it had happened, and wanting to do something about it, that he'd missed this very small detail.

If the door was closed, then Leo couldn't run inside. Then Ruby wouldn't have any reason to toss her red rubber ball for him and get herself hurt. Still, because history had a way of attempting to stay the course, she might get hurt in some other way, so they needed to be vigilant when the little family passed on the sidewalk. Closing the door would surely help in all of this, just the same.

"Good idea," said Finn. "Let's do it. Stand in front of the doors, in case someone tries to open them from the inside."

With a nod, Artie closed the doors, exposing his slender wrists from his shirt cuffs while Finn stood in the street and scanned it up and down.

Turning north, he saw a little family of three on the sidewalk, coming close. The woman had a broad hat and was dressed in a slender skirt and blouse, while her husband in a straw boater with his pencil thin mustache, leaned solicitously toward her, taking her hand.

Ahead of them was Ruby. She wore her sailor dress, the waist of which was quite low. Her skirt furled to her knees over her white stockings, and her trim little boots skipped and danced on the flagstone pavement as her beloved dog, Leo, raced around her heels.

They were coming up the sidewalk quite slowly. It was easy to see that all were distracted by the beautiful evening, of being together in the early summer air between one gentle rainstorm and the next.

Leo was quite excited, being not on a leash, and without even a collar, and was dancing, his mouth open, tongue lolling, eyes bright. This was a well-loved dog, and it clutched at Finn's heart to think of him pining for his young mistress, of having no one to love him as well as Ruby did.

Someone tugged at the hotel door from the inside, the manager perhaps, and Finn nodded at Artie.

"Here they come," he said. "Keep that closed."

With a nod, Artie held onto the curved brass handles with both hands and dug his heels in. Leo raced ahead of his little family and up to the hotel's door and sniffed at Artie's feet.

Artie let go of the door handles, which flew open, the manager sputtering at the two of them, his hands on his hips. But instead of Leo racing inside, Artie scooped the little dog up and held him close to his chest, where he wagged and wriggled, glad to be held. Ruby, with a gasp, dropped her red rubber ball, but as it bounced away and she turned to chase it, he reached out to her and waved at the parents.

"Don't chase it," Finn told her, tugging on her starched sleeve. "Come and get Leo, now. See? Artie's got him safe for you."

"What are you doing with my daughter?" asked the father, with some indignation as he came close, his wife in tow. Any father would have been suspicious at seeing his only daughter being approached by a strange man. The mother, at her husband's side, clutched his elbow and reached out, pulling Ruby close to her, embracing her shoulders.

"Mr. and Mrs. Hopkins," said Finn, quickly, finally remembering their names from the newspaper article. "Her dog was about to race in the hotel lobby, and Ruby's ball has fallen into the street? See?"

He pointed to where the red rubber ball had rolled across the wooden plank that went over the shallow gutter, still filled with rainwater. There it rested a little ways from the edge of the street in a curl of mud.

"I could see she was about to chase it," he said. "Didn't want to do that and get hurt."

Just then, a large Model T ford swerved close to the gutter, tires just missing the red rubber ball, and then with a loud *haooooga*, barreled back into the middle of the street and drove away, leaving slaps of mud behind.

From the way he drove, the driver was drunk, which explained to Finn how it must have happened. Only it wasn't long ago, it was *now*. Now was when it had happened, now was when Finn had stopped it, with Artie's help. But would the father, quite concerned, think that Finn had done something wrong?

"It's true, Mr. Hopkins," said Artie, still cradling Leo and lavishing him with petting. "It was quite a near thing. If not for my friend here—"

"Oh, it's you, Artie," said Mr. Hopkins. "You're the one who brings the paper to my office every morning."

"You take the *Harlin Advocate* and the *Rocky Mountain News*," said Artie, nodding. "And sometimes the *Erie Echo*."

"For the local farm report," said Mr. Hopkins, nodding back.

Tipping his hat to Artie, he crossed the wooden plank to retrieve the red rubber ball from the street. He wiped it off with his hands before putting it in his pocket, and eyed the scene. "Looks like a near miss you fellows saved my daughter from."

"She could have gotten hit by a car," said Mrs. Hopkins, looking pale from beneath the brim of her wide hat. "Oh, I don't think I could have borne that, my dear." She hugged Ruby close and kissed the top of her head, and smoothed her curls. "You are the light of my life."

"And Leo, too," asked Ruby, tilting her head back to look up at her mother.

"And Leo, too," said Mrs. Hopkins. "Though surely we should get that collar and leash and teach Ruby how to control him a bit better?"

"Yes," said Mr. Hopkins.

It was easy to see that perhaps earlier he'd denied that the dog needed a leash and was quickly changing his mind with the evidence presented to him. Just as he'd changed his mind about the danger Finn might have brought to his daughter, once he knew the truth. "You're right, my dear, as you usually are. I'll purchase one in the morning."

Rather than lord it over her husband that she had been right and he wrong, Mrs. Hopkins tipped up her chin for a quick kiss, more of a buss, as they were on the street with plenty of people around.

"I am," she said with a smile, with no ire whatsoever. "Now maybe we can talk about buying that bit of land for a farm, where Ruby and Leo can have all the room to romp and play in."

"And I can get out from behind a desk," said Mr. Hopkins, smiling down at her, as though this was a conversation they'd had many times. "With spring coming on, I'm in the mood for green fields—"

"And harvest moons," said Mrs. Hopkins in a sing-song kind of way, as though she'd been quoting something they both knew.

Mr. and Mrs. Hopkins must have suddenly realized they had an audience standing quite close, for they both looked up as though they were small children who'd been caught with their hands in the cookie jar. Feeling rather bountiful, like a beloved grandma who could not bring herself to scold, Finn smiled.

"Sounds like a plan to me," he said.

127

"I'll take that little one now," said Mr. Hopkins.

He walked up to Artie, who came down from the steps and handed over Leo, who wriggled into Mr. Hopkins' grip and licked the bottom of his chin. Ruby reached up and patted Leo's white behind, while Mrs. Hopkins wrapped her arm around Mr. Hopkins' waist, her other hand on Ruby's shoulder.

"Thank you so much," she said. "Sometimes I think I'm not ready for town life, and this just tells me there's too much going on for me to rest easy. But thank you for saving my Ruby and her Leo."

"You are welcome," said Finn.

"Yes, quite welcome," said Artie.

Artie stayed at Finn's side as Mr. Hopkins tipped his hat and led his small family, his *intact* small family, down the sidewalk, where they crossed the street to the bank, and went along Third Street, as if headed for their own home. All safe and accounted for, all untouched by a barely-averted tragedy.

"That's a job well done," said Finn, puffing out his chest as he smiled at Artie.

Now that Ruby was saved, he'd go back to his own time, and probably see that Ruby's portrait was gone, and her notebook, too. Nobody at the hotel, not even Mrs. Brice, would have any memory that she'd ever been as notable as to be included in the tableaux about ghosts.

Since Finn had saved Artie from death by knife, it only remained that when Finn went back whether time or the universe would determine that Artie would yet die, maybe this time by even more brutal means. If that happened, if that's what he found out when he went back up those back stairs into the nighttime of his own time, with sheet lightning flickering on the far horizon, then he would just have to make another foray to 1912 and save him.

Then again, if time and fate kept upping the ante and moving the fatal day of Artie's death forward in time, one day each time, what would he do then? Stay in the hotel forever, always making notes, always updating his Ghost Force application? He didn't want to think about that just now, so he patted Artie's shoulder, moving close as he went up the stairs and into the hotel.

"You going to be okay?" he asked Artie as they walked through the lobby and quickly to the back door. "That guy had a knife."

"Don't I know it," said Artie. "Those meatheads—"

He stopped as if he was considering whether to trust Finn with the full story, but when they arrived at the back door of the hotel, and Finn's hand was on the nickel-plated knob, he reached out. Maybe he would have grasped Finn's hand in his, or maybe he just was reaching out to stop him. Either way, Finn turned to look at him, his heart pounding, even though the main danger had passed for now.

"What about 'em?" asked Finn. "We could call the cops and let them know—"

"We can't," said Artie. "Horace and Ricky would only tell them exactly what I don't want anyone to know."

Finn didn't ask what that was because he already knew. He'd seen that kind of look on faces before, both men and women, for even in his own time some people still took umbrage with different ways of loving. For the most part, he'd only ever encountered acceptance for who he was and who he loved, who he wanted to love. But back in the day, back in 1912, it was probably a well-guarded secret by those who feared for their very lives at being different. And maybe that was the worst tragedy of all.

CHAPTER THIRTEEN

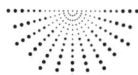

They stepped out into the now-empty alleyway where the wind rushed past Artie's ears. A strange energy swirled around his feet, as though he was caught in a small storm that wanted him to pay attention to it. It was a feeling he was only now recognizing from his other encounters with Finn, like Finn carried some kind of lightning with him, disbursing it with open hands and an open heart, leaving behind energy for anyone who needed it.

Well, Artie had needed it, and still he needed it now. Hiding in his rented room wasn't the answer to his problems, only he didn't know what was. Maybe Finn knew. Maybe Finn could tell him, if only he knew the right questions to ask.

"You going to be okay?" asked Finn. "They're going to keep coming for you, you know."

"I know," said Artie, and his heart sank. This was where they came to every time they met. Finn would go away, and Artie would be alone, never sure when Horace would attack again. Never sure if Finn would come back. "Thank you for the help. And that little girl. How did you know what would happen to her?"

"Another long story," said Finn with a small smile as he dipped his chin and looked at Artie quite gently.

"I'd like to hear it sometime," said Artie, his voice low, meaning it with all of his heart. This strange young man had been there when Artie needed him, but would he be again?

"I've got to go," said Finn. "I need to get ready for tomorrow."

But even as Artie wanted to ask him what he meant, Finn turned to open the door, only it wouldn't budge. Artie had seen the way the manager had looked at them both as they'd tramped through the hotel, eyebrows raised, hands on his hips. Vagrants and hobos weren't well-dressed enough for the Harlin Hotel, and certainly that kind of odd foot traffic would be frowned upon, so it made sense that the door was locked now.

"Do you have a room in the hotel?" asked Artie, suddenly thinking now that it was strange that Finn kept appearing through this one, single door. "You must be rich," he said, trying to make a little joke of it.

"I do have a room," said Finn, tugging on the doorknob, frowning. "On the top floor. It's got a great view, it's got—"

Blowing out a breath, Finn frowned at the door, and then looked at Artie. "I'm going to go around front, see if I can get in that way."

"Do you want me to wait?" asked Artie, for not only did he owe Finn, it might be safer if he wasn't ever alone so that Horace and Ricky didn't take another chance at backing him into a corner.

"No," said Finn, but he didn't sound so sure. "I have to go. I'm so sorry."

With that, Finn raced down the alley onto the sidewalk, disappearing from view. Leaving Artie all alone in the alley that, for now, was mercifully empty save for the tin trash cans, scraps of trash and paper, and the ever-present-smell of urine.

Alleys were never salubrious spots, even on the best of days, and yet he found himself frozen there. It was almost as if he was rooted where he stood, waiting for something to happen to him.

What he really needed to do was to go inside the boarding house for dinner, eat as fast as he could, and then lock himself in his room for the night. It wasn't a pleasant prospect, but until he could make up his mind about taking the train north, it was the best he could do.

It wasn't a handful of minutes before Finn came back around the corner. His face was flushed as he raced toward Artie as though he felt he'd left him unattended and was rushing in to save him yet again. Only there was nothing to save him from, as he was quite alone and safe for the moment.

"What happened?" asked Artie. "Did the manager throw you out?"

"The hotel didn't change—I don't have a room," said Finn, shaking his head. "I got all the way up there, but it's just an attic storage now—"

"A what?" asked Artie. He knew what an attic storage was, he just didn't understand how a hotel room could turn into storage at a moment's notice. "Maybe you were on the wrong floor?"

"I checked all the floors," said Finn. "I think it only works if I go in the back door and up the back stairs, but I don't know—I'm so fucked. The manager yelled at me and told me he'd call the cops if I went in there again."

"Uh—"

Artie wasn't used to being the one doing the rescuing, but he sure owed Finn for more than once being there when Horace and Ricky had been intent on teaching Artie a lesson about how to be more like them. Which, them being who they were, was the last thing he wanted. The other last thing he wanted was to see that expression on Finn's face, a sort of lost look, like everything good in the world had just vanished.

Overhead, the sky was growing darker as the sun settled behind the clouds that rolled along the tops of the mountains to the west. The colors of the brick buildings on either side of the alley were dusking to purple and blue, and a bit of a breeze brought the chill of early evening with it.

It might rain sooner rather than later, but that was the way of early summer, and nothing to fret about. Yet it wasn't fun to sleep out of doors, and if Finn didn't have his hotel room, he'd need somewhere to stay.

This idea of offering to help was more pleasurable than it ought to be, as Artie knew well enough not to reach out to anyone—or trust anyone. Yet, they'd gotten along, they'd shared a meal. Finn had been so nonchalant about Daisy and Maude being in a relationship, and he needed help. Needed *Artie's* help. And, if Artie helped Finn, then maybe Finn would answer all those questions constantly whirling in Artie's head.

"You can stay with me," said Artie. "I can spot you two bits for dinner. Mrs. Clarkson probably won't charge you for sleeping on my floor tonight, and maybe she'll maybe loan us a blanket and pillow."

"You'd do that for me?" asked Finn. His blue eyes were wide and he looked a little pale, as though focusing on what Artie was saying to him was harder than it ought to be. "You don't even know me."

"I know you well enough," said Artie with a shrug. "Besides, every time I see you, you're saving someone, like you're a hero. And you saved me, twice now. I owe you."

"You don't," said Finn, but it seemed like he meant something else with these words, for his blue eyes were dark, like he'd lost something very dear to him. "But I'm going to take you up on that, and maybe the door will be unlocked in the morning."

The door being unlocked in the morning wouldn't change a damn thing except maybe expose Finn to more of the hotel manager's direct wrath. Not that Finn deserved that, as he obviously wasn't a hobo or a vagrant.

"C'mon, then," said Artie with a wave. "We'll settle things with Mrs. Clarkson, and then we can eat."

Artie led the way into the back door of the boarding house, into the little mud room where they washed their hands and faces as the smells of cooking drifted along the narrow hallway. He offered Finn some of the Macassar oil Mrs. Clarkson kept for boarders, but Finn sniffed at the bottle, and then waved it away. Checking for change in his pocket, Artie went into the dining hall with Finn close at his heels.

They went into the dining hall and sat at the table with all the other boarders, with Horace and Ricky at the head where they always were. They glowered at the two of them as Mrs. Clarkson came up to them, apron strings flying and a huge bowl of boiled carrots in her hands.

"You're late, young man," she said. "And who's this?"

"He's my friend, Finn," said Artie, jerking a thumb over his shoulder, completely unaffected by her scolding tone, as he knew she meant well and was just busy. "I've got two bits for his meal. He's going to stay with me tonight, sleeping on the floor, if that's okay."

"If it's just for one night," she said. "I can loan you a pillow and blanket. Now, where's them two bits?"

Artie handed her a quarter and led the way to two empty seats at the end of the table. They sat down, bent their heads for prayer, and did their best to keep up as the bowls and platters came around.

It was just the usual meal, beef stew, boiled carrots, biscuits, butter, and honey. Mrs. Clarkson set a generous though simple table, so Artie couldn't understand why Finn looked so astounded as he took servings of the food and put them on his plate.

"What is it?" asked Artie, bending close, enjoying the excuse to be near.

"Everything smells so good," said Finn. "I've never seen carrots that bright before."

Artie leaned back to look down at his pile of carrots, which were early spring ones, and had no idea how to respond to this.

"And why is everything so brown?" asked Finn.

"So brown?" asked Artie, completely bewildered by the question.

"The walls are brown, and the tablecloth, it's not plastic, it's—"

"It's an oilcloth tablecloth, young man," said Mrs. Clarkson as she sat down at the head of the table. "And brown's a good sturdy color that doesn't show dirt, so if you've a mind to eat at my table then you best keep your eyes in your head."

"Sure," said Finn with a gulp. "I mean, yes, ma'am."

It was when the boarders around the table settled into their meal that Artie realized how out of place Finn looked. Sure, in the alley, both times, he'd seen that Finn's clothes were too tight, or made of a finer material. And sure his hair was cut differently, and he had broad shoulders and carried himself differently. But now, with ten other folks Artie could compare him to, Finn stood out like a marble carving in a field of corn. His teeth were white and straight, and he had a glow of good health, and certainly the height to match. Not that anyone around the table looked sickly, no. But Finn was different and there was no getting around that.

As the meal progressed, Finn ate heartily, finishing everything, and looking like he enjoyed the apple crumble that Mrs. Clarkson served. After they'd eaten, Mrs. Clarkson handed them two blankets and a pillow with a clean pillowslip, and then turned to the dishes with the hired girl.

Quickly, Artie slipped up the stairs to his room, with Finn quick on his heels. His heart was pounding, not because of the stairs, but because he was going to have Finn in his room all night. It might mean nothing to Finn, but it meant something to him. To have that companionship, that quiet conversation. With another fellow. A fellow who was, maybe, possibly, like him. Or, at the very least, one who wouldn't turn away if Artie, at long last, opened his heart again.

Horace and Ricky didn't follow them up the stairs, as they might have done had Artie been alone, but he had Finn with him. As for how long he'd be safe with Finn at his side, he had maybe a day, which might be enough to decide, in the end, that going to Wyoming was the best, safest thing to do.

But he was tired of this, tired of looking over his shoulder, tired of being afraid. Why couldn't he be like other fellows? Why couldn't he look at a girl, take her hand, and ask her to marry him? Because that was just another way of hiding, that's why, and it wouldn't be fair to the girl. Still it was strange, all of it.

Once they got to the room and Artie placed the extra bedding on the end of his bed. Artie stared at Finn, and Finn stared back, seemingly nervous about something, even though they were quite safe.

"Thank you for the meal," said Finn. "I'll pay you back somehow."

"Aw, think nothing of it," said Artie, waving the offer away. He went over to lock the door and considered moving the dresser in front of it; he actually started doing it, then he stopped. "I usually block the door, you see. To keep them from coming in while I sleep."

"That's rough," said Finn. "How long has this been going on?"

"This is the second night," said Artie. "After you rescued me the first time, I figured it was smart. I have to work in the morning and can't never sleep with one eye open."

Finn looked around the room, which held the bed and the dresser and a single table, with no chair. "No books?" He asked gently.

"I have a compass," said Artie, feeling a tad desperate to keep Finn interested enough to stay. "Here."

Going to the as yet unmoved dresser, Artie pulled out the small brass compass and carried it over to Finn. He popped the tiny button with his fingernail to open the compass, which, instead of gently pointing to true north, lazily swung back and forth back and forth before settling on Finn.

"That's not north," said Finn.

"I know," said Artie. "But I don't know why it's happening. Stand over there, and I'll try it again."

Finn moved to the door, where he could have easily gone out and slipped away, leaving Artie on his own. But he didn't. He stood there and patiently watched while Artie spun around and then settled the compass in his hand as he stopped.

"It still points at you," said Artie. "That's the darnedest thing I ever did see."

"Where did you get the compass from?" asked Finn. "Maybe it's defective."

"I don't know," said Artie. "I've always just had it. Maybe someone gave it to me at the orphanage when I was little and I just kept it."

Finn looked at Artie, keeping his hands at his sides like a soldier at attention. But on his face was something else, a sweep of something gentle and kind and sympathetic all mixed all together. He seemed to be assessing Artie and his situation all at once, coming to some conclusion he wasn't yet ready to share with Artie.

"Beer's legal, right?" asked Finn. He walked over to the bed and leaned over it to look out the window. "Why don't we get some beers and come back here and drink it. You said the saloon was pretty skanky, but maybe we can buy beer to go."

"We could get a bucket of beer," said Artie, slowly, thinking this through, not letting himself linger over the statement that beer was legal, when of course it was. When would it not be? "We could go sit on the roof."

He fully expected that the suggestion would be dismissed out of hand, but Finn nodded.

"Can we afford that?" he asked. "I'm afraid I don't have any money."

"It's fifty cents for a bucket of beer, and ten cents to take the bucket," said Artie. "We get the dime back when we return the bucket. We could grab two of those glasses from Mrs. Clarkson, if we're careful not to break them."

"Okay," said Finn. "And if we see those guys, should we run for it or fight?"

Artie liked the way Finn thought, and smiled. He was willing to fight or run, also, whatever the situation called for, but it was nice having someone on his side who was also trying to think through those things.

"Either," he said. "But I think you and I could take 'em together."

Checking his pocket for change, Artie unlocked the door and headed down the stairs, Finn close at his heels. The dining hall and kitchen were still winding down from dinner, so it was easy to slip out the front door and go across to the saloon, which, even at this early hour, was hopping with people, mostly rough-looking men, and blaring with music.

Artie led the way to the little side door and slipped in, with Finn following, quickly bought small bucket of beer, and walked out again. On their way across the street, they narrowly missed getting run over by a spider-wheeled automobile.

Back at the boarding house, Finn grabbed two small glasses, and then they were up the stairs again, without ever encountering Horace and Ricky.

"Which way to the roof?" asked Finn as he trotted up the stairs next to Artie.

"This way," said Artie. "Those fellows don't care to think what's above their heads, but this little door here—" Artie opened a small door at the end of the hallway on the top floor. "This door here leads to the maintenance stairs to the roof. The view is beautiful—"

He stopped, thinking how nice it was to have someone to share this with. How he could spend time with a guy who somehow had stepped into his life just when he needed him. Who marveled at spring carrots, and wasn't afraid—not of anything.

CHAPTER FOURTEEN

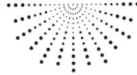

S eeing Artie just where he'd expected him to be had been surreal, as had saving Ruby, and having dinner at the boarding house, eating the freshest carrots he'd ever tasted. He'd traveled back through time on purpose, *again.* He'd done what he came to do, only now he couldn't get home. Was it forever? Would he be trapped in 1912, growing older and older each year until the future came around?

Mom and Dad and Mia would miss him, for sure, and it made his heart ache to think of missing them. He didn't want to stay in 1912, he wanted to go home, but until the back door of the Harlin Hotel was opened, he was stuck.

It was odd about Artie's compass, too. There couldn't be anything particularly magnetic about him, but maybe the back stair had been charged in some way, like with too much electricity, or maybe it just happened to pass through a space-time vortex.

All of these unfamiliar notions were making his head ache, so he concentrated on following Artie up the narrow, dark stairway to the roof of the boarding house, a flat, tarred surface with only a few vents and one electric wire running from a wooden pole and down to the street below.

Finn went up to the edge of the roof and looked down at the street, which was nearly empty. There were a few streetlights, but they were spaced very far apart. They were also quite dimly lit, as though the town itself was going to sleep, and nobody expected that anybody would want to be out when it was bedtime. There was a Mayberry feel to it all, with the slow sleepy bark of a dog, the chug of a train down by the tracks with its carefully patterned whistle warning travelers to stay clear as the train passed to the west. The low chatter from an open window somewhere.

Along the distant horizon stretched the edges of the mountains against the starry sky, which Finn could see quite quite clearly due to the lack of smog and the fact that there was hardly any light pollution. What a sky it was, dark, midnight blue, pale at the western edge, like a flair of fine, faint lace. To the south, across the silver ribbon of river, the far horizon reached dark and long, and above that flickered the sheet lightning, a long-distant and silent dance of light.

"Sure is pretty," said Finn, as he felt Artie come up beside him.

"I like to sit up here," said Artie. "Now that it's nice. I arrived in town in winter, and was mostly in my room, but then found those little stairs. Horace and Ricky never come up here."

"They're meatheads," said Finn, echoing the term Artie had used for them earlier, liking the old-fashioned feel of it on his tongue.

"I was thinking of heading north," said Artie, quite out of the blue. "It's nice that you're here, that you rescued me from them, but you can't keep doing that."

Finn turned to look at him.

"Can't I?" asked Finn aloud, though the question was for himself.

Artie had died three times, once by being shoved off the roof, the next by getting beaten to death, and the next by being stabbed to death. Finn had saved him each time, it seemed, just by showing up. Each time, Fate seemed to up the ante and move Artie's death forward by exactly one day.

It was as if Artie was meant to die, so what was Finn to do? Stay in the hotel forever and come down each time to rescue Artie from what was coming at him? How long would Horace and Ricky keep it up? How long could Finn keep it up? He had no idea.

"Is there a spot we can sit and watch the sheet lightning from?" asked Finn. "I can imagine you've been on your feet all day."

"It's nothing to me," said Artie, but he led the way to the other side of the roof where there was a hump beneath the tar where they could prop themselves, knees bent.

As they settled on it, the bucket carefully stowed at Artie's feet, they slowly drank their slightly warm, slightly flat glasses of beer and watched the evening come down.

A million questions raced through Finn's mind as to what he should do. The beer, for all it was flat and warm, was pretty potent and made his head swim a little. Along the far, dark horizon, sheet lightning raced, and he made himself focus on that and how he could fix all this without screwing everything up. Or was he crazy imagining that he was some kind of superhero who could mess with time and be able to brave out the consequences?

"I've got a penny for 'em," said Artie, gently.

"For what?" asked Finn, dragging his attention away from his own muddled thoughts.

"You're thinking mighty hard for a fellow who just saved the day," said Artie. "Actually, we saved the day. You an' me together. Twice."

"It's more than that, it's more," said Finn, though he couldn't really explain what he meant without saying what he knew, that Artie's death throes got more horrible each time they happened. "Never mind me," he said with a shake of his head. "What do you do when you're not helping me with rescues?"

"I sell papes, penny a piece," said Artie. He smiled, as though pleased with himself. "Extra, extra, read all about it."

"Oh, so that's where the shouting was coming from—" Finn stopped himself, but at least a part of the nighttime sounds that had led him down the back stairs were now identified.

"You're a paperboy," said Finn with a nod.

"No," said Artie, a little stern. "I'm a distribution assistant. I work for Joe Moody at the depot. He buys the papers off the daily train in the morning, and I sell them to the newsies, who sell the papes on the corner. I've got two newsies now, though maybe I only have one, on account of Bobby Ross can't be counted on."

"What does he do, steal from you?" asked Finn, barely able to focus on the conversation on account of the worry spinning in the background of everything.

"No," said Artie. He took a swallow of his beer. The nighttime had settled down enough so that it was quite dark and the starlight reflected in his eyes, on the rim of his glass. "His mother likes him at home. Stanley is my go-to kid. He's always on time and sells the heck out of those papes."

"Papes?"

"It's the lingo for newspapers, if you're the business," said Artie. It felt like his mouth was running a mile a minute, now that he had someone to talk to. "I really want my own shed, you know? I want to buy the papes directly off the train myself and distribute them directly to the newsies instead of going through Joe Moody. He's a good guy, you know, but I want to be my own man. I'm hoping to buy his shed off him one day."

"That sounds like a pretty good dream," said Finn. Maybe it was a simple dream by modern standards, but in 1912, Artie was prepared to do everything he needed to get there.

"As long as those creeps leave me alone." Artie nodded as he finished the last swallow of beer in his glass.

Artie poured them both another glass of beer, which meant the bucket was empty. That was fine. Too much more of this kind of strong beer, and Finn knew he'd be talking up a storm, getting chummy, curling up beside the nearest warm body like a cat seeking affection. At least he wasn't a mean drunk, and it didn't seem like Artie was either, for he smiled at Finn while he drank his beer.

A comfortable silence settled between them as the sheet lightning shifted away and the stars came out, one by one. There was so little light pollution, almost none, that the Milky Way twisted overhead like a white ribbon, dotted with darker places between faraway galaxies, drizzled with diamonds.

It was glorious to see the nighttime sky like this, and made it worth it to have come back in time. But he didn't want to stay in 1912, not by a long shot. Home was home. Home was Mom and Dad and Mia and the bees and the lavender. What was he thinking, wanting to move away from that? Ghost hunting passion or no, he was a fool—and he wanted to cry.

"Are you okay?" asked Artie. "Maybe we should finish up and then we can get some shut eye."

"Sure," said Finn.

He swallowed the rest of his beer, blinking back the tears. Then, lightheaded he stood up and offered Artie his hand. Artie took it, warm and sure, and together they made their way down the tiny stairs, latching the access to the roof, and tiptoed to Artie's room. Artie put the bucket by the door.

"We need to take those glasses down and wash 'em. And I need to wash up and pee," said Artie. "I expect you do, too."

"I'll wait," said Finn.

He was a private person that way, and everything was feeling quite intimate already. Sitting on the bed, he ran his fingers through his hair and waited for Artie to go downstairs and then come back.

When he did, Finn snuck down the hallway to the bathroom, which turned out to be large and old-fashioned, the white tiles and paint glinting in the overhead bulb, from which dangled a chain. He got a drink of water from the faucet, peed and washed his face and hands, drying them on the communal rolling towel, thought about germs, then headed back to Artie's room.

There, Artie had made a bed for Finn on the floor, and even as Finn stepped inside the room, Artie locked the door, and shoved the dresser in front of it as quietly as he could.

"I'm sorry," he said. "I know you're here to protect me, and I appreciate that, but I wouldn't want those fellows busting in, you know?"

"I get it," said Finn.

His head was really swimming, but the darker thoughts were being shoved aside by the fact that Artie was so near. The fear of not being

145

able to get back home mixed Finn's awareness of everything Artie was doing.

"You should get some rest," said Artie. He was quickly unlacing his boots, and taking off his socks and trousers and shirt, which left him standing in a pair of neck to thigh cotton underwear that in the light of the simple overhead bulb showed everything. Every line of Artie's body, every curve, shifting across his bare collarbones, tracing across his upper thighs.

Artie looked at him and blinked slowly, as if realizing that, in his seeming comfort of being with Finn, he had just bared himself almost to the skin. Making himself vulnerable for whatever Finn might say.

"My underwear's a little different," said Finn, as he got undressed, though that probably wasn't the only thing. All of his clothes were different, and the fact that he was half a head taller, and had more meat on his bones was another. Artie was trusting him, all without words, so it was up to Finn to not break that trust, to make Artie feel at ease. Though it was hard, with all the dark thoughts crowding inside his head.

He laid his folded jeans and socks on the top of the dresser, where Artie had placed his compass, and kept his t-shirt on because while it wasn't exactly cold in the room, it wasn't warm either. Besides, Artie was covered from neck to thigh, so Finn would do likewise.

Finn tugged at the elastic of his briefs, just to make sure he was decent, and also because he was consciously aware that both of them were together in a small, rented room in the year 1912, and he needed to touch something that came from the future, and the elastic was the only thing. Did they even have elastic in 1912? His mind continued to whirl, even as Artie nodded at him, as though to tell him that everything was going to be all right.

"I'll turn out the light," said Artie.

As he crossed the room, he passed quite near Finn's shoulder, so Finn could feel the warmth of his skin. Yet again the idea of how strange this all was surged over him. Only a few days ago, Artie had been a rough, badly reproduced portrait in a tableau about the ghosts that haunted the Harlin Hotel. Now he was here in this room with

Finn, more real than anything Finn had ever expected, beautiful and pale and determined.

After turning out the light, Artie got into his narrow bed against the wall and shifted around. Finn crawled into his little bed on the floor, laid his head on the starched pillow, and tried to fall asleep.

Without his phone or his laptop or the internet to distract him, he would have thought that he'd fall asleep quite easily. Except now the beer was wearing off, and the silence all around, the lack of noise from the street, was letting all the thoughts, *all* of them, stream through his head like a cinematic movie.

What would happen if he never went home? Everyone would be miserable and he would be beyond grief.

What would happen if Horace and Ricky busted in on them while they were sleeping? There would be a fight, and maybe fate would decide that both Finn and Artie would breathe their last and nobody would ever know what happened to him. Worse, nobody would be there to mourn Artie, because there was nobody who would care, nobody but Finn.

He sat straight up in bed, clutching his t-shirt, gasping. His chest ached with a deep, sinking longing—for home, for something familiar. For Dad's voice on the phone telling him to come home, come home to the farm.

"Are you all right, Finn?" asked Artie, also sitting up.

Finn could see the outline of Artie's shadow in the half-darkness. See the gleam of his bare arms, and he sensed that Artie was looking at him.

"I'm scared," he said, admitting it full out, he who was never scared of anything in his life. "I think I'm homesick, and it *hurts*—"

"I never get homesick, on account of I don't have a home," said Artie, quite slowly. "But I do know what it's like to be scared."

"Do you?" asked Finn, his fear mixing with his appreciation that Artie seemed to care about him the way he cared about Artie.

"I do," said Artie. "I'm afraid of all kinds of things, so I know what it's like. Why don't you—" He paused, and took a slow breath, as though he'd come to a decision after a long conversation with himself.

147

"Why don't you bring your pillow up here and sleep with me? That floor has to be as hard as all get out. We could—we could keep each other safe."

Having never heard a better idea, Finn leaped up, grabbing his pillow and one of the blankets. He laid the blanket out over Artie, in the dark, and then put the pillow in the space Artie had left beside him.

Then, as the last dregs of the beer faded away from his system, taking with it the question as to whether this would lead to something he might not be ready for, he slid into the narrow bed. The mattress was a little hard, but the sheets were clean and soft, and the pillow the perfect cushion for his head. Beside him, Artie made room for him, scooting close to the wall, his back to it as he lay on his side, hands beneath his pillow.

"We'll look out for each other," said Finn, echoing what Artie had said earlier.

"I've never had nobody looking out for me before," said Artie, low, soft, and it seemed that every ache and sorrow in the world was cradled in those words.

"Now you do," said Finn, stoutly, doing his best to chase away the terrible loneliness of his homesickness, focusing on Artie, who was right there in the bed with him. "Until I figure a way to get home, you're kind of stuck with me."

It might have been his imagination, but he felt Artie smile, felt his body relax in the darkness. Saw the shimmer in his eyes. Saw the curve of his neck was a shadow against the wall, his bare wrists tucked beneath his pillow.

Finn rolled on his side facing Artie, but their knees bumped, so he rolled the other way, and settled his length beneath the covers. Behind him, he felt Artie scoot closer, felt the gentle weight of Artie's forehead between his shoulder blades.

Then came the slight press of Artie's clasped hands against Finn's spine, as though Artie was snuggling as close as he dared, as though Finn was the first bit of human comfort Artie had known for a good long time.

He was glad to do it. Glad to be someone to someone. Even if he never got home, he had this, what he was sharing with Artie—human comfort in the darkness. But he wanted to get home, wanted to get home more than anything else, except to save Artie from the fate that awaited him.

Could he do both? Could he? His mouth was dry and he longed for a drink of water, but it was too late at night, and he didn't want to wake Artie up just for a simple drink of water. He would wait until morning and trust that his mind, once it wasn't addled with beer, would come up with a solution that would work for everything.

CHAPTER FIFTEEN

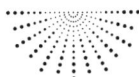

The morning found Finn with a muzzy head, bordering on a headache, and an armful of Artie. He hadn't meant to get so cozy in the night, but there he was, with Artie tucked in his arms as if he'd always been there and always would be. Warm and breathing slowly, softly, his breath whispering against Finn's neck. He wanted to stay like this forever and he wanted to go home at the same time. But it was hard to let go, hard to move away, as Artie woke up and looked up at him.

It was Artie who broke the embrace, Artie who scrambled over Finn and out of bed, and who stood there in his cotton underdrawers that showed Finn how hard he was breathing, how panicked.

"I'm not, you know, one of those fellows," he said, eyes wide as he tugged at his underwear, as though wanting to hide his morning erection. "One of those fellows who likes other fellows."

"Natural as breathing," said Finn, as he adjusted himself under the covers. "And besides, who cares if you are. I'm one. So what?"

Though even as he said it, the weight of Artie's words hit him. Artie had, in a way, made a confession. Nobody who wasn't worried about being gay ever defended themselves against it. Artie just had. And Finn had responded in kind. *Yes, I'm like you.* Which obviously wasn't making Artie feel any calmer about it, the way he was so quickly getting dressed, his movements stiff and jerky.

"It's okay, really, it is."

Finn got out, tugged at his white briefs, and got dressed, too. Maybe if they were both dressed, Artie would stop stumbling about the room as though he was still drunk, maybe he'd stop shaking.

"I shouldn't have told you," said Artie. "Please forget I said anything. Please?"

Finn helped him move the dresser out of the way, almost dragging the heavy piece of furniture over his sneakered foot in his haste to get through to Artie before he fell apart.

"I'm not going to tell anyone, ever," said Finn. He reached out to touch Artie on the shoulder, anywhere, and when he did, his hand felt warm against Artie's cool skin. "I know in 1912 it's a big deal, and you could get arrested, I know all about that."

"I could get beaten up," said Artie. He patted Finn's hand and gently pushed away, and went to stand by the door, looking at Finn with wide, worried eyes. He jingled the change in his pocket. "That's why Horace and Ricky were after me. Somehow, they found out. Somehow Horace knows Cecil, and I told Cecil, before I knew that I shouldn't."

"Sounds like you think trusting anyone at this point would end in disaster," said Finn. "But not with me. I won't tell anyone, I promise. You think I'd out you like that?"

Something in Artie's expression told Finn that Artie was on the verge of asking him what he meant by that, but outside the windows, a pair of church bells were ringing, each a slow echo of each other that tolled across the rooftops.

"Hell," said Artie. He tugged on his suspenders, and buttoned the last of his shirt collar buttons. "I've got to go meet Joe Moody at the depot, and get those papes moving."

"I'll come with you," said Finn, not wanting to let Artie out of his sight. "But what about breakfast?"

"I never have time," said Artie. "I usually get a cup of coffee from

Mrs. Clarkson, but I'm late as it is. Grab that pillow, would you? We'll take the bucket back this afternoon."

In some haste, Finn grabbed the pillow, while Artie bundled up the blankets beneath his arm. Quickly checking that the hallway was empty, they hurried down the stairs to where Mrs. Clarkson was in the kitchen. Handing off the bedding, Artie led him out the back door to the alley, which, in the bright morning sunshine, only looked marginally better than it had the night before.

Finn stopped to tug on the back door of the hotel, but was firmly locked. His heart sank, but at least he would be able to stick around and make sure Artie was safe from those thugs, and that was worth it. He hurried after Artie and caught up with him.

Together they headed down the alley to Third Street, past the looming factory on the left, which would be replaced by condos by Finn's time, and the squat, almost elegant brick building on the right, which, in the future, held an internationally renowned cheese shop. Then they went down Main Street to where the sidewalk ended at the railroad tracks.

Artie led Finn to a small, rough shack that was dwarfed by the larger brick building that was the train depot. Inside the shack, bright with the morning sun coming through the bare glass windows, was an older man with greying hair. He wore a brown jacket that was greasy along the edges, and he was sorting through piles of newspapers that showed where they were from by a large, flopping label that was tied to a rock with a sturdy string. *Harlin Advocate. Rocky Mountain News. Trinidad Times. Brighton Banner.*

None of the newspapers were even remotely recognizable to Finn, except maybe the *Rocky Mountain News*, which had closed down ages ago. Only now, in the past, it was a going concern, and the daily morning paper was a fast-moving business.

Finn thought to offer assistance, but Artie and Joe knew what they were doing, so the best he could do to help was to hold the handle of the sturdy handcart to keep it level as Artie rolled the papers and filled it up. When they were finished, Joe Moody wiped his glistening forehead with a large handkerchief.

"This fellow going to keep helping you?" asked Joe, his words clipped, like he was from back east. "I can't pay him unless he helps you sell more papes."

"It's just for today," said Artie.

"Well, give him fifty cents, then," said Joe. "I can spare that, at least."

Fifty cents in Finn's day wasn't a lot, but back in 1912, it would keep him in coffee, at least. Maybe he could buy both him and Artie breakfast later. He would just have to ignore his growling stomach till then and focus on the work in front of him to keep the panic away. Focus on the work instead of the fact that he'd just spent the night with Artie, he and Artie in each other's arms. That was a first. His dates with other guys, very few, ended with brief fumbles standing up, and never with a sleepover. Artie was different, in every way possible.

The sun was bright, the packing plant bustling with men, steam coming from the pipes. Artie hustled them past the packing plant and the power plant both, shoving the cart uphill, only letting Finn take his place beside him when he insisted.

"The two of them work at the plant," said Artie, tightening his fingers around the handle of the cart. "I try and lay low so maybe they'll forget about me."

Finn knew well and good that, until the end of time, or so it seemed, Horace and Ricky would be coming for Artie, each time nastier than the last. They would never forget about him. He didn't know the words to explain any of this, so he stayed quiet and concentrated on helping Artie push the cart up the hill, which felt quite steep, until they reached the front of the Harlin Hotel.

There, a boy with brown hair and shining brown eyes waited for them. He wore knee pants and long stockings, lace up boots, and a jacket that was open, showing his suspenders. He looked like a charming picture, like he knew what Finn's expectations were about how boys looked in 1912 and wanted to live up to them.

"Hey, Artie," said the boy, waving his cap, coming up to them on the corner.

"Hey, Stanley," said Artie, his smile quick and easy. "This is Finn. He's helping us today, okay?"

"Hello, Finn," said Stanley, bright and breezy. "Am I going to get a dime again today?" He asked, moving on to obviously more important matters. "You can get a lot of candy for a dime, you know."

"I hope you're not spending it all on candy," said Artie. He ruffled Stanley's hair, and then began pulling out rolled newspapers and placing them, end up, in the green canvas sack that Stanley wore around his shoulder. "I'll write that down, so go and sell papes. I'll come back and help after my rounds."

"Thanks, Artie," said Stanley. He put on his cap and tipped it in Finn's direction, but it was easy to see he was an industrious lad and not distracted by new people.

Carefully looking both ways, he hopped over the open ditch and crossed the dirt street until he got to the other side. Which was, to Finn's surprise, not the Dickens Opera House, but a bank, which seemed regal and old fashioned even for 1912. Stanley unfurled one of the papers, scanned the front page, and then held it like a banner.

"Extra, extra!" shouted Stanley in a clear voice. "Earthquake in Alaska, shots fired in Hungarian Parliament. Read all about it! Penny a paper!"

All of this was long ago history to Finn, but instead of focusing on that, and how it made him all stirred up inside, he concentrated on helping Artie push the cart up the street. They went along in the sunshine, going quite slowly as though there was no rush. They stopped at various businesses, handing out papers to the butcher, the barber's, the shoe shine boy, the grocers, the milliners, all one after the other.

Everyone was working, seemingly cheerful in the clear June morning. It was so different than the town of Harlin that Finn knew in his own time, where people grabbed their coffees and jumped in their cars and raced off to work, with nobody talking to anyone they didn't have to. In his own future, there were no cheery hellos, not even grumpy ones such as they received at the end of the block where the downtown area began to turn residential. If it was always like this, would it be so bad to stay behind in 1912?

When the downtown started to turn into farmland, they crossed the street and began the trek south, walking in the shade of the two story buildings, some wooden, but mostly brick. When they stopped in at Ziegfeld's Diner to drop off a stack of papers, Finn saw that up ahead a block, Mr. and Mrs. Hopkins, with Ruby and Leo in tow, were going into a store.

As they got closer, Finn realized it wasn't a store but a real estate office. The Hopkins family was probably looking at farmland, so they could get away from the bustle that was Harlin. To the Hopkins family, Harlin was a bustle, but to Finn, it was slow and sedate, friendly and nice, the way a small town should be. If he had to stay in 1912, there were worse places to be, for sure. The thought made him want to go home, now more than ever, but he couldn't leave Artie behind when he was in danger.

Finally, they stopped at the corner in front of the bank where Stanley was selling the last of his papes, taking a penny for each, which he stuck in his pocket.

"Got any papes left?" asked Stanley. "And did you see? You're on page three! You're a hero. Why didn't you say?"

"Heroes don't say that they're heroes," said Finn, quickly, as he could sense Artie's embarrassment.

"Take a look anyhow," said Stanley. He grabbed a copy of the *Harlin Advocate* from Artie's cart and snapped it open, like someone who'd been handling large sheets of newsprint paper his whole life. "Says here, lookit: *Young Artie Larkin, risking life and limb, scrambled down to the roaring bank of St. Vrain Creek to aid the trembling and pale Daisy McKee, who had lost her handsome fiancé on the tragic sinking of the RMS Titanic*—say," said Stanley. "Do you reckon she was going to try and drown herself in the river?"

"She was," said Artie. His voice was low, as though he was concerned about the attention Stanley's high, clear voice was bringing, and how people coming out of the bank slowed to listen.

"They took your picture an' everything," said Stanley. He pushed the paper in front of Artie and Finn so they could take a good long look. And there, just like in the portrait over the lion-legged table, was the picture of Artie, nice and clear and sharp, as though the photographer had taken extra pains with it. "You should clip it and save it for your grandchildren, Artie," said Stanley, happily closing the paper and handing it to him. "Then you can tell them the story of when you risked life and limb."

"That I will," said Artie. "Here's a penny for the paper, mister." He laughed a little as he handed over a copper penny, and also a bright, shining dime. "And this, in case I forget. Come by the shack later for your weekly pay, okay? Joe Moody will have it for you."

"Sure thing," said Stanley, handing over the pennies in his pocket, of which there was quite a lot. "Do you need any help selling the rest? Looks like you still got some in your cart."

"They printed extra," said Artie. He pulled out a notebook and a stub of a pencil from his back pocket, and scribbled in it before putting it away. "You run along and buy that candy. Enjoy yourself. You earned it."

With a wave of his cap, Stanley was off, making a beeline for one of the shops along the street. Artie turned to Finn.

"We can sell these quick, and then we can go get something to eat at the diner," he said. "But we have to shout to sell."

"Okay," said Finn, but he felt dubious about the whole thing.

If he wanted to avoid affecting the past in any way, and he was well beyond that already, then standing and shouting on a street corner would surely not be the best way to avoid attention. Still, if they wanted to go eat, they needed to sell papes. He picked up a copy of the *Brighton Banner*, a less popular paper, it seemed, scanned the headline for something interesting to shout about, and raised it high, feeling foolish, but having fun.

"Extra, extra," he said very loudly. "Body of steward aboard the *RMS Titanic* recovered. William Thomas Kerley's body recovered and buried at sea!"

A woman in a wide straw hat perched above her forehead must have felt sorry for him, for she stopped, fished out a penny from her curved, beaded purse, and bought a copy of the *Brighton Banner* from him. Then she swirled her skirts to get past him and went up the street in her summer gloves and pointed shoes and large hat. Looking at her was like seeing something in a picture, and for a moment he felt dizzy, stumbling against Artie.

"Are you okay?" asked Artie. "We're almost done. Hold that paper high, hold it high, and shout!"

Finn did his best, half-laughing, half shaking his head. In another half an hour, all the papers were sold. Artie took a copy of the *Harlin Advocate* and tore out the page that the article about him was on, which he carefully folded and put in his back pocket. The rest of the paper he handed to the shoeshine boy on the corner, and then led the way to Ziegfeld's Diner, just up one block.

Finn's stomach was growling, and his head felt light, his feet unsteady beneath him. Was this happening because he was stuck in the past and his body was adjusting? Or was he still in his room, in the dark, in the early hours of the morning, having a complete brain wipe-out and just imagining that he was here?

It was hard to argue with the reality before him: the curve of Artie's shirt-clad shoulder just ahead of him, the determined way he pushed the empty cart ahead of him. The way the sunshine poured down on the street, bathing everything in a layer of golden light. The smell of the muddy street as it dried, the odor of shoe polish as the shoeshine boy flicked his rag in the air. The smell of someone smoking a cigar in the open doorway of the barber shop across the street.

Everything mixed together felt so real that he could not deny he was here. And as much as he wanted to go home, and he did, so very much, he wanted to make sure of Artie before he left. Artie deserved to live, deserved to have a life that wasn't ended by tragic violence simply because he was who he was and loved in a way that was against the law in 1912. If Finn could do nothing else that was good, he would do this, he would make sure Artie was safe, but how?

CHAPTER SIXTEEN

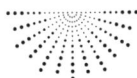

Z iegfeld's Diner wasn't too busy, as it was just before lunchtime when they got there, so they were able to find a booth by the windows. The waitress quickly brought them paper menus. Artie scanned his menu, even though he had it memorized and already knew what he wanted, to give Finn time to settle himself.

There seemed to be a secret behind Finn's blue eyes, a sense of worry that grew as the day wore on. Surely he must be concerned about getting back to his hotel room, though why he didn't just go in through the front door was beyond Artie to figure out. It was as though there was something in his mind that wouldn't allow him to access his room through the front door. Though this kind of delusion normally made Artie feel uneasy, Finn had helped him out on more than one occasion, so Artie would see this through.

Besides, having Finn around made him feel safe, not just from Horace and Ricky, who seemed to loom around every corner, but about everything. His life. His future, and where it might lead.

He'd never met anyone as easy with himself as Finn, someone who could admit *I'm like you* and then go on with the conversation as if he'd not said something amazing and unexpected. As though loving who you loved was a matter of easy free will and not a battle to be fought.

To live like that, to think like that, was a kind of miracle, a beautiful, energizing, sparkling miracle that Artie didn't want to let go of. He couldn't, and wouldn't, force Finn to stay, of course not. But if he could be around him for just a little while, learn from him, bask in his brightness, he'd be far and away along to making a better life for himself. He'd be one his way to a life that didn't involve scurrying from one town to the next, learning to hide so well that he became afraid of his own shadow.

It was hard to put any of this into words, of course, it being made clear to him only so recently, but now that Artie knew, now that he was thinking about it, he wanted to do something with that and make a better life for himself.

"I wish I could be like you," said Artie, the words slipping out.

"What do you mean?" asked Finn, all of his attention settling on Artie.

"Just that—" Artie stopped to consider what he wanted to say, now that he'd started saying it. "You say what you want to say and you don't care what other people think."

"Oh, I do care," said Finn. Then he smiled. "I mean in general, but I do care. I care what you think."

The expression on Finn's face warmed Artie through to his bones. It was nice not to be alone, even if only in this moment, this short time shared between them.

"The chopped steak and gravy is good," said Artie, his cheeks growing hot as he drew Finn's attention to the menu. "It comes with fried potatoes. I have that sometimes."

Finn looked up from his menu, as though glad to have something to distract him from his unknown, unnamed worries. "That sounds good," he said.

"And it might be too early in the season for rhubarb pie," said Artie. "But it's pretty good if they have it."

"Okay."

In the end, they both ordered the same thing, chopped steak with gravy, and the rhubarb pie, of which there were exactly two slices left. Artie got a glass of milk and drank it right down, then a cup of coffee to go with the pie. As they ate, the silence grew between them, but it was on the comfortable side, as though eating together helped settle Finn's soul, somehow, just as being near Finn helped settle Artie's.

"I figure after lunch, I'm going to take money to the bank for Joe, and then I'll put this clipping somewhere safe," said Artie, wiping his mouth on a napkin. "But you probably want to go home, don't you, and not stick around to help me."

"Guess I'll stick around till that back door opens," said Finn, but his voice trailed off as he looked out the window. "I got back before, so I should be able to again."

"What?" asked Artie. He shook his head, a little sorry that he asked, for Finn looked at him like he'd said something he shouldn't. "You know, you helped me, so why don't you tell me what's wrong and maybe I can return the favor."

"You wouldn't believe me if I told you," said Finn. He ducked his head, smiling a bit as though at a joke only he knew, but the smile was uneasy. "There's nothing you can do, but I appreciate the offer."

Artie paid the waitress when the bill came and left a dime as a tip. Then, with a nod to Finn, they both got up and went down the street to the distribution shack, where Joe Moody went through the motions of pretending he hated banks, but then paid Artie and handed him cash in a red canvas sack.

Their errand to the bank was quick. All the while, Finn looked at everything with round eyes on the verge of surprise, as though he'd never seen any of it before, never dealt with a teller with a green shade over his eyes as he tucked his white shirt sleeves into protective cuffs as he counted out money behind a set of solid brass bars. Never held a door open for a pair of ladies going into the bank, nor jumped the open ditch to get into the street to cross it.

"We'll just stop in my room," said Artie. "I need to leave the clipping and some of this money."

"Okay," said Finn.

He followed Artie in the back door of the boarding house, and up the flights of stairs to his room on the third floor. There, Artie paused, but then shrugged; Finn knew his darkest secret of all, so him knowing where he stashed his money probably wasn't more of a stretch of trust.

Bending down, Artie flipped up the floorboard, and took out the tin box full of money. He added most of the cash from his pocket, saving back two bits so maybe they could both get some root beer later, and put the clipping on top of that before putting the tin box back in place and laying the floorboard back over it.

"That's my bank," said Artie, standing up and wiping the dust from the knees of his trousers. "I trust 'em less than Joe Moody does and that's saying something."

"What about your compass?" asked Finn. "Why don't you keep that in there too?"

"I like to hold it," said Artie. "Don't know why, but I do. Here, let's see if it's still doing that crazy thing."

Going to the tall dresser, Artie pulled out the compass and walked over to Finn as he opened it with his thumb. There, the brass gleamed in the low light as the needles swirled around before the painted red end came to rest once again on Finn. Circling around Finn, Artie walked slowly, slowly, both of them looking as the needle shifted and swirled, always pointing at Finn.

"Are you magnetic?" asked Artie, putting the compass in his pocket.

"No," said Finn with a small laugh that drew Artie to him like a lodestone. "At least I never thought I was."

"Until now," said Artie. "Say, do you want to go get a root beer at the ice cream parlor? I mean, I usually go work at the newspaper office for more work, but sometimes they don't need me."

"Sure," said Finn, seeming pleased to be asked.

Normally Artie's simple room seemed a safe haven. But now that Finn had shown him a different way to think about things, the room seemed too small. With Finn at his side, the world was a different place with rules they could make for themselves.

They headed down the stairs, giving a nod to Mrs. Clarkson as they headed out the back door and to the alley. There, Artie planned to take the shortcut and head up to Fourth Street, pausing briefly as Finn stopped to tug on the back door of the Harlin Hotel.

"Still locked?" asked Artie.

"Yes," said Finn. He gave the door another tug. "Damn it."

"Maybe it'll be open later," said Artie.

He found he wasn't unhappy that the door to the hotel was locked, though he did wonder, again, why Finn didn't just go around the front and upstairs to his room on the third floor. If he lived at the hotel, as he claimed, then why couldn't he just go to his room? Artie wanted to ask, but the expression on Finn's face was so unhappy, so lost, that he couldn't bear the thought of upsetting Finn further. And, for now, it meant that he had Finn's company for a little while longer.

"Let's go to the print shop first and then get those root beers," said Artie.

He had visions of them having root beers together, and then maybe taking a walk through the park afterwards. Though his mind conjured up ideas about them holding hands as they walked, the place where their hands might join became a fuzzy spot inside of the image, because of course men couldn't hold hands in public. Couldn't be anything more than friends, not ever.

"Sure, where is it?" asked Finn. Then he added, bumping his shoulder against Artie's, "You're such a hard worker."

"Just up Main Street," said Artie, his cheeks feeling warm at the compliment. "Just past the diner."

Silently, Finn followed him back down the alley and up Main Street to where the print shop was. There, Norm Ector was at the broad table just behind the front counter, a pencil stuck behind his ear while he went over a bill of lading for newsprint.

"They're charging way over budget," said Norm, almost to himself. When he saw Artie at the door, Finn close at his heels, he took the pencil from behind his ear and pointed it at them. "Don't have any work today, Artie. This damn company wants to charge a nickel more a roll, which is highway robbery. Try tomorrow, all right?"

"Sure, Norm," said Artie. And while he was sad to lose the extra fifty cents for a few days, it meant that he had more free time. Time to spend with Finn, before he went back to wherever it was he'd come from. "See you later."

As they went out to the sidewalk, with the sunshine pouring down like gold about their shoulders, Finn looked a little glum about the mouth. Artie determined to do something about it. Even if it meant exposing himself in the worst way, he wanted to make Finn happy, wanted to change that frown to a smile. Wanted to spend time with him, just be with him. With that idea in mind, he took a deep breath and just made himself say it.

"That's an afternoon free," he said, smiling. "We could—we could go for a walk in the park, and then get a root beer float afterwards."

"A root beer float?" asked Finn, blinking at Artie as though his mind had been dragged to attention from far away, from somewhere that Artie couldn't follow.

"Yes," said Artie. "The ice cream parlor is right across from Ziegfeld's Diner, and it's a real swell place to go, especially when it's warm, like this afternoon is going to be."

"Sure," said Finn. He ducked his head and looked up at Artie through his dark eyelashes. "I've not had a root beer float in ages, actually. Lead the way."

Artie jingled the change in his pocket, more pleased than he'd been in a long while. Finn wasn't anything like Cecil, and he sure wasn't anything like Hector. He was handsome and kind and his presence was a gift Artie didn't deserve. But he was here now, and they were going for a walk in the park, after all. Would they be able to hold hands? That remained to be seen, but Artie was willing to risk it.

CHAPTER SEVENTEEN

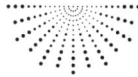

The simple idea of going for a walk in the park distracted Finn from the worries racing through him, like a mad things that didn't know where to stop and catch a breath. The only way to get home was to go through the back door of the hotel and up the backstairs—it was the only way.

As long as the back door was locked, he was stuck in 1912 and he didn't want to be. He wanted to go home to Finnwood Farms. That certainty was an ache in his belly that just wouldn't go away, and the pain of it kept forcing its way to the surface of his consciousness over and over.

At the same time, he couldn't ignore Artie—and he didn't want to. The look on Artie's face was hopeful, and Finn found he was pleased at the idea of this simple date. He loved the gleam in Artie's blue eyes, the way he was poised on the tips of his lace-up boots, full of energy. These were the things that he could gratefully grab onto, a distraction framed in Artie's lithe form, and the curve of his mouth just on the edge of a grateful smile, as if only waiting to see if Finn would say yes. So he did.

"Sure," he said, searching for the words as he imagined someone might say in response in the year 1912. "That'd be swell."

Artie looked so pleased, a faint rose coloring his cheeks, that Finn felt bad about hesitating in saying yes. A walk in the park, how simple that sounded. A root beer float afterward, such a nice treat. With a nod, as Artie leaned toward him, Finn found himself smiling.

"It's just up Main Street and over one block," said Artie, and together they began walking. Side by side, their hands almost brushing, as though Artie had moved too close and Finn had let him.

The people walking along the sidewalk in the afternoon sunshine were all dressed quite nicely, as though they were proud of where they lived and wanted to share their best selves. Everyone walked slowly, except for the two little girls who raced by, giggling, their lace-edge skirts flying, their curls and ribbons bouncing.

In the street, two Model T Fords, both black with spidery-spoked wheels, went past each other like two matrons doing a stately do-se-do. A horse drawn cart carrying a load of barrels of beer headed along, kicking up a bit of dust and leaving behind the scent of yeast, of horse sweat, and leather oil.

Everything was slow, everything was quiet, even though it was the busiest part of the day in Harlin. Dad had a box of old pictures, inherited when they bought the farm, of how Harlin had looked back in the day. The previous owner had collected the pictures and then given them to Mom and Dad when they bought the property, as a kind of inheritance of memories. Dad sometimes said that the pictures should be in the local historical society's museum, but then, each time, he'd put the box away quite carefully and mumble something about considering it another day.

And now, Finn was there, *inside* those old photographs. What if he'd ended up in one Dad's photographs? He'd never really looked at the photographs when Dad would bring them out, being too busy with college, or his friends, or his ghost hunting pursuits.

Maybe, when he got back—*if* he got back—he'd take the time to sit and listen and look, scanning each photograph for evidence of himself. It was too much to consider, and he looked up to realize that he was falling behind Artie, who, in his pleasure to have the afternoon off, was hurrying ahead.

"Sorry," said Finn, racing to catch up until he was at Artie's side, matching his stride, their shoulders brushing. "I was in my own thoughts."

"I don't mind," said Artie. "That's what a walk is for, thinking."

They passed from the downtown area into the more residential area, where grand homes were set back from the sidewalk and the trees, still young and planted seemingly only a few years ago, spread their new leaves, tender and green. Finn took a deep breath. The walking was helping, definitely, and Artie's quiet companionship felt like a balm that was soaking all the way through him, letting him relax his shoulders.

They crossed Main Street at Longs Peak Avenue, a truly busy intersection in his day, but a quiet one in 1912. As they passed beneath the shade of stately oaks that grew around the edge of a wide, open green space, Finn truly felt Artie's delight at their simple outing. He wanted Artie to be as happy as Artie made him. Could they hold hands in this old fashioned place?

It was almost too perfect a setting as they walked along the flag-stone sidewalk that went around the park, with mothers pushing fancy strollers in front of them. An older couple sat on one of the wooden park benches placed along the paths that wandered through rose gardens and patches of daisies amidst the green lawn. In the center of the park was an open pavilion where, no doubt, a brass band played on Sunday afternoons, as people strolled the park after church —all of it was like a drawing come to life. Only here in 1912 it was real.

He was so distracted by the thought that all of this would change by the time his own time rolled around, and everyone now in the park would most likely be dead—

"Are you okay?" asked Artie. "Do you want to sit for a while on one of the benches?"

"Sure," said Finn, making himself pay attention to the fact that Artie was doing his best to show Finn a good time. Doing his best to cheer Finn up, when all Finn could do was mope and worry. He wasn't in his own time and didn't belong here. Whatever was in control of the time traveling stairs—be it fate or magic or magnetism —knew that.

He followed Artie to the nearest bench, and they sat together in the shade of a large oak tree, whose branches overhead spread the most delicate shade, while still letting in sparks of sunshine and blue sky. Finn took a breath and relaxed against the curved back of the bench, then looked at Artie, who was looking at him.

What a sweet face Artie had, with blue eyes so full of a hesitant expectation. Life was slow in 1912—it just was—and here they were in a park, sitting on a bench, with Artie looking pleased just because he had the afternoon off.

Was he also pleased that Finn was with him? It was possible, though it was still hard to struggle through the idea that, in Finn's own time, Artie was a ghost. A beautiful, blonde-haired, blue eyed ghost with a sweet mouth and a tender look about him, but he was a ghost just the same.

Even if Finn was able to save him and have it stick, when he went back to his own time Artie would still have died. Maybe he'd die in his own bed years later, but he'd still be dead and Finn would have to move on without him. All of this rose up inside of him and, heart breaking, he crumpled forward, resting his head on his knees, hands on the back of his neck, just trying to breathe.

"Finn."

Artie moved closer until their thighs were touching, his warm body curling over Finn's, as he wrapped his arms around Finn's shoulders. Finn shuddered as the warmth of the connection soaked into him. He leaned into Artie's arms, moving his head to Artie's knee, letting himself be held. He'd never been held like this, never felt so weak, so needy, dependent on just one other person for this simple creature comfort.

It was as though he'd been alone his entire life, without even knowing it, and it had taken him going back in time to 1912 to realize it.

"Finn, it's okay, it's going to be okay." Artie's breath whispered across Finn's cheek and he turned toward it, grinding his forehead into Artie's thigh, struggling not to cry.

"I just want to go home," said Finn. "But I don't want to leave you behind."

"I don't—" said Artie but then he stopped, his arm still around Finn's shoulders, his hand cupping the back of Finn's head, a warm, gentle touch. "I don't understand. You could go anytime you liked. Are you—are you asking me to go with you?"

With a groan, Finn sat up, scrubbing his eyes with the back of his hand, scrubbing hard until he saw spots. He didn't need to drag Artie into his troubles like this. Artie didn't deserve them and had enough of his own.

"I don't know what I mean," said Finn. "I just know that I care about you and I'm worried, so worried—"

He scanned the park and saw that one of the mothers with her fancy stroller was looking at him, her eyes wide, her mouth screwed into a horrified frown. He knew quite well what she was seeing: two men embracing in a park on a sunny afternoon. To her, it was not only horrifying, it was illegal.

How different from his own time, when gay couples could stroll and hold hands and kiss pretty much anywhere and nobody really cared. Well, some people cared but they were idiots and assholes, but he needed to stop letting his mind race on like this.

"Maybe we could get that root beer float now," he said, focusing on Artie, on the here and now.

"Sure," said Artie as he stood up. Just as he held out his hand to assist Finn to his feet, he snatched it back, wincing as though he'd just been stung. "Sorry," he said, shrugging as though to dismiss his impulse of kindness as foolish. "I want to help, but I don't know how."

"I'm supposed to be the one helping you," said Finn with a small laugh. "How about that root beer float?" he said in lieu of anything that he was thinking, because being with Artie was the most important thing.

Artie jingled his coins in his pocket as though pleased at the prospect. In his eyes was that low gleam again that Finn could only interpret one way: Artie was, in his way, seeing this as a date. He was courting Finn, 1912-style, with a walk in the park and a really swell treat at the ice cream parlor afterward.

The kindness of this rippled through him, easing the twisting ache of his worry like a sweet, soft balm. So, when Artie started walking, Finn rushed to be at his side, grateful in ways that he couldn't express. Deep inside of him, the warmth of Artie's company was helping to soothe him.

They headed back to Main Street and walked in the shade until they got to the ice cream parlor. The front of it wasn't as fancy as Finn had imagined it would be, but it was painted white, with a huge picture window and a pale pink awning over the door. As they went in, the bell on the door jingled and the man behind the counter, wearing a starched apron and white, peaked cap, smiled at them.

"Hello Artie, and friend," he said. "What can I get you this fine day? The usual?"

"Two, please," said Artie as he went up to the white marble counter and plonked down a quarter.

"You can have a table, since there's two of you," said the man.

Two more people came in as Finn and Artie took a round table, a wooden one, painted white, by the window. The whole of the ice cream parlor gleamed, and Finn tried to recall what the shop would become in his day. It might be a yoga studio or it might be a breakfast cafe, he wasn't sure. All of his landmarks had melted into something else, leaving him without any references.

The only thing that seemed familiar now, was Artie himself, who sat across from Finn, pleasure lighting up his features. He was sitting straight up, in anticipation for the root beer float, perhaps, but his smile was directed at Finn, and Finn alone. What would it have been like to meet a guy like this in his own time? One whose idea of a good time was so charming and low key that all of his attention was on his partner. What would it be like to really get to know Artie, his likes and dislikes? To see his sweet face in the light of morning? To have someone like that by his side, forever and for always?

Finn dragged his attention away from Artie, so expectant and hopeful, and looked out at the street. There, afternoon shadows made interesting patterns on the street, swirls of dirt rising up as a cool wind whisked through the center of town.

Passersby on the sidewalk held onto their hats—straw boaters, broad brimmed summer hats, a workingman's cap—and hurried, moving faster as though they hoped they could outrun the wind. Then, the wind paused and the sun sparkled from behind the clouds on the windows and brickwork of Ziegfeld's Diner across the street.

"Here you go, gentlemen," said the man as he delivered their root beer floats from a tin tray with scalloped edges, placing them on the table.

The mugs were tall, though not frosted as they might have been in Finn's day, and the root beer was dark, swirled through with melted ribbons of vanilla ice cream. Finn could smell the vanilla, strong as anything, and the tang of the root beer, crisp like it had just been made. Or made locally, which, no doubt it had.

He was going to drink his root beer float and then they would go back to the alley behind the hotel so he could try to get home. If that didn't work, he'd have to figure something else out. Like how to get a job when he had no idea how to do that, and a place to live, unless Artie was going to continue being kind and let him stay at his place with him.

Would they share the same bed again? Finn liked to cuddle, and it had taken all he had not to curl around Artie and hold him close as the darkness came. If they slept together again, he would not be able to resist.

"How do you like that root beer float?" asked Artie. His lower lip was daubed with ice cream, and he was licking his spoon.

He was a picture—a sweet, charming picture. He was also, in Finn's time, quite deceased; when Finn went home, he was going to have to leave this adorable young man behind him, forget him, and move on. It made him want to cry.

"It's delish," said Finn, focusing on his root beer float. As he noticed Artie's confusion, he corrected himself. "It's delicious. It's very good."

"Really?" asked Artie. "You were frowning so hard there, I thought you didn't like it."

"Really," said Finn, nodding. It wasn't right to make Artie worry, not when he had his own problems to think about. "It's just so much fresher than any I've ever tasted. The root beer, I mean. So good, like they make it in the back."

"Well, they do, actually," said Artie. "Every week they make a new barrel."

Of course they did. That's how it was in 1912. You made things yourself. You walked everywhere. You put up with a Main Street that was made of dirt, and you read newspapers to find out what was happening in the world, getting ink on your fingers and calling it good.

"It's the best root beer float I've ever had," said Finn, and this was not a lie. It was. And the company, how ever poignant the moment, was the sweetest.

CHAPTER EIGHTEEN

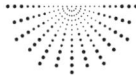

A s they walked back to the boarding house, it wasn't hand in hand as Artie secretly wanted, but it *was* side by side. He'd been able to distract Finn from his worries with root beer and ice cream, too, and now Finn seemed more relaxed, more at ease. Of course he wanted to go home, a place where he must feel loved and safe, and while Artie had never had a home like that, he could imagine what it might be like.

But for now, they headed up the back alley and went into the boarding house to wash for dinner. Artie wasn't near hungry enough to make the most of the lamb stew that Mrs. Clarkson was dishing up as he and Finn took their places at the end of the table. But he did his best, and made sure that Finn got his fair share as he handed over a quarter to Mrs. Clarkson for the meal.

"Is he going to stay again?" she asked as she brought over a plate of sliced bread. "If he's moving in, I'll have to raise your room rate. Maybe I won't double it, but I'll have to raise it, especially if I put in a second bed for him to sleep in. It's only fair."

For a moment, she stood there, wiping her hands on her long, no-longer-white apron and studied the table for anything that might be missing. The smell of boiled potatoes wafted from the kitchen on a slight breeze, along with the odor of the tin pan beneath the ice box, which told Artie that it had not been taken out and cleaned in a few days.

At the far end of the table, Horace and Ricky plowed into their stew like cows in a feedlot while giving both Artie and Finn glaring, side eye glances that were probably meant to scare, and did. They now knew that Finn had slept in Artie's room and probably would again. They also knew, full and well, that there was currently only one bed in the room. It was as though he'd shown up in his underwear to the dinner table, for now the two bullies had more ammo for their attacks.

"Yes, ma'am, if that's okay." Artie looked at the lamb stew in front of him, and the slice of bread that Finn had kindly gotten for him, and knew he was going to have to force himself to eat or waste the money he'd paid for the meal. "And I don't know about the second bed—"

"We'll know in the morning," said Finn, quickly.

It was obvious he meant that if he got to go home, wherever that was, they wouldn't need a second bed. At which point, Artie would be alone once more.

"I'll give you one more night, then," said Mrs. Clarkson. She walked back into the kitchen, skirts furling around her ankles as she shook her head. "Sometimes I'm too kind for my own good."

Artie had to agree; she ran the nicest boarding house he'd ever lived in, and she'd let Finn stay the night. She'd even loaned them extra blankets. Too bad there was nothing she could do about Horace and Ricky outside of the boundaries of the boarding house.

They ate their dinners slowly, still full from their treat at the ice cream parlor. Sitting next to Finn, it was hard to keep himself from looking over at him, at the serious expression on his normally cheerful face, and the way he concentrated on his food, as though that was all that was keeping him from slipping away into thoughts he didn't want to have.

The impulse to comfort him was strong, but Horace and Ricky were always watching. What if there was a place that he and Finn could go? A place where nobody watched and nobody minded, and he could comfort Finn the way he had in the park. Wrap his arms around Finn's shoulders and draw him close, maybe kiss him on the cheek, on the mouth—

"You coming?" asked Finn.

Artie looked up. He'd eaten only some of his meal, and Finn was standing next to his chair, arms on the back of it, looking at Artie as though he'd been doing it for quite some time. Waiting so patiently, so calmly, not cross at all. If only all of Artie's world could make him feel like Finn did, in that moment, like he was someone worthy of waiting for.

"Yes," said Artie. He stood up and pushed his chair in and hastened to follow Finn out of the dining room and up the stairs to the third floor. There, alas, Horace and Ricky were waiting on the landing, as though they'd been planning this ambush all through dinner. Their shoulders were up and they were blocking the way. Horace's eyes glinted.

Artie shivered. He wanted to move behind the protection of Finn's body, but that was the coward's way out, so he stood at Finn's side.

"You should let us pass, fellows," said Artie, pretending that the encounter was just an accident, and nothing Horace and Ricky were doing on purpose. "That was such a good meal—"

"What do you mean, you little shit," said Horace. "Inviting him to stay? Now everybody will know a faggot lives under this roof. No, two faggots."

"Two faggots," said Ricky, ever the echo.

Artie never wanted to run away more, to protect Finn from having to witness Horace and Ricky backing Artie into a corner and beating him up. He didn't want Finn to see him like that, didn't want Finn to have to be involved and maybe get hurt, too.

Why did any of this have to happen? Once Finn left, and surely it would be in the morning, Artie was going to get that train ticket on the *Shoshone Zephyr* and head north first chance he got. It didn't matter that, other than Horace and Ricky, he had a pretty good setup because there was no escaping encounters like this one, hard as he tried.

"Two faggots?" asked Finn, perfectly calm and casual, surprising them all into stillness. "Just the two?"

"What d'you mean?" asked Horace, growling, his hands becoming fists, his lank hair sliding across his forehead.

Artie wanted to know what he meant by that, too, for if there were other homosexuals living at the boarding house, how was it that he'd never met them? All three of them stared at Finn as though he'd said something astonishing, which, actually, he had.

"It's like this, guys," said Finn, so nonchalant, chin lifted, a confident gleam in his eyes. "Maybe you're looking under the bed because you've hid there yourself. You ever think about that?"

"What?" asked Horace.

It was easy to see that he was completely confused by the analogy. But Artie got it, in that heartbeat of silence that followed Horace's question. Finn was suggesting that Horace was accusing them because *he himself was a faggot.*

Artie's jaw dropped at the shocking newness of this idea.

"You're only worried about Artie being faggot because you are," said Finn, going on, bold as anything. "Otherwise, why should you care? He's not done anything to you. I mean, has he? Well, he hasn't, which means you're chasing him all over town trying to do some damage because when you look at him, you hate yourself for being like him. Now, what do you think about that?"

The air on the third floor landing suddenly seemed quite still and quiet, as though waiting for Horace's response. It could be explosive and they'd have an all out brawl then and there. But, to his surprise, Horace scraped his hair out of his eyes, and glowered at Ricky, as though all of this was his fault.

"You guys are nothing but punks," said Horace, mouth twitching as if he didn't quite know what to do with himself.

"Yeah, punks," said Ricky.

"Dumb, stupid punks," added Horace for good measure.

With a hard scuffle of his work boots, he turned and shoved Ricky ahead of him, like they had plans to make and places to be. As though

Finn had not just stuffed them both into a box and put them neatly on the shelf.

"That was—" said Artie, barely daring to speak it out loud. "That was spectacular. How did you do it with just words?"

"Bullies are like that," said Finn, a smile playing across his mouth in such a way that made Artie want to kiss him, right then and there. "They're afraid of who they are so they lash out like that. He might or might not be gay, but he's certainly freaking out about it."

"Gay?" asked Artie, blinking. "He seems pretty miserable most of the time, not very gay at all."

"Gay is a nicer word than faggot, wouldn't you agree?" Finn turned to look at Artie, his eyes full of a sudden and inexplicable laughter. "Gay. That's what you and I are. Gay. Happy as birds in a tree. Gay. So very gay."

Unable to share this very private joke but nonetheless quite happy to have been rescued once more, Artie patted Finn's solid shoulder. He was grateful to have an excuse, however thin, to touch this man who was brave and smart and kind, all at the same time.

Finn went still beneath his touch, but he didn't pull away. His eyes darkened as he looked at Artie, shimmering with all the secrets he seemed to have. Places he needed to go, places where Artie didn't know he could follow.

"I've had about enough of today," said Finn. "What about you?"

"We could go up on the roof and watch the evening come down," said Artie, not knowing if this would be enough. "We could get beer again, if you want." He'd be willing to fetch and carry for Finn, if only he could see him smile again.

"No, I'm good," said Finn. "But sitting on the roof would be nice. There are no streetlights to block out the stars."

Of course there wasn't, but Artie didn't know how to explain this when it was so very obvious. Maybe where Finn came from, there were more lights, like in the city, that made it hard to see the night sky. But that would mean he'd be asking questions that Finn wouldn't want to give answers to. He always seemed so private about where he'd come from and how he'd ended up in a hotel in a small town like Harlin.

They scrambled up the stairs to the roof, Artie keeping an eye over his shoulder the entire while for Horace and Ricky until they shut the trap door. The roof was flat and covered with tar. In the summer it would be unbearable at this time of day, toward evening, with the tar bubbling along the edges, heat rising in waves, but now, in June, it was pleasant. Sure, there was the smell of tar, but it was faint, from a distance.

They went over to the low hump they'd sat on before. Artie was so very content to sit beside Finn again, alone on a rooftop, watching the evening come down.

The sunset over the mountains to the west was dipped in purple along the edges, turning to darker blue higher up, fading to rose lower down. A slight smell of pine trees, cooling in the dusk, came to Artie like the promise of summer, the promise of something good.

To the south could be seen the flicker of lightning that brightened as the sun sank lower behind the mountains. Long shadows draped the southern horizon, beyond the packing plant, beyond the train tracks and St. Vrain Creek, beyond the low, sloping, green-speckled hills where crops were pushing their way up through the soil.

Artie sighed and turned to Finn, wanting to join him in embracing such beauty. To enjoy the refreshing drench of a cool breeze that took away the smell of tar and replaced it with the sweet scent of rain coming toward them.

Finn was hunched, shoulders rolled forward. His eyes were dark and troubled; on impulse, Artie reached over and pushed his hair from his forehead.

"I miss home," said Finn, flicking his eyes to Artie and then away. But he didn't shrug Artie's hand off or move away as though he disliked the touch. Instead, he leaned into it, and Artie let his hand linger cupping Finn's cheek, fingers tracing the line of Finn's jaw.

It felt so bold to be this way, touching another man as though he had every right to. As though it wasn't completely against the law to feel this way.

The last person he'd touched had been Horace, when they'd fought. And before that, Cecil, when they'd joke together in the communal bathroom while cleaning up.

He'd brushed against Cecil and, oh-so-accidentally, had flung his arms around Cecil's shoulders. It had taken almost a whole minute before Cecil had shrugged him off, laughing half wildly, as though the whole thing had been an accident or a joke. But it hadn't been either, not to Artie.

And now here he was, making tentative, new steps when he'd promised himself over and over that he'd never reach out to another human being. Never open his heart, never have the urge to whisper sweet promises and imagine what it would be like to kiss Finn so very gently. Which was totally confusing.

His encounters before with strangers, or men he'd barely met, had been rough, tumbled gropings and sweaty exclamations. Could love between two men be like this? Like he'd imagined? Like he'd seen when he'd paused to watch a young couple share sweet kisses beneath the shade of a spring umbrella?

He was imagining all of this, of course he was. Finn wasn't interested in Artie that way, however expertly he'd defended Artie, told him that *gay* was a nice word to describe what they were, and said it like it was nothing to be such. So instead of presuming, Artie said nothing while they sat there and watched the sky grow dark, the stars coming in tentative sparkles to the east—then more came, and more, covering the blue black blanket above with them, as all the while the sheet lightning zagged and ran to the south.

When it got really dark, a chill wind started blowing at their backs, announcing that rain was on the way.

Finn stood up.

"Shall we go in?" he asked, and to Artie, it seemed that the question was an invitation to more than merely going inside.

Artie wanted the evening to last forever, but of course they had to go in and get ready for bed. He had work in the morning, and Finn was probably going to try the back door of the hotel once more, as though it was his only hope.

"Sure," said Artie. He took Finn's hand and let Finn help him up, and together they opened the trap door and went down the narrow stairs.

"I'm going to wash up," said Artie.

He was pleased when Finn followed him to the bathroom on the third floor, but didn't let himself imagine it was because Finn couldn't bear to be parted from him. There, they rolled up their sleeves and washed their hands and the back of their necks, drying their damp skin on the communal towel.

This was all done in silence, as Artie had no idea what to say, how to ask Finn not to leave the first chance he got, and no idea at all what to do with his own anticipation of sleeping with Finn again. Surely Finn wouldn't insist on sleeping on the floor, when the bed was so much more comfortable? Not to mention that the night before they'd slept in each other's arms, in only their underwear—a far better encounter, that simple thing, than Artie had ever known before.

When they got to Artie's room, he saw that Mrs. Clarkson had, all on her own, left them two extra blankets and a pillow on the bed, rather than taking them away when she cleaned. He'd have to pay her in the morning for Finn sleeping in the room, and after that? He had no idea what would happen.

He had no idea what would happen now, except that they would go to bed, hopefully in the same bed, and at least he'd have that. One night. One more night.

As though to sweep away Artie's dark thoughts and distract him, Finn began to get undressed, taking off his strange canvas shoes, shrugging out of his denim trousers. He laid his clothes on top of the dresser and raised an eyebrow at Artie as though to ask him what was taking so long.

In response, Artie hurriedly took his clothes off, folding them anyoldhow on top of Finn's clothes and for a moment they stood there, together, half naked. The outline of Finn's shoulders beneath his thin cotton shirt was a complete distraction. Plus, it was hard to drag his eyes away from the curve of Finn's hip in his strange, oddly tight underwear, where the dark shape of his private hair could be

seen as a shadow, and the line of his sex oddly erotic for all its innocent stillness.

Jerking his eyes up, Artie gasped at himself, at his boldness. At the
fact that, yes, Finn had caught him staring.

"There's nothing wrong with it," said Finn.

Artie wasn't sure what part he meant. The fact that they were
standing together in their underwear? Or the fact that Artie had been
looking and looking and looking some more? His heart raced wildly
the entire time, wanting what it shouldn't want. Could never have.

"With what?" Artie asked, making himself ask. Feeling brave and
desperate all at once.

"Looking," said Finn, in his straightforward way. "Wanting."

"I don't know what I want," said Artie, and it was true. If Finn
meant to go home at the first opportunity, then there was no point in
Artie unlocking his heart and letting it have its way.

"I just need to sleep." Finn shook his head, hands on his hips for a
minute, fingers digging into the cloth above his hips, tightening the
outline of his body in that brief instant, making Artie's mouth water.

Artie turned away, toward the bed, where he fussed like an elderly
aunt, placing the two pillows side by side above the folded down
sheet, and laying out the extra blankets. Then he got in, scooting
toward the wall so there would be room enough for Finn.

"Can you get the light?" asked Artie.

He told himself he wasn't breathing too hard, that he wasn't strung
tight from head to toe. He was, he so was, but Finn made it easy as he
always did, flicking off the light and climbing into bed next to Artie
like it was the most natural thing in the world.

As his eyes adjusted to the low gloom, he could hear the snap of
elastic as Finn must have felt his underwear riding up and tugged it
down. All at once, Artie's whole body shuddered.

"You cold?" asked Finn as he shifted down in the bed, his head
resting on the pillow next to Artie's pillow.

"No," said Artie, but it was a lie. A lie he had to keep telling both to
himself and to Finn. "It's just different, is all."

He wasn't sure what he meant by that, but Finn, ever so casually, yawned and rolled on his side, flopping his arm over Artie's waist as though he meant to keep them close all through the night.

"G'night," said Finn.

"Good night," said Artie, a little disappointed that there wouldn't be more, but content to have Finn near, so close.

He was lying on his back, but he turned his head on the pillow so that his forehead brushed Finn's forehead, and there was a gleam in the dark, Finn's eyes looking at him as though Finn knew every secret Artie meant to keep to himself.

After a while, as Finn's breathing grew steady. His own heart began to slow to its normal rhythm, and he turned in the bed. Finn's arm was still over his waist, and he rolled on his side, facing the wall.

Now Finn's body was close behind him, close and still and warm. Safe with the scent of Finn, salt and soap, floating over him, like another layer of protection. He didn't know how this was all going to look in the morning, but for now, he was going to sleep in another man's arms, a memory he knew would have to last him a good long while after Finn left.

CHAPTER NINETEEN

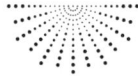

Morning didn't come upon Finn like it did in his own time, with a blaring alarm and the jangle and movement of traffic. Instead it came softly, with the low glow of the dawn on the horizon pushing through the half-curtained window with gentle urgency. A yellow and pale gold light, tinged blue at the edges. And from somewhere, not too far away, the clang of the packing plant bell.

As he shifted in bed, only a little bit awake, he realized that he had Artie in his arms. He was also wrapped around Artie's body a little too close to explain away. And that, in return, Artie was tucked close against him, his head beneath Finn's chin, his nose buried in Finn's t-shirt. He was warm all over and sleepy-still in Finn's arms.

It was delicious and good, making Finn feel like he could stay this way forever, until time passed and Harlin grew and changed and suddenly it would be his own time, with him and Artie together. It was an impossible thing to wish for, surely it was. He had to go home to his own time at the first—the *very first*—opportunity, and he would have to leave Artie behind him. Didn't he?

Artie made a low sound, tucking himself close to Finn as his whole body seemed to tighten in a form of pushback against actually waking up. Finn knew the feeling, and sighed a deep breath, wishing it could all last longer.

But then, as Artie tilted his head and looked up at Finn, the sleepy haze in his blue eyes was enough to make Finn swear that he wouldn't be able to resist this little moment between them. His cock was rising hard against his belly and while he would normally just tug at the elastic in his briefs, his arms were full of Artie, and he didn't want to let that go. The perfume of the heat of their bodies, tucked together for most of the night while they slept, filled his lungs, twinged in his belly, made him groan out loud.

"I don't know, Artie, I don't know."

Finn shook his head, not certain of what he didn't know, only that it would be the kind thing to do to say no to what his body was asking, to those questions in Artie's blue eyes. It would be kind because he would be leaving as soon as he could. That it would hurt him was one thing, but that it might hurt Artie? Impossible. Not permitted. The last thing he wanted to do.

He tried to move, to unwrap himself from the delicious warmth that was Artie, but Artie tightened his arms around Finn's waist, and as Finn looked down at him, his mouth trembled.

"Please," said Artie. "Just—please."

It was hard to say no to the plea in Artie's voice, the hope in his eyes. Finn knew that he should say no, but just then Artie surged upward in Finn's arms until their hips touched, their chests, the whole length of the two of them soft and connected beneath the bedclothes. The sensation ran a thrill through Finn's body and up the back of his legs, tightening him all over, his cock rising against his belly, tight in anticipation.

"You know I can't stay," said Finn, low, urgent. "If I can't get home, I don't know what I'll do. I have to go."

"I don't care." Artie's voice broke on the words and he leaned in, silently pleading, maybe for a kiss, maybe for two kisses and every-thing else that followed.

If Finn had felt lonely, every now and then in his own life, there was no loneliness compared to Artie's. He'd been stuck in a world that considered him a grotesque sin, all the while knowing he could be arrested at any minute just for being himself.

Would it be a worse torture to say no or to say yes? Finn couldn't decide, and maybe Artie, determining that Finn's stillness and lack of saying no was a kind of yes, rose and softly kissed Finn on the mouth. As though he'd been waiting for that moment his whole life, a sweet little sigh, a butterfly kiss.

He pulled back, looking up through his eyelashes, the glimmer of blue in his eyes like a flash of faraway hope that maybe he was already letting go of because he knew he shouldn't have done it, not without Finn saying—truly saying—yes.

"Yes," said Finn. "Yes."

He tightened his arms around Artie, and held him close. He dipped into the curve of Artie's neck to kiss him there, sweeping his mouth along muscle and skin, inhaling Artie's scent. It was like finding something he'd lost, so long ago it was beyond memory. Finding something he'd not known he wanted until that very moment. The warmth of Artie, the soap and salt scent of him.

A breathtaking giddiness followed as Artie unclasped Finn's waist and lowered his hands to cup Finn through his briefs, then swept down and trace the back of his thighs and up again. As though Artie was memorizing the shape of Finn, leaving traces of wishes and shivers behind.

"Have you been with anyone before?" asked Finn, his voice quiet.

"Yes," said Artie. "When I lived in Denver, sometimes I'd go to East Colfax, you know, where there are men like me."

This was a little bit of a shock, as that part of Denver was grotty in Finn's time, and must not have been much better in 1912. He felt a ripple of sadness at the image of sweet-faced Artie haunting basement bars and back alley hangouts, looking for human connection, accepting it where he found it even if it was for only those briefest of moments to find relief. He let go of Artie to scrub at his eyes and then gathered Artie to him again.

"Whatever happens," said Finn, wanting Artie to understand him completely, but not wanting to freak him out. "Whatever happens, this moment, this now, is real. Understand? Being with you now, I mean it with all of my heart. No matter what the day brings, what we're sharing is real."

"Of course it is," said Artie.

Finn knew, then and there, that Artie didn't understand him, but then how could he? He might understand, should Finn ever leave him and go back to the future, leaving no trace of himself behind except for an odd, small mention in a local newspaper that would go out of business long before Finn was ever born.

This made his mind whirl, and unsettling feelings began to creep beneath his skin. To fight them off, he dipped his head and kissed Artie back, tracing the curve of Artie's mouth with his tongue, letting himself linger.

In response, Artie, bold beneath his innocent face, swept his hand from the back of Finn's thigh to the front of him. His fingers tucked into the waistband of his briefs, the edge of his nails sharp against Finn's warm skin.

Finn shivered and closed his eyes, waiting for that moment when Artie would touch him. Thankfully he did, curling his fingers around Finn's cock, a sweeping sure moment that spoke of experience that had to have been without any love behind it.

The lonely slag of trading sex for sex with no other connection, horrible and cold, had no place in a morning-warm, sundrenched bed. Besides, Finn didn't want that here, not between him and Artie, who now seemed a bundle of precious want and desperate need. He was shaking as he slowly swept his hand up and down Finn's cock, slowly, oh so slowly.

Not wanting Artie to be lonely, Finn attempted to reach out to do the same for Artie, but Artie stopped him.

"No," said Artie, softly. "I just want to focus. On you."

He was a little stunned when Artie let go of Finn's cock to push him gently back. Then when Artie skimmed his briefs from his hips, he gasped, mouth open as Artie kissed his way down Finn's front, placing butterfly flicks of affection, his fingers spread across Finn's ribs as the kisses went down and down.

There, just where his cock, hard and pink, grazed his bellybutton, Artie paused and looked up through his lashes. His precious ghost was waiting for Finn to say yes or no. While Artie'd obviously done this before, it was a little sad to think that everyone else he'd done this to had been a stranger to him, a momentary connection of flesh to flesh that, in the moments that followed became no more than a shadow of a memory, a tingle of physical release that was not, in the end, something to fill the dark corners of his soul.

Artie's mouth on his cock, the feel of a warm tongue swirling around, was a shock to him, a pleasant buzz that grew up his spine. He knew he should stop, but he didn't. He just let him go on doing what he was doing, clasping his fingers around the base of Finn's cock, treating Finn to what felt like a wave of affection and caring that felt quite undeserved.

The bed shuddered beneath them, not loud enough to wake the neighbors maybe, but loud enough to add to the sense of secrets being exposed and truths coming out into the light. They should come into the light; they all should, because nobody like Artie should have to hide in plain sight.

Finn sighed and sank beneath the waves of pleasure coming from the movement of Artie's mouth, the careful way he kept Finn in place, a hand on his hip while Artie's head bobbed, slowly, carefully, up and down. Artie's mouth left traces of pleasure behind, a ribbon of warmth, a curl of love, festooned with the bright sparkles behind Finn's eyes when he closed them.

His whole body was tight and ready, drawing up into itself as the final curve of sizzle and excitement pulsed in his groin, in his belly. Artie sped up, hunkered in the bed between Finn's trembling thighs, the bedsheet barely draped over his hips as he bent forward, pleasuring Finn the entire while.

With a final lick, he swallowed Finn whole, all the way down to the root of his cock and sucked hard, then soft, hard, then soft. When Finn came, it was with a burst of white heat that came up from his spine, his cock pulsing as Artie swallowed gently, gracefully, and never once did he leave Finn alone in his pleasure as he came.

Artie's hands were always on Finn, cupped around his hips, the root of his cock. Now, as Artie sat back, he stroked Finn's thigh and belly, lying down beside him once more as he pulled up Finn's briefs and set him to rights. Then he pulled up the bedsheet and covered them both as the bedsheet floated down like an enormous snowflake coming to rest on the quiet earth.

Finn sighed in his throat, tugging Artie to him, an exhaustion dragging his eyes closed even as he wanted to keep them open so he could figure out what Artie needed. What Artie wanted.

"Let me take care of you, now," said Finn, his voice rough.

"We don't have time," said Artie. "That's the packing plant horn. The work day is starting and I need to get down to the depot."

"Two minutes, at least," said Finn, more disappointed than he ever could have imagined at Artie's work ethic. "I'll get you off, quick. Please? Let me hold you and take care of you."

He wouldn't hold Artie there if he didn't want to be held. At the same time, he wasn't one of those who would take their own pleasure and then dance off, as if the partner who'd just pleasured them was of no consequence. He'd had so few encounters in his life, he was practically a virgin, but he knew, beyond a doubt, that he wanted to take care of Artie, to give him pleasure before he raced off into his day.

Artie made a small sound as he turned into Finn's neck and buried his face there, arms wrapped tightly once more around Finn's waist. Maybe he wasn't used to having pleasure offered like this, wasn't used to making out in his rented room in a boarding house, with thin walls all around and who knows who listening.

"I'll be quick," said Finn, ducking his head to whisper into the tender curves of Artie's ear. "We'll be quiet and quick, okay?"

"Okay," said Artie.

Artie swallowed, and there was a pink blush along his jawline—as though he was not quite sure he could accept, but had been, at the same time, unable to resist Finn. As much as Finn liked to consider himself irresistible, he certainly wanted to give to Artie what Artie had given to him, the feeling of being lovable enough to slow down for.

He plucked at the tiny buttons on Artie's neck-to-thigh cotton underwear, smiling when finally Artie started to help him. Artie's fingers trembled in his haste, and he felt warm next to Finn, as though his desire to be touched was building a fire within him.

Finn undid the last few buttons at the crotch of the underwear, and pulled away the cloth until Artie was bare from his collarbones all the way down to his upper thighs, where, in the bright sunshine, the hairs shone faint gold. His cock was curled against his belly, rising up from the thatch of dark hair.

"C'mere," said Finn.

He pulled up his hand and licked his palm, and gave it to Artie to lick, enjoying the sight of Artie's pink tongue, the hard feel of it against his hand. Then he reached down to grasp Artie's cock, settling it in his hand and getting the heft of it, getting to know it as he rested there, while Artie's cock grew taut and the thin skin shaded to purple and rose.

He licked his palm again and took Artie's cock and stroked him slow and careful, then brisk, brisk. All the while, he kissed Artie, sweeping his tongue over Artie's sweet mouth, licking a little, giving him butterfly kisses on the nose and stronger kisses on the lips. Stroking and kissing and putting his heart into it so that on the day he left, back to his own time—which must surely come soon—Artie would have this moment to keep with him. Finn would have it, too, to take home to the farm, where he might remember it until it faded away into a ghost of itself.

He was crying and had to blink it back. Had to focus on Artie and his pleasure, and not on the future that would be a vast, Artie-less wasteland. The rest of his life would be devoid of this secret pleasure, this stolen moment, this warm, sun drenched hideaway place where the two of them would ever be, forever together in each other's arms.

Swallowing hard, he concentrated on the glide of his hand over Artie's cock, on the tension he felt in Artie's body, building like a secret thing coming into the light at long last. When Artie came, Finn slowed his motions, going lighter and lighter, enjoying the pulse of Artie's seed over his knuckles, storing the moment away forever.

With a grunt, Artie pulsed into Finn's hand and then, with a sigh, he collapsed, boneless, in Finn's arms. His arm came up and he covered his eyes with his wrist, a bit like a delicate damsel who'd just been rescued, his cheeks flushed, his mouth rosy. When he looked at Finn, an expression of sleepy pleasure glinted in his eyes.

"That—" began Artie, but then he stopped, shaking his head as though he could hardly believe what he'd just experienced. "*That*— thank you, Finn. It's never been like that for me before."

"Like what?" asked Finn, whispering, kissing Artie's forehead as Artie rolled into his arms.

"Like the other person cared," said Artie.

"Of course I care," said Finn, and he very much did. But how would it look when he was able to go back to his own time once more? Artie would think that he lied and there was really no way to fix that. "Of course I do," he said, anyway, in spite of all the confusion in his head.

"And now, work," said Artie with a final kiss to Finn's mouth, his hand warm on Finn's cheek.

Work. Artie was being practical, as he must have been his whole life, with only himself to rely on, to depend on. Only himself, all this while. It made Finn want to cry all over again.

"I got some change," said Artie. He sat up, scrubbing at his face with his hands. "We can grab some coffee from Mrs. Clarkson and maybe stop by the diner for some breakfast rolls."

Knowing full and well that Artie usually went without breakfast, Finn knew what a treat this was. It was something special to celebrate this morning they'd spent together.

As to whether there'd be another, he had no idea. He would either be trapped in 1912 forever, mourning his Mom and Dad and Mia until the day he died. Or, he'd go home and be lovesick so hard that Dad would wonder whether he'd caught something and would try to get him to talk about it. Talking about it would mean letting it go, and Finn didn't want to do that, not ever. He wanted to be with Artie forever, only he didn't know how to do that.

CHAPTER TWENTY

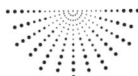

As they walked down the alley to go down to the depot where, no doubt, Joe Moody was already grouchy due to Artie being late, Finn checked the handle on the back door to the hotel. For a moment, he froze as the door swung partway open. Ahead of him, walking blithely on, was Artie, already focused on his work for the day, confident that Finn was only steps behind him.

What should he do? Call Artie back and try to hurriedly explain to him where he was going and why? Or just leave and cut it to the bone, quick, like a mercy killing? He could not, would not stay in 1912 forever, and could not count on the doorway through time being open whenever he wanted it to be. There was no way to predict when, if ever, this chance would come again.

He wanted to think what his Dad would tell him to do, but Dad had never been in a situation like this. As Artie turned the corner onto Third Street, he was gone from Finn's view. In that moment, Finn opened the door all the way and stepped into time, his heart breaking the whole while.

Dizziness struck him, the sensation of going down in an elevator at high speed until everything came to a jerky stop. The first floor of the hotel was near dark, as though it was the middle of the night. A growl of an engine, something modern and sleek, passed in the alleyway behind him as he shut the door. He inhaled the smell of the air conditioner, the tart modern cleaner that had been used to mop the hotel's foyer, the bleach used in towels and sheets. All around, he sensed the quiet air, the old-fashioned feeling the hotel evoked with ease, the old-fashioned feeling that it did quite well.

But the hotel didn't know the brown color of sturdy tablecloths or brown paint on every wall, or acidy tasting cups of coffee. It didn't know what it was like to walk everywhere and to jump the ditch to cross from the flagstone sidewalk to the dirt of Main Street. Or what it felt like to hold the hand of a young man who was so alone in his world that it made your heart break to think of it.

That was the way Finn's heart was breaking now as he climbed the back stairs to his hotel room. The old fashioned key was still in his pocket and still worked. He went in and sighed at the cool, crisp air that completely hid the smell of rain from the outside. Went to the window and looked at the haze of lights that spread into the sky, completely blocking the glint of stars on the spring-swollen river as he gazed at the sheet lightning on the horizon.

Nothing would ever be the same now that he had known Artie's world and shared it with him. Nothing.

He checked the clock on his phone. It was only fifteen minutes later than it had been the last time he checked. Just like the first two times, though it gave him no pleasure at all to recognize this pattern.

Going over to his EVP, he turned it on and listened to the quiet hiss of blank tape. Then he heard the pained sounds of a body hitting a wall, and unanswered screams from the alley, garbled amidst the interference created by the afterlife. He clicked it off with a hard thumb and wanted to shatter it against the wall, but he didn't. Someone might want it. He'd give it away, that's what he'd do. Or maybe Dad would want it—

He dialed Dad's number before he could stop himself. It was only after midnight, and sometimes Dad stayed up reading. Though, in the spring, he got up with the sun to tend to his bees and his lavender bushes, to make the most of the day. In the evening, he would sit on the back patio, a half circle of flagstone lovingly laid out by the previous owner, and watch the sky darken over his fields, while Mom mixed up a small batch of gin and tonic for the two of them to enjoy.

With Mia home, she'd want something a big sweeter. Maybe Mom would offer to make that, too, so Mia and Dad could enjoy the silence of a cool summer evening together, the scent of lavender coming with the sweet smell of faraway rain coming closer.

Tears dripped like hot mercury down his cheeks and he swiped them away just as the line clicked as Dad picked up at the other end.

"Hey, kiddo," said Dad, his voice gruff because it was late. "What's up? You getting scared by the wee ghosties and things that go bump in the night?"

"A little, Dad," said Finn, never so glad to hear Dad's voice, to hear the ready joke waiting in the wings, to feel Dad's calm presence washing over him. "I—I think it might not be working. I'm not ready. The application is due tomorrow, only I'm not ready."

"You might be more ready than you think you are, son," said Dad, a tone of seriousness in the words now that he knew there was a problem and that all was not well. "Do you have your notes? Do you have your photographs and such? You'll come home tomorrow and write it all up, then submit that application. It's all you ever wanted, right?"

A moment of silence fell as Finn flicked his eyes up to the window where the tall structure of the new condo building blocked light from the buildings behind it, reflecting the other light in its own windows. It was an eyesore, really, and not in keeping with the home town charm that Harlin liked to project. It wasn't old fashioned, and not Mayberry at all but more an adjunct to Boulder, the high-browed cultural center of the Rocky Mountains. It was just a mini Boulder, really. Nothing special on its own.

"Dad, I don't know what to do." Finn wiped away more tears, scrubbing at them hard.

"Like—" Dad paused, being careful with Finn's feelings, as he always was, as he was with everyone, really. "Like not being a ghost hunter?"

"It's not that," said Finn. "I mean, it is in a way. Like, maybe I'll write those stories, like you said. Write books. Do local hunting, help out with those cemetery tours and stuff like that. Like I've been doing."

"That's always an option." Dad paused, like he did, not wanting Finn to do what Dad thought best but more what Finn himself thought best. "But if you got in, you'd travel the country in that Scooby-Doo van, remember? You could still swing by the farm every once in a while, help me with the honey—"

Dad was describing Finn's dreams, as he interpreted them, for Finn. Reminding him what he'd been so excited about. Finn made a choking sound that came right up from his chest so hard and fast he could hardly breathe.

"You need to do what you need to do, son," said Dad, quiet and serious. "Why don't you give yourself some time to think it over. Nighttime is no time to make important decisions. After all, there will be other groups like Ghost Force that need your particular talent, right?"

There might be but there might not be. Ghost Force had seemed such a perfect fit when he'd started out, something exciting and novel. Plus, traveling around in a van chasing after ghosts, whether or not the van was painted in obnoxious psychedelic colors with hippie flowers plastered all over, sounded like a blast, a huge amount of fun and adventure, and a whole lot of not staying on the farm.

"Get some rest." Dad paused, and it felt like he was nodding at this wise advice. "Get some rest, come home tomorrow, and just finish filling out that application. Do what you set out to do. Then, later, you can change your mind and turn it down if you like."

"You think I should," said Finn, amazed that Dad was so casual about the fact that he would get offered the position. "You think I should turn it down."

"I think you should do what you need to do." Dad's voice was kind but firm. "This is not the only crossroads you will come to in your life, you know. Every now and then, life will offer you an opportunity, but it's hard knowing which way to go, left or right. It's easier to know when you get there, to that point, because your heart, your gut, will tell you what you should do. But you're not there yet, kiddo. You've got a bit to go yet. So hop in the shower, take a walk around the block—"

"At midnight?"

"—do whatever you need to do to get your equilibrium back. Okay? And try not to worry." Dad yawned, a huge, lion-like growl that he liked to exaggerate to demonstrate that he was the leader of the pack, which he was, except when Mom was, and they tended to trade off, as needed. "When you get there, you will know what to do. Okay?"

Dad yawned again, not exaggerated this time, but a real, sleepy yawn.

"What were you doing when I called?" asked Finn, scrubbing a hand through his hair.

"Eating the last of the ice cream and hoping the sweetness would erase the suckingly bad taste in my mouth from watching—"

"No, Dad, please," said Finn, almost laughing. "Tell me you didn't try watching it again? It's never going to get any better, even with Idris Elba doing his best. And his best is mighty good, as you know."

"I do know, I do," said Dad, putting on an air of being more despondent than he was. "It is so very terrible, but I do like squinting my eyes, and imaging I'm there, slinging a gun, looking for The Man in Black so I can save the world." When Finn laughed, he added, "Hey, it could happen. Anything's possible, you know. There are more worlds than are dreamt of in your philosophy."

"That there are, Dad," said Finn, feeling more somber now, his heart aching as he thought of Artie looking for him and never finding him. "Okay. I'm going to take a walk around the hotel, and look for my ghosts and think my thoughts."

"Ghosts, as in plural?" asked Dad with a yawn. "I thought there was only one."

"Uh—"

Finn's mind stopped as though he'd slammed on the brakes extra hard. But really, Dad's question made sense, at least in this reality. He'd saved Daisy and he'd saved Ruby, both with Artie at his side. Which left only Artie as the hotel's resident ghost, the only one that Finn had been unable to save.

"Yeah," said Finn, his voice cracking. "Just the one ghost."

"Well, sometimes one ghost is enough," said Dad. "Imagine how puffed up with pride that hotel would be if they had three ghosts! Imagine the racket."

"Yeah, imagine that." Finn clutched the phone with both hands, not wanting to drop it as he reeled with the idea of how Dad thought he'd only ever existed in his current timeline, but actually Finn had changed everything for him, four timelines ago. Thank all the stars in the sky that the only thing that seemed to have changed was how many ghosts now haunted the Harlin Hotel. "Thanks for the pep talk, Dad."

"Any time, son, any time. Get some rest. See you tomorrow."

"I will, Dad. Bye."

Finn clicked the phone off and put it on the night table with a thunk. He wanted to sink into the bed and rest his head on the pillow and imagine that all of this was a dream, a bad and very complicated dream where, while it might have been scary or weird, he'd never fallen in love with a ghost. But he *had*—he'd fallen so hard he was willing to give up his ghost hunting dreams and was considering going back again to see if saving Artie one more time would save him forever.

Remembering his promise to Dad, he shook himself and washed his face and hands in the bathroom. He left the light off so he didn't have to see his own hollow-eyed expression. Then, with his old-fashioned room key in his pocket, he went down the elevator to the lobby, intending to sit in one of the cozy looking but not very comfortable chairs, and mull in the darkness until he was relaxed enough to sleep. To fall asleep believing that this would all look better in the morning.

In the lobby, he waved to the sleepy, slightly bored nighttime clerk, and nodded at the young couple still flirting in the small tapas and wine bar just off the lobby. He went straight up to the tableau with a lack of resistance that felt like it came from everywhere all at once. It was as though his obsession with ghosts had now narrowed down to this one moment.

The lion-legged table had, finally, been replaced with a tall, narrow retro looking stand, upon which was laid a single three ring binder. And on the wall was a single portrait of Artie, the crystal clear photograph that Finn recognized from the newspaper article.

Artie was as beautiful as ever he had been, with that sad gleam in his eye, with only the barest edge of hope traced into his features. The curve of his cheek was still the same, the long lines of his thin neck, all of it beautiful and desperate and lost, all at the same time.

Finn had left him to his lot in life; although he was desperate to save him, Artie had been unable to outrun fate or Horace and Ricky, which were likely the same things. They'd been on a vendetta, zeroing in on Artie for being too different—or, perhaps, too much like them.

Finn turned his attention to the single notebook, flipping it open with quiet dread. It was still as thick, still stuffed with the horrible recountings of the screams of Arturo Larkin racing up the backstairs, the feeling of darkness, of malevolence when anyone dared open the back door. The difference was that Artie's story was a lot longer and more dramatic. The headline was brash and eye-catching: *Young newspaper Delivery Boy - Dead by Axe.* And in the byline it said: *Murderer Still at Large.*

By axe? It was too horrible to imagine his beloved Artie dying like that. Alone and scared, with no-one to look out for him.

Nobody was there to counsel Finn, nobody knew what had really happened. If Finn went back and saved Artie yet again, Artie would still die, one day forward into his own future.

Maybe it would be by poison, or getting run over by a Model T that had chanced a new route down the back alley. Maybe Artie's deaths would move out from the alley and he'd be killed by getting run over by one of the many trains that passed through Harlin in 1912. Drowned in the river. Eaten by wolves—

Finn stopped himself so hard and fast from going further down this unproductive path that he almost bit his own tongue. There seemed only one way to save Artie—one desperate, surely-it-won't-work kind of way. Was he ballsy enough to try it? Was he brave enough to risk failure? There was only one way to find out.

CHAPTER TWENTY-ONE

A rtie could still feel the trace of Finn's kisses, his touch, the taste of him on his tongue. Such a marvelous morning could only have been a dream, except for the fact that his body knew what it felt like to be loved, to be cared for, and his heart was full.

The bright morning sunshine streamed down on the alley as he made his way to Third Street and reached into his pocket, realizing that while he had change, they'd not stopped to grab any coffee from Mrs. Clarkson.

The boarding house had been stuffy anyway, and maybe he and Finn could head to the diner and grab a quick breakfast before going down to the depot. Surely they had time? Surely Finn would want to continue working with Artie and delivering papers, or maybe he'd want to get a different kind of job? It was hard to know, so Artie slowed, his hand on the sharp brick corner of the hotel, and turned, looking for Finn.

Finn wasn't there.

Artie looked up and down Third Street, squinting to look harder, but Finn wasn't there, either. He wasn't in the alley, wasn't standing near the back door of the boarding house, pausing on the low wooden step as though he wasn't sure which way Artie had headed. As though he didn't already know that Artie was going to work at the depot, the same as he had the morning before.

Retracing his steps, Artie went back up the alley. All at once it seemed that the sunshine had dimmed, and the smell of trash and urine rose up at him, making the alley less a pathway to a beautiful morning and more like a one way march to the way his life had always been, before Finn. Just work and putting money beneath the floorboards and hiding from Horace. A very pure and simple hell.

But surely Finn was close. He couldn't have gotten far, couldn't have gone all the way up the alley to Fourth Street, not in the time it had taken Artie to walk to the flagstone sidewalk at the south end of the alley. There wouldn't be any reason for him to go into any of the back doors of the shops along the street, but maybe he'd finally been able to open the back door to the hotel and slipped in? That was it, it had to be.

Artie hurried to the back door of the Harlin Hotel, turned the knob, and yanked the door open. It opened just as it would if it were unlocked, but when Artie stuck his head in, the manager at the far end of the hallway, standing by the front desk, shooed him away with a wave of his hand.

Finn was nowhere to be seen.

He'd always said that he needed to go home, first chance he got, and while Artie had half-believed him, he'd mostly shrugged that off as just talk. Or maybe that had been his own hope talking, the belief that Finn wanted to be with him, to stay with him.

Kisses that sweet, and a touch so caring had left Artie feeling like he'd been petted and stroked the right way for hours. They could not have been based on falsehoods. Could not have felt so true and right if Finn hadn't meant them. Being with Finn had been different from encountering men like himself on East Colfax as night was from day, as desert from dewdrop.

Nothing that felt that right and good could possibly make him feel the way he was right now. As though he'd been kicked in the stomach and left on the ground in a groaning heap. Turning what he and Finn had shared into an alleyway encounter of the worst sort—a fumbled, buttons-yanked-open kind of sex, standing up, the lid of a trash can kicked away because it made too much noise.

He hadn't wanted that when he had lived in Denver, and now, after Finn, he wanted it even less, but it was what he was left with. An empty heart, and a body traced with memories of the sweetest kind.

How could he go on with Finn's touches still soaking into his heart, so new, so gentle, and so fine? But that's what he was left with, the hard reality of it all having been some kind of joke, a trick.

The blast of the horn from the packing plant told Artie how late it was. With his whole being on numb instinct and habit, he finally let go of the knob on the back door of the hotel and sprinted to Third, and then down the hill to the depot. There the second train of the morning was already arriving, telling him how hard he was going to have to scramble to catch up.

Joe Moody's mood was as predictable as could be.

"What the hell, Artie?" asked Joe with a growl. He gestured to the stacks of papers, all tied in bundles with hard string, the fresh newsprint leaving greasy stains on the wooden floor. "These papers are piling up. They don't sell themselves, you know. I've a mind to dock your pay."

"You'd be right to," said Artie, doing his best to submit to the scolding.

Joe didn't know the half of it. Joe didn't know that Artie's heart had just been ripped out of his chest, leaving an empty shell and long jagged scars behind.

He had to ignore that. He had to work. Save more money. Buy that ticket out of town. Today. By that evening, he'd be on the *Shoshone Zephyr* and headed well the hell out of Harlin, bound for someplace north, where nobody would know him or care to know him.

"Here," said Joe as he shoved a stack of papers in Artie's direction. "Get started, and share my apologies for your lateness with Stanley, though you should have more than one newsie working for you. Why don't you have more newsies, eh?"

Joe Moody was as mad as Artie had ever seen him, and he had to hustle to sort and roll papers to load his cart so he could head out quick and avoid more angry words. He just just couldn't take that right now. He was sweating by the time he started pushing the hand-cart up the hill to Third Street. He hurried past the packing plant as though Horace and Ricky were watching from one of the thin windows, only to find that Stanley was just about to abandon his perch on the steps of the bank and head home.

"I'm sorry, Stanley," said Artie, hurrying to bring the handcart to a hard stop in front of the steps. "This is my fault. I have a dime for you, a whole dime. I'm sorry I'm late."

"S'okay," said Stanley, in that amicable way he had, giving Artie a sweet smile as he swept his cap off, smoothed his russet colored hair, and then tucked his cap back on. "I was just worried, is all. You're not usually late. And where's your friend? Where's Finn?"

"Finn had to go," said Artie, trying not to choke on the words. "It was sudden like, you know. But important. He wouldn't have gone if he didn't have to—"

Artie stopped. It was all a lie. He had no idea why Finn left unless it was because he'd grown so quickly tired of Artie that anything else, anyone else, was a better choice.

"Anyway, it's just you and me this morning. Here's your papes. The usual?"

"Give me some extra of the *Rocky Mountain News*, I think," said Stanley, sounding wise. "I think I can be a little bold and take on something new, eh?"

"Sure," said Artie. "Sounds good."

He concentrated on setting thick rolls of newspapers in Stanley's green canvas bag, and then helped the boy loop the strap around his neck, and across his front. He handed Stanley a shiny new dime, and then another nickel, just because.

"Get yourself an ice cream, on me, today," said Artie because there was no reason Stanley should suffer just because Artie was a heartsick fool. "And I'll write it in the book."

"Will you help me sell any extra papers?" asked Stanley, as if second guessing his bold move of taking on more than he usually did.

"Sure thing," said Artie. "I'll do my route and come back, just as I always do."

With Stanley's broad smile and his energetic shouting of *Extra, extra, read all about it*, Artie headed up the street, walking in the sunshine, trying to focus on his work.

It was an ordinary day, nothing different about it. Sure Finn had left him, but he still had his work and his own plans.

If he left on that train—*when* he left on that train—would he leave a note for Stanley? Would he tell Joe Moody where he was going?

Maybe he shouldn't do any of that. After all, he didn't want to leave a trace of himself behind and have someone like Horace telling tales about him that would follow him all the way up to Wyoming. So what if his heart was broken into bits? Didn't mean he had to be stupid about how he moved on, leaving Harlin in a dust cloud at his heels.

In the meantime, he had to hustle, so when he'd finished with his usual route, sweating in the sunshine, he dropped off the handcart and ran to the bank for Joe Moody, then went to the print shop to beg work from Norm Ector. Anything to put extra money in his pocket for that train ticket later. To keep busy. To keep himself from feeling the edges of his ragged heart that would never heal.

By the time he was done in the print shop that afternoon, his ears were ringing with the racket of the presses and his nose was clogged with the smell of grease and ink. Hungry and tired, he staggered back to the boarding house, richer for the day with money in his pocket, but his soul was all the poorer for it.

Keeping busy was only part of the answer. Escaping all the memories that Harlin now held was the other part of what he needed to do. He stumbled his way to the boarding house, slipped through the back door, washed up at the kitchen sink, then got to his place at the table, late again, but only just.

"Where's your friend?" asked Mrs. Clarkson as she began handing out tureens of stew and plates of cornbread. "You owe me a quarter, by the way."

Artie slipped her a quarter, put his napkin in his lap, took some food on his plate, and ate it, hardly tasting anything. He was operating at the lowest levels, a kind of automatic response that he'd trained himself for, oh, so long ago, it seemed. Sleep, work, eat, sleep again. Work some more.

These were habits that had gotten him through the toughest of times, though now it seemed unable to distract him from missing Finn. Even without Finn's comforting bulwark against loneliness and Horace's angry glares, Artie simply missed him.

Before, he'd not ever known a connection like that, a gentle hand leaving traces of affection—of caring—behind. Now he did, and the loss was all the more painful for it. But maybe Finn was somewhere in town, only Artie hadn't been able to find him because he was so distracted by the need to work, to earn money.

Focusing on his dinner, on the last swipe of cornbread across his plate to soak up the stew, Artie ignored the bitter conversation going on between Horace and Ricky at the far end of the table. They were arguing over something, though it was unusual for the two young men to not be in total agreement with each other. It gave him plenty of space to slip away from the table, unnoticed by either of them, to slip up to his room. There he lifted the floor board and tucked his money for the day inside. It was just like any other day, except what should he do now? Bar the door with the dresser again? Go down to the train station and buy that ticket like he'd planned? Or should he look for Finn again?

At a loss, he went to the dresser, hands on the edges as though he meant to shove the dresser in front of the door and call it a day. He'd wait till morning, then decide whether or not he'd get that train ticket and head out. Give his heart a rest from the ache welling inside like an overflowing well of darkness and hurt.

Shifting his hands, he reached inside the top drawer and pulled out the compass. He opened it with a click as he went to the window and knelt on the bed, pushing aside the thin curtains to look out.

It wasn't dark enough for the sheet lightning, not dark enough for the stars to come out, but maybe that was a good thing. Seeing all that, the light against the dark, would only remind him of what he'd shared with Finn. What he'd lost. How much more it hurt, having known Finn.

With a sigh, he clicked the compass closed and lifted the closed compass to his forehead, letting the coolness of the brass soothe his forehead, the wash of metal soaking into him. If only he could find Finn, and they could talk this out. He'd tell Finn, when he found him, that he was sorry for whatever he'd done to send Finn away and that he wouldn't be so needy.

He wouldn't insist on taking the lead all the time, the way he'd done that morning, bossing Finn around, making him let Artie give him a blow job. Or maybe that wasn't it at all. Artie had no idea, but he needed to find Finn and he needed to do it now. Before his nerves gave out. Before he had to leave town, all on his own.

How could he find Finn? He looked at the compass in his hand and opened it, quite silently, imagining it could tell him. To his surprise, the needle spun around in that crazy way it had, even without Finn in the room. Then it settled and pointed to the E. E was for east, where the hotel was. Where Finn *might* be.

Artie tucked the compass in his pocket, straightened his shoulders, and opened the door. It was still light enough outside. He still had a chance, if only he would try.

CHAPTER TWENTY-TWO

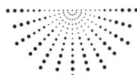

S lipping down the stairs, Artie made it out of the boarding house without being spotted. He felt sweaty all over and uneasy as he stumbled across the alley to the back door of the Harlin Hotel, rushing so Horace wouldn't catch him. He wouldn't have come into the alley at all, if not for the compass as it pointed in Finn's direction.

Boldly, instead of opening the door and merely taking a look inside, he swung the door wide, and strode in, like he had every right to be there.

His intention was to go up the backstairs to the room on the third floor where Finn said he was staying. Only the manager spotted him and crooked his finger to make Artie come to him.

Artie did, only half-unwillingly because, after all, maybe the manager would know where Finn had gone.

"You can't keep coming in here like this," said the manager, his mouth a bitter frown. He waved at the elegant lobby, at the two ladies in broad hats who were having little glasses of sherry, at the clerk behind the shiny, wooden reception desk who was checking in a rich looking fellow in a swank coat. "I have customers, and they've no wish to see your grubby person mingling among them."

"I'm looking for my friend," said Artie, talking fast so he could find what he needed to know before the manager threw him out. "His name is Finn. He's the fellow who rescued Daisy McKee and Ruby, too."

"I know full and well who he is," said the manager, but he dismissed this information as though it was yesterday's news. "While you have proved your worth to society, that doesn't mean you can tramp in here and leave stains and odors behind."

Artie looked down at himself. There was a swipe of ink across his button-down shirt and he'd missed a spot when he'd washed up for dinner. Of course the manager would already think that Artie, a common man, was the lowest of the low, surely not fit to even think about stepping inside the Harlin Hotel. But he had to try, just the same.

"I want to go up to the third floor," he said. "Finn has a room there, he told me."

"There are only quarters for the staff on the third floor," said the manager, his hands on his hips like a washerwoman whose laundry has just been trampled. "You have no business being up there and neither does he, rescue or no rescue. Now, get out before I call the cops."

The manager was the kind to make good on his threat. If Artie kept at it, he'd be in jail for trespassing before nightfall. He opened his mouth to apologize, but the glaring look the manager gave him warned him off.

Finn wasn't in the hotel, that was plain to see, and it was doubtful that he ever had been, or else surely the manager would be singing a different tune. Something like, *yes, the young man is staying here, but that's none of your business.* Snapping his mouth shut, fists clenched, Artie made himself turn and walk down the hallway to the back door.

Every footfall felt like doom and gloom. He'd failed his stay in Harlin in so many ways. Letting himself grow complacent. Letting himself trust. He'd never trust again, that was for sure, though deep in his heart he knew that if he ever had a second chance with Finn, he'd do better. Be better. Make it better. With everything he had.

The alleyway, when he stepped out into it, was brightened by the indirect sunlight, odd sparkles of light showering the brick, the slick of grease in the low part of the alley, even the tin trash cans.

He paused and let the door to the hotel swing shut behind him, only to be confronted by Horace, who stepped out of the shadows as though he'd been waiting for Artie all along.

The angry look on Horace's face was normal, the greasy hair over one eye was normal. Sweat stains from his labor at the packing plant, all normal. That he was alone with an axe in his hands, was not. He swung it like a bat, like he was Ty Cobb aiming for the outfield.

Artie backed up until he banged into the hotel door. Someone was pushing from the other side as Horace came at him. Unsure of which way to jump, Artie stumbled to the side, barely ducking in time to miss the swing of the axe, which glinted in that strange, off-cast sunlight that came from somewhere, everywhere.

When he was out of the way of the door, it swung open and there was Finn. Dressed as he always was, in those too-tight clothes, those strange canvas shoes. He looked tired, exhausted, bleary-eyed as though he'd been awake for days. But his shoulders were back, his chin up, and he looked confident, the angle of his jaw determined.

In his shock, Artie stumbled forward, stepping on Finn's canvas shoes. Finn scrambled to stay upright, and grabbed Artie around the waist.

"Fuck off, Horace," said Finn, startling Artie to his very core. "You can just *fuck* off with that axe and whatever else it is you have planned. And Fate, you can fuck off too. He's mine. I'm keeping him."

Horace came right up to them and it seemed there was no room to run as he swung the axe. Artie ducked and tried to push Finn back behind him, out of the way.

The axe whistled in the air, and as he raised his arm, he felt the axe slice through his shirt sleeves, felt the cold touch of metal, and slammed back into Finn. Finn held onto him, holding him upright while he tugged at the doorknob.

"Damn it, open," said Finn. Then, swallowing, he ducked his chin and spoke to the door as though he felt it could hear him. "Please,

please open. I can't help him like this, I can't save him. You let me come back, so let me help him."

The light in the alley dazzled Artie's eyes, as though the sheet lighting had come upon them, even though it wasn't yet full dark. The knob gave a hard, metallic sounding click, the back door came open, and Finn dragged Artie through the open doorway, and slammed the door shut, locking it hard. That left them in darkness, a whisper of cool air rushing past Artie's ears.

His arm throbbed, and he clasped it with his other hand. The warmth of blood pulsed through his fingers, but it didn't hurt, at least not yet. But they were safe in the hotel, at least until the manager came and threw them out and explained that the back door was locked for a reason.

"Did he hurt you?" asked Finn, his voice hushed, his arm still around Artie's waist.

"Maybe," said Artie, the shock of it rolling through him like an echo that was only going to grow stronger.

"Let's go to my room and take a look."

Finn led the way up the stairs, which seemed to be the back stairs of the hotel, though they were lit and carpeted, just as fancy as you please. On the third floor there were more hotel rooms, not the rooms for the staff that Artie had pictured. It was also lit and carpeted, everything freshly painted and seemingly new.

Finn took a key from his pocket and unlocked the door, which opened onto a darkened room. Through the windows, Artie saw a spread of lights as though the city was on fire or that the Fourth of July had come early.

Finn clicked a switch on the wall, and now the room blazed with light, dimming the lights on the other side of the window in comparison. The room was richly furnished with thick drapes, a monstrously sized bed, complete with half a dozen pillows, and carpeted from wall-to-wall, like a rich person's home, the kind Artie had been inside a time or two to deliver papers.

Along one wall was a low dresser, and on top of that was a thin, rectangular box that had a little red light along the bottom of it. To one side was obviously a bathroom, though it seemed as big as a bedroom, with a little yellow light glowing like a candle stuck in the wall. On a small, circular table were a few metallic looking items that he couldn't identify, and on some kind of stand was a little black box, whose red light blinked on and off slowly.

Finn went over to it and clicked something, and paused there, looking at Artie.

"This is some room," said Artie slowly, with his hand still gripping his wounded arm.

"Yeah," said Finn, and while he still looked tired, his eyes glowed with happiness as he looked at Artie. "Look, I'm sorry about all of this, all of it, and I can explain. But first, let's look at your arm."

Touching Artie gently, Finn guided him into the bathroom, where he flicked on the overhead light and made him sit on the closed toilet.

Artie blinked at the brightness, at the arrangement of white and blue tiles along the walls and the enormous shower curtain that partially hid an equally enormous bathtub. Everything sparkled like polished diamonds, everything was sleek and new.

"Roll up your sleeve," said Finn, ignoring the sumptuous surroundings as he bent and unbuttoned Artie's shirtsleeve, to slowly roll it up.

There was a single slice in the shirt, and a single red line in Artie's arm that went along the outside of his forearm, from wrist to elbow. The wound was shallow, dotted with blood, but the evidence was clear. Horace hadn't been messing around. Another step closer and he would have shattered Artie's arm. Another swing and he could have done real damage.

"How is it nighttime?" asked Artie, blinking as Finn grabbed a washcloth and ran it under the tap, then took some soap and carefully cleaned the long cut. "It was just after dinner when Horace came—"

"I don't think this needs stitches," said Finn, making soothing noises as Artie winced at the sting. "But I'll put some antibacterial cream on it, and cover it. We'll keep an eye on it."

"But Finn—" said Artie, as Finn carefully dabbed some cream on the cut and used half a dozen bandages to cover it. Then he rolled Artie's sleeve down slowly, as though putting off some task he dreaded more. "Why is it nighttime? And how did the door open just when we needed it to?"

"Have you had your tetanus shot recently?" asked Finn. "Were they even invented in 1912?"

"What?" asked Artie, completely confused now. "What's a tetanus shot?"

"Probably not," said Finn, almost absently. He straightened up, throwing away bits of bandage wrapping, rinsing the stained wash-cloth beneath the tap. "Look, can you wait here? I'm going to go check something and then I'm going to be right back. Then I'll explain—I'll explain everything."

Finn took Artie out into the main room and settled him on the sumptuous bed. Taking a blanket from the enormous closet, he wrapped it around Artie's shoulders. Then he grabbed something from a little brown box in the corner, a bottle of orange liquid.

"Here," he said, screwing open the lid and handing it to Artie. "Drink this. I don't care if it is five dollars, you need something for shock. I'll be right back."

Taking the bottle, Artie sipped out of it as he watched Finn leave. The liquid tasted faintly of oranges, and something acidic. Though it made him cough, it gave him some energy.

Looking around the room, his eyes were drawn to the black rectangle on the low dresser, and the clock that he saw on the night-stand. The numbers looked funny, as though they'd been drawn in straight lines in green ink, and announced that it was 3:09.

Was that in the morning? In the afternoon? It was hard to tell. Only that it felt like everything was upside-down, and if Finn didn't come back, he didn't know what he should do. Go back down the stairs and brave Horace's wrath like an idiot? Or wait and sneak back into his room, grab all his money and hightail it for Wyoming?

Both of these options, and many more like them, all entailed running or hiding or a combination of both, and that wasn't a life worth living. Not at all. The only thing that held a promise of anything good was Finn himself, and that was worth waiting for. Another five minutes at least.

Besides, Finn had come back for him, a protective hero who'd shouted at Horace, and even, it seemed, at the heavens as he'd pulled Artie out of a very bad spot. He'd come back for Artie because he cared. He'd tended to Artie's cut like he cared, and he very probably did. It was hard to stay angry, though he still ached that Finn had left him without a word.

If Finn would tell him the truth about where he'd gone, Artie knew he would believe him and forgive him. He just wanted to know. He wanted to know what was between them. A dream, perhaps, or a happenstance meeting? A morning shared beneath the bedclothes? Something more?

Artie wanted something more, but his belly clenched with the thought of being let down again, of being betrayed. But maybe if he trusted, if he let himself trust, just this one time. Just one more time. Maybe it would be okay. Maybe.

CHAPTER TWENTY-THREE

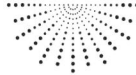

I n the quiet hours of the early morning, the hotel was sleeping as
Finn tiptoed down the stairs to the lobby. There he found a
sleepy night clerk again, completely absorbed in his laptop and
oblivious to Finn's quiet tread. He went into the lobby and looked at
the tableau, quietly lit by a single soft lamp.

The lion-legged table was returned to its old place. The row of
portraits was back as well, all three pictures in their wooden frames,
all as before. Except, rather than being the stiff, creepy and, in Daisy's
case, badly colorized, they showed slightly different photos.

Finn clicked the other table lamp on so he could take a look.

Daisy's portrait was of her as a young woman, smiling in black and
white. Sitting next to her in the picture was a young blonde woman,
who was identified in the little placard below the photo as Maude
Slater. The two women were holding hands, and while their smiles
might be the polite kind that young ladies affected in 1912, happiness
streamed from their eyes that nothing, not even years, could dim.

The next portrait was of little Ruby, with her dog in her lap, a
happy, lively photo that was blurred around the edges because Leo
had been in action, wiggling in her embrace. Ruby was alive and
laughing, her curls bouncing, joy filling the picture frame.

215

The last portrait was of Arturo Larkin, with the same somber expression, the same round cheek, and thin neck where it rose from the workingman's collar of his shirt. It was basically the same picture as Finn had seen earlier, but there seemed to be a smile around Artie's eyes. A sense of something. Of expectation. Of hope.

Below the portraits was a single three ring binder, emblazoned with the title, *Famous Hotel Guests*. Astonished, Finn scanned the information.

Daisy McKee had still been engaged to Gerald, and had lost him in the *RMS Titanic* disaster. Daisy had been saved from a tragic death by the heroism of Arturo Larkin and his friend, Finn. But Gerald's sister, Maude Slater, had not been on board the doomed ship, as luck would have it, unlike what had been previously assumed. Maude had joined Daisy soon after the fatal sinking, and the two of them had shared a Boston Marriage to the end of their days, running a dressmaking shop in Harlin.

Ruby's story was the same as he'd remembered it, though now the story was that Ruby had *almost* been hit by a drunk driver in a Model T Ford. She'd been playing with her dog who had *almost* run into the lobby of the Harlin Hotel, except a young man by the name of Arturo Larkin had shut the front door to the hotel and scooped up the dog to keep it safe. Ruby's parents, the article read, then determined to move out of the busy town and purchased a farm north of Harlin.

As for Arturo Larkin, he'd been the young man who had rescued Daisy from a horrible fate, who had also saved Ruby from an accident in the street. Then he'd mysteriously disappeared on June 7, 1912, sadly mourned by those who knew him.

A memorial service had been held. His gravestone, paid for by his boss, Joe Moody, stood over an empty grave in Harlin Cemetery, now in the center of town. The final page of the notebook indicated that the tableau was a rotating one and that every three months or so, new famous guests would be presented.

Standing quite still, Finn closed the notebook. His heart was beating in his chest; he could hear the whisper of the ventilation, and the creak of the old hotel from somewhere overhead.

It was as though, when he'd asked the door to open, the hotel—or something, some energy—had answered and opened it for him, changing time because he'd asked it to. Leading him and Artie straight back into the future where it was the middle of the night. To a hotel where there were no ghosts, nor likely ever had been. Finn's application to the Ghost Force fell around him in tattered ruins, but he couldn't care less. He had his prize.

As for everything else, like what he'd tell his folks and his sister, that would have to be dealt with, but not right this minute. He needed to make sure that the cut on Artie's arm wouldn't get infected, and he needed to figure out what he'd do when the sun came up. Just that. Between now and then, how was he going to explain everything to Artie in a way that wouldn't freak him out? He needed to explain in a way that would make Artie want to stay with Finn till the end of time.

Slowly, almost dragging his feet, Finn went upstairs to his room. Artie was on the bed, his boots leaving faint traces of dust on the counterpane, a half empty bottle of organic orange juice in his hands. He'd been half dozing, but sat up when Finn came close, and shut the door behind him.

"Everything is strange," said Artie. "Why does everything feel strange? Am I dying?"

"No," said Finn. "Long as we keep that cut clean, you'll be fine. As for everything else—"

Finn paused, and then sat down on the edge of his bed, placing his hand on Artie's calf. Artie's eyebrows rose, but he didn't pull away.

"Tell me," said Artie. "Please tell me. You had a story, you said. A long one. Can you tell me now?"

"I know it's going to sound strange," said Finn, beginning as simply as he could. "But remember how I knew that Daisy was going to try and kill herself at the river? And how I knew about Ruby getting hit by a car in the street?"

"Yes," said Artie. "I did wonder how you knew, and how you, well. How you were so easy when you told me about Daisy and Maude. Two women, loving each other. But I never said, because I didn't want you to think I thought you were strange. I thought you were—"

217

Artie snapped his mouth shut over everything he probably thought he shouldn't say. Finn knew it was up to him to explain, to get everything out in the open so Artie wouldn't feel like he was about to step into a trap.

"I'm from the future," said Finn. "That is, this is the future. *Your* future. I came back to the year 1912 though the staircase, which seems to be like a doorway into the past, a time portal."

"That's crazy," said Artie, sitting straight up, his face white.

"But it's true," said Finn. "How do you think I knew about Daisy and Ruby and you, all being in trouble? The first time I went back in time was an accident, when I stopped Horace and Ricky from taking you up to the roof to throw you off. After that, I came back to save Daisy, and Ruby— and especially *you*, if I could, even if it meant that the hotel had no ghosts. Then I got stuck there."

"You saved me four times." Artie flung off the blanket from his shoulders, and put the bottle of orange juice down on the nightstand, sloshing it, shuddering as he moved away from Finn to the far side of the bed. "Four times I would have died, had it not been for you."

Finn stood up, but stayed where he was.

"He's tried to get at you before," said Finn, trying to be calm, even though the urgency of getting Artie to believe him was making his chest hurt. "He might have thrown you off the roof that first time, beat you up the second time, came at you with a knife—" Taking a deep breath, Finn slowed his words. "Each time I came back, your death changed to something even more horrible. I couldn't let it keep happening—I didn't want to lose you. Didn't want you to be a murdered ghost howling your head off in that alley, scaring people. So I traveled back in time to save you."

"Time travel is impossible." Artie almost spat the words, gripping his fists to his belly. "It's a thing for stupid stories. And ghosts don't exist. Everybody knows this. Are you and Horace—did you and Horace plan this to spook me? To scare me so you could catch me off guard?"

"No," said Finn, low, doing his best to keep his voice steady. His hands came up, a silent plea. "I promise you, I'm not in this with

Horace or anyone. I just came to the hotel to get recordings and pictures of ghosts so I could apply to the Ghost Force team and be on a YouTube channel."

"A what?" Shaking his head, Artie scanned the room as though looking for a way out. "You think you can hunt ghosts? Like a ghost hunter? So you can hunt me? Does that mean—does that mean I'm a ghost?" His face white, Artie looked at his hands, curling and uncurling his fingers. "Am I—am I *dead*?"

"I'm not hunting you. And you're not a ghost. Not anymore." Defeated, Finn hung his head. "I went about this all wrong. Okay? I'm so sorry, but in my time, in the present, now, the hotel is, or *was*, haunted by three ghosts. They were famous for it; they got guests because of the hauntings. The ghosts were Daisy, Ruby, and you. But each time I went back, I saved someone. The first time was Daisy, and when I returned to my own time, the hotel only had two ghosts: you and Ruby. But, you have to understand, you died worse the second time I came back, and then the third. Each time Horace killed you, and each time, he did it more violently. Do you see? Each time I went back, it was the next day, and you suffered more than you had the last time. I couldn't let it go on, even if it meant the hotel had no ghosts at all. And now it doesn't, because I brought you into the future."

Artie didn't move from where he stood. The air in the room felt cool on Finn's skin, on the back of his neck, and his heart was still beating hard. He had a strange feeling that this moment would decide whether Artie trusted him or not, and if he didn't, he was likely to go back down those stairs to meet his fate.

It didn't matter that the camera on its sturdy tripod probably held absolutely no data at all, and that his EVP recorder was full of blank tape. That his camera showed only the hotel room he'd taken photos of. That his notes were probably about the weather and what he ate.

What was he doing at this hotel in the first place if not to hunt ghosts? What was he going to say when he went home, that he'd changed his mind? Well, maybe he had.

What was more important anyway, being a famous ghost hunter or saving the lives of three people? He'd brought happiness to Ruby's parents and her little dog, Leo. He'd brought happiness to Daisy and Maude, and maybe to other people, each act stretching out through time in ways that Finn found he was unable to wrap his brain around.

"You left me without saying goodbye," said Artie, and in his eyes was a look of such sadness that it almost broke Finn's heart.

"I'm sorry," said Finn. "I was scared I wouldn't be able to get home and then I was scared I wouldn't be able to save you. I was so *scared*—"

He'd done the right thing, of course he had, he just had to get through the next few minutes. He just had to convince Artie of the truth. Artie didn't have anyone to leave behind, to mourn him when he was gone, except a handful of people who'd interacted with him on his newspaper route. Joe Moody. Stanley Sullivan. Maybe Mrs. Clarkson at the boarding house. He didn't know what to do about that, but he knew he had to convince Artie that he was safe.

"Artie," said Finn, gently, taking a step forward, but keeping the bed between them. "I only ever wanted to hunt ghosts for a living, you know? But since I met you before you were a ghost, I'm seeing everything differently. I went through time to save you and when that wasn't working, I brought you back here where you will be safe. I'll see that you are. It's a different world, now. Guys like you and me, and gals like Daisy and Maude? It's all okay. People can be together, and love each other."

"What do you mean?" asked Artie, seeming distracted by this new idea. "What do you mean it's okay?"

"It's not perfect, but it's not illegal." Finn took another step closer. All he wanted to do was wrap Artie in his arms and convince him he was safe.

"It's not?" asked Artie, voice rising as though this was an outrageous thought. "Men can hold hands with other men and everything in public?"

"Sure," said Finn. "Just like everybody else."

"And walk through the park together?"

"Yeah, sure," said Finn, smiling, remembering their sweet and gentle walk through the park, the root beer floats they'd had together. "And share a meal, and buy a house together. Take care of each other."

After a long pause, Artie wrapped his arms around his middle and sat on the far side of the bed, head hanging down.

"I don't know if I believe you about all this," he said. "But you did save me and you knew things, too. Things nobody could know were going to happen. And my compass."

Artie reached into his pocket and pulled out his compass. Clicking it open with his thumbnail, he held it flat in his palm. Finn crept close, going slow, until he was on the same side of the bed as Artie held up the compass, and together they watched as the needle spun slowly, and pointed away from Finn and toward true north, just as it should do.

"You're not magnetic anymore," said Artie, the words a little shaky. "Is this really the future?"

"It is," said Finn. "And I'm not going to hurt you. I'm not going to let anyone hurt you."

As Artie's shoulders slumped, his lower lip trembled. On impulse, Finn sat on the bed and wrapped his arms around Artie.

Expecting to be rebuffed, he breathed a long low sigh as Artie snaked his arms around Finn's waist and held on, his whole body trembling. Finn let them stay that way for a long while, petting Artie's back, waiting until Artie grew still within his arms. He thought about Artie's life, living like he had, with nobody to turn to, no solid connection, nobody he could count on as belonging to him or belonging with him.

"I'm going to take you home with me," said Finn. He pictured how Dad would receive Artie, with open arms and a hearty welcome. That's how he always was, with friends, people he knew, even strangers.

"Home?" asked Artie, voice muffled by Finn's t-shirt. "Don't you live at the hotel?"

"No," said Finn, dipping his head to lay his cheek on the top of Artie's head. "I live on a farm my folks have. I was going to hunt ghosts as a way to get away, but maybe I'll stay there for a while, just to think things through. You can, too."

"They won't mind?" The words came out small as Artie trembled in his arms.

"No, they won't mind," said Finn, pretty sure that they wouldn't mind him bringing a friend home. As for how he would manage everything else, like getting falsified papers for Artie or keeping the fact that he traveled through time from his Dad, well, that all would have to wait for later. "But listen, it's the middle of the night, though, and I think I'd freak everybody out if I went home now. So why don't you and I—" He stopped, going through his options. "We're going to listen to an audio book, okay? And lie in bed and just breathe till the sun comes up. We don't have to rush, there's no need to hurry."

"An audio book?" Artie lifted his head, the bandage clinging beneath his sleeve as he pulled away a little, without entirely letting go. "What's that? I know what audio means but how can a book be audio?"

"You know how you listen to someone read a story out loud? Well, there's a machine that can capture it and play it back."

"Like a Victrola?" asked Artie, scanning the room. "But you don't have one."

"Just like a Victrola, but smaller." Finn let go of Artie long enough to grab his tablet from the bedside table and showed it to him, still in the curve of Artie's arms, as though Artie was afraid to let go. "You turn it on, and here, I'll scroll. Look. So many audio books to choose from. We'll do something simple, like fairy tales, or, I know—Bill Bryson. He tells such good stories, it'll be a good way to ease you in."

"Whatever you think," said Artie, and it was easy to see that he was glad to have something to concentrate on other than his own thoughts. "This must all be a dream. Horace really killed me with that axe, and I'm dreaming on my way up to heaven."

"You're very much alive," said Finn. He kissed Artie softly, on his mouth, his nose, his forehead, so glad he'd gone back, so glad he'd brought Artie back with him. "I promise you, you're alive, and you're here with me. Safe. I won't let anyone hurt you, ever."

Artie nodded with a gulp, his eyes only on Finn, his grip around Finn's waist tight as though he feared he might fall.

"Lie on the bed, here." Finn lay the tablet down to plump the pillows, then got up to turn up the heat. "We'll listen and doze, and when it's light out, I'll take you home. To the farm. Dad grows lavender and collects honey from the bees, and Mom paints tinware and they sell everything at the farmer's market in summer. It's good. You'll like it there."

Finn turned off the main overhead light and, leaving the bathroom light and the table side lamps on, lay on the bed next to Artie. Artie moved close and tipped his head till it was resting on Finn's shoulder. The motion made Finn sit up and adjust himself so that Artie could rest in the curve of his shoulder with his arm around him, safe and warm. Then he tapped the tablet and found a good travel story, doing his best to be relaxed so that Artie could relax, could truly feel safe. Everything else could wait until morning, true morning.

CHAPTER TWENTY-FOUR

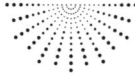

S unlight was pouring into the hotel room when Artie woke up. When he realized that he was wrapped around Finn like a blanket, he tried to untangle himself, the desire to stay safe and warm warring with the deeply-ingrained habit of keeping his distance. He felt Finn's hands on him, trying to make him stay with a soft, insistent tug, but he pulled away and stood up between the bed and the window, where the drawn-back curtains showed an entirely different view than the one he would have expected.

The small town of Harlin, where the hotel was one of the tallest, grandest buildings in town, now stood in a sea of buildings much the same height. Where the street sloped downward to the railroad tracks, buildings occupied every inch. The packing plant was gone, and in its place was a taller structure that looked like apartments. The edge of the brick power plant could still be seen amidst the other buildings, almost hidden, and it gave him comfort to see the familiar pattern of color and shape.

"You okay?" asked Finn from behind him.

"It's all so different. The town is so huge."

Artie turned to look at Finn, who'd gotten out of bed still fully dressed just like Artie was. His clothes were rumpled and he looked tired.

Artie had a flash of what it must have been like for Finn, going back through time over and over, trying to save Artie each time, and succeeding, only to find out that his fated death was again rescheduled for the next day. He didn't quite understand how hunting ghosts worked into all of this, but it seemed that Finn had a project he was working on, only now he couldn't because there weren't any ghosts at the hotel any more.

"It has grown," said Finn. "But look, why don't we check out of here and go to the farm. We'll be there in time for breakfast."

Still feeling a little shaky, Artie nodded slowly. He was hungry, but that sensation was somewhat overshadowed by a sense of underlying uncertainty. If he was here, was he safe from Horace? If he wanted to, could he go home to his own time? But did he even want to? And what was Finn to him, now that he was the only person Artie knew in the entire world?

"How will we get to the farm?" asked Artie, trying to focus on something simple. "Will we walk? Is it far?"

"I've got a car—an automobile," said Finn. "Let me just pack up my stuff, and we'll go. I'll try to explain how stuff works, but if you want to know, just ask. I don't want to overwhelm you."

For all he seemed so calm, Finn's hands were shaking as he pulled things out of the sleek-looking dresser and put them into a large suitcase with wheels and a long handle. He carefully packed his little black box on the tripod, and the other silver things, into a special, padded case.

Going into the bathroom, he came back out with what looked like milk. There were other bottles, too, that said shampoo and conditioner; it all seemed rather fancy, yet, at the same time, these were just things that people used in his own time, only they were in different containers. That helped Artie feel a little calmer; if he could recognize what things were used for, then what they looked like wasn't as important.

As Finn stacked his cases by the door, he looked around the room as though wanting to make sure he wasn't leaving anything behind. Lastly, he looked at Artie.

"Come over to the window for a minute," he said, and when Artie obliged him, they stood shoulder to shoulder as Finn described how the town of Harlin was now set up.

He explained about street lights, and electricity, and pollution, and traffic. He pointed out how women dressed—which was shocking given the tightness of their trousers and the shortness of their skirts— and how men dressed, much like Finn did, with tight clingy fabric, and artfully cut hair.

Then he turned Artie gently to face the room and explained about television and radio, how the room had a ventilation system, and how to turn it up and down. It was almost too much, and Artie lifted his hand to get Finn to stop.

"Why are you telling me all this?" asked Artie, his head spinning.

"Because—" Finn ran his hands through his hair, and shook his head. "You need to be able to fit into the future. I don't know how I'm going to explain you to my parents, so if you at least seem like you belong, it'll help. They're good people and very open minded, but I can't imagine what they'd say if I told them, hey, here's my new friend and he's from 1912. You know? So maybe if you can fit in a little bit, I can figure out a way to explain you to them."

"We can't tell them the truth?" asked Artie, though he realized how odd this story would sound to anyone but the two of them.

"Maybe we can, one day," said Finn, his eyes looking a little sad. "I hate to lie to them. I just need to find the right way without them thinking I'm crazy."

"What will we tell them when we get there?" asked Artie. It seemed like a lot of lies were piling up all over the place.

"That you're my friend," said Finn. "That I met you through the ghost hunting group I'm in, which is kind of true."

"You are my friend," said Artie. "My only friend, now."

As though the weight of the words suddenly rested on his shoulders, Finn paused, his head bowed. Then he pulled Artie into his arms and kissed him softly on the cheek.

"There seemed like nothing else I could do but take you with me," said Finn, almost to himself. "I couldn't keep standing by and reading about you dying over and over."

"I'm not angry with you," said Artie while the warmth of Finn's body soaked into him. "I'm not, but my mind won't stop spinning around."

"Mine either," said Finn. "Listen, we'll check out and go to the farm, just take it one step at a time, okay?"

"Yes," said Artie.

If it was all so confusing in this single room, what would it be like once they were outside of it? What he needed to do was focus on letting go of Finn, on taking the handle of the special padded case that Finn handed to him, on following him down the hallway to a pair of metal doors that slid open when Finn pressed a round button with an arrow on it.

"This is an elevator," said Finn.

"Oh," said Artie, a little surprised. "I've heard of them, and seen pictures in the newspapers, but never seen one in real life. Are they safe?"

"They are," said Finn. He stepped into a tall box that was as nicely decorated as the hotel room had been. "C'mon. We'll get through this, you and me. Just stay close, and if you have any questions, just ask. I'll do everything I can to explain it all to you."

With his eyes feeling very wide, Artie stuck close to Finn as they went down in the elevator that shuddered more than he would have liked. When the elevator stopped, they stepped out into the lobby, which looked, oddly, much the same as it had on the day they'd raced through it to save Ruby from getting hit by a car. There was a long table next to a wall, and Finn paused to pull Artie over to it and to show it to him.

"That's Daisy and Maude, now happy together," said Finn, pointing. "The telegram arrived before she could kill herself, as you know. And there's Ruby and Leo, and that's you. The information says you disappeared that day."

"Did they look for me?" asked Artie, almost whispering, his eyes wide as he looked at the photograph the reporter had taken of him just the other day. Only now, in the future, the picture looked a little rough around the edges.

"They figured you died, somehow, or disappeared. They had a memorial service, and there's a headstone with your name on it." Finn dropped his arm and turned to Artie. "But you're here now, with me. You're safe. You didn't die."

"No, I didn't," said Artie, trying to sound more confident than he felt.

They went to the wooden desk where Finn checked out, chatted with a tiny, well-suited lady he called Mrs. Brice, and leaned against the counter as casually as if he were home. While no actual money changed hands, Artie watched Finn hand over a small square and sign a slip of paper. For comfort, Artie reached into his pocket to jingle his change, and to curve his fingers around his brass compass. Except for the clothes he stood up in, it was all he had.

"Let's go," said Finn. He tipped the suitcase and began walking, the suitcase rolling at his side. Artie hefted the padded case for a surer grip, and followed him outside.

There, the street was sleek and new with broad sidewalks that now covered the ditch on each side. The street was no longer made of dirt, but of some kind of white asphalt. Shiny cars whizzed past, going at high speed in both directions.

When the light turned red, all the cars stopped. Pedestrians crossed in front of the rumbling, growling cars, seemingly unafraid. So many people carried little thin boxes that they held up to their ears, and in their other hands, they carried large cups that they constantly sipped from. The sound of the cars roared in Artie's ears, and he had to stop and close his eyes.

"Are you okay?" asked Finn's voice, quite close. "You want to wait here? I can bring the car around."

"No," said Artie because what he wanted to do, really wanted to do, was to go up in the elevator and down the back stairs to his own time. But Horace no doubt was waiting there with an axe in his hands.

"Just keep close," said Finn, hugging Artie with a quick, warm arm around his waist. "We'll make this quick and be home in no time."

Briskly walking, Finn let go of Artie and led the way along Third Street, where Mrs. Clarkson's boarding house had been replaced with a cream-colored brick building that announced itself as an Elk's Lodge. The saloon across the street from the boardinghouse was now a building that sold flowers. The whole area was built up and contained a variety of businesses like a tattoo parlor, a second-hand shop, and others that were vaguely recognizable, as well as grand houses with enormous green lawns.

Artie stuck close, and stopped when Finn stopped at each corner, until finally they arrived at an automobile that belonged to Finn. It was dark blue, with four doors, thick black tires, and many more running lights than Artie was used to seeing on automobiles.

Finn pressed a button on a little black square he pulled from his pocket. When it clicked, he opened the back end of the car to reveal a space for their luggage.

"Lift that in there," said Finn as he arranged the wheeled suitcase in the space. "Here."

Finn helped Artie with the cases, then took him to the side of the automobile, where he opened the door and helped Artie with a strap that went over his waist and another over his shoulder. The inside of the automobile smelled funny, like he'd been shut up in a paint shop or something, and he wrinkled his nose against it.

"You'll like the farm," said Finn. "I promise, it's a lot quieter than downtown."

As Finn slammed the door shut, Artie nodded, thinking he would just look at his hands while Finn drove. That was what he did, studied his hands, and his feet, and looked over at Finn's feet and hands as they managed all of the multiple controls of the automobile.

Finn seemed handy at the wheel, though Artie peeked at him only once, then dropped his gaze from the glowing green-tinged dials. Surely they were going a whole lot faster than any automobile he'd ever seen, but he made himself trust in Finn's ability to get them where they were going.

Finally, at long last, after many long moments of listening to the tires whine against the street, and the honking, and the chuff of engines all around, as the buildings dropped away he realized they were headed out of town. Artie lifted his eyes to see the green countryside all around, sloping away to young cornfields and stretches of alfalfa grass, and he felt his shoulders relax a little. When Finn took a dirt road headed east, and headed slowly up a slope to where a white farmhouse stood behind a row of trees, he took an even deeper breath.

"Is that the farm?" asked Artie, gazing at the fields, thinking how nice and peaceful it looked, how empty. Much different than Denver, or even a small town like Harlin.

"That's Mike Johnson's place," said Finn. "He just grows alfalfa and hay for farmers. We're along here, just over that rise."

Now that he could watch where they were going, Artie soothed himself by looking at the dirt road as they went up a slight hill and down the other side, where there was a farm nestled in a small valley. It had a white-painted farmhouse much like the one they'd passed, but there were more trees ringed around it, two outbuildings—one large, one small, both painted red—and several rows of white boxes. Beyond that was a creek with a curved wooden bridge going over it, and past all that was row upon row of purple bushes growing on a hillside.

"That's us," said Finn, slowing to turn into the driveway, which was edged on one side with lilac bushes and on the other by a mailbox. "Finnwood Farm welcomes you."

The driveway curved in front of the white farmhouse, and when Finn finally stopped the engine, he let out a long, slow breath. When he turned to look at Artie, his eyes were very blue and wide and full of hope.

"The farm is a good place," he said. "You'll see. Sometimes I don't know why I ever want to leave, but then I do. I get itchy feet, I guess. But we'll stay for a little while. We'll figure it out."

"Sure," said Artie, swallowing hard.

He looked over Finn's shoulder to where someone was coming out of the screen door on the screened-on porch of the farmhouse. He

JACKIE NORTH

was an older man with Finn's same features and broad shoulders, a bit of a belly beneath his white shirt, and dark glasses.

As he came toward the car, Finn leaped out and rushed to give him a hug, leaving Artie with his heart feeling sore, his soul a little lost.

How could he find a place here, when Finn already had a family that cared about him? Back in his own time, there was nobody to care about Artie, so why should the future be any different? Still there was nothing for it but to somehow unbuckle himself from the straps and get out of the automobile to face this new life that he wasn't altogether sure he wanted.

CHAPTER TWENTY-FIVE

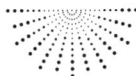

I t was good to hug Dad, and to have Dad tousle his hair before stepping back to bend over to see who else was in the car.

"You done at the haunted hotel, then?" asked Dad. "And I see you brought a friend. Well, bring him in, Mia's just making pancakes."

"She's here?" asked Finn. He'd forgotten about that and was now somewhat panicked at the thought of having to introduce Artie to so many at once, and to have to lie about it till he could figure a better way to tell the truth.

"Sure, got here yesterday, like I told you." Dad went around to the back of the car and opened the trunk but didn't say anything, though he must be puzzled as to why Finn's friend wasn't getting out of the car yet. "Need help with these?"

"Sure," said Finn. He went around to the passenger side and opened the door to where Artie sat amidst the half-undone tangle of buckles. As he helped him out, he was surprised that his only shook slightly. "It's okay," he said to Artie. "Dad says come in. Mia's making pancakes, so we're in time for breakfast."

This is what he would have said to any guest, but to say it to Artie, now, sounded a little inane, as if they were ignoring the bigger picture that this was going to be Artie's first meal in the future. Artie looked scared, his face white.

Dad would know something was wrong the second he laid eyes on him. Luckily, Dad was busy taking Finn's luggage inside, so Finn had about three minutes to help Artie through this.

"Listen," he said. "You're safe here, you know that, right?"

"Yes," said Artie, his head bowed, his voice faint.

"Do you—" Finn paused, not really wanting to ask the question, but knowing he needed to give Artie that option. "Do you want me to take you back? I will, if you want me to."

What he didn't add was how much he wanted Artie to stay. How much he wanted to keep Artie safe, here in the future, where he wouldn't be chased by some maniac with an axe, or looked down at for being who he was.

"You know, at any time, you just ask, and I'll take you back." He bent close, but didn't reach to touch Artie, to comfort him, as he wanted to. "I'm sure I can get the stairs to work the way they did last night. Or maybe I can't. But I'll try, if you want me to."

"Don't you want me to stay?" When Artie looked at him, Finn felt his heart cracking, just a little bit, at the expression in his eyes, the sad slump to his shoulders.

"Of *course* I do," said Finn. He hunkered down so he wasn't looming over Artie, but instead, looking up at him. Gently, he placed a hand on Artie's knee, and was so very moved when Artie, quite gently, covered Finn's hand with his own. "I don't want you to be scared. I want you to stay. I want to *beg* you to stay, but I don't want to force you. You should be able to decide what you want, for yourself."

To his surprise, Artie leaned forward until their foreheads were touching, though he didn't move any other part of his body, only let his hand stay where it was, resting on top of Finn's hand.

"I wasn't sure," he said. "I don't want to be any trouble."

"You're not," said Finn. "You're never any trouble to me."

While he wanted to say more, Dad had come back out of the house and was looking at them through the driver's side window. His eyebrows were raised, as though he was some nosey next door neighbor who had suddenly come upon them buck naked and dancing the hootchy-kootchy on the front lawn. But that was Dad's way, and with a laugh he straightened up and waved at them to come in the house as he walked back in through the screen door.

With a squeeze to Artie's hand, Finn stood up and helped undo the seatbelt the rest of the way, then stood back as Artie clambered to his feet. He shut the car door, no need to lock it way out in the country, and led the way to the house slowly, letting Artie look around at the surrounding countryside, all lush and lovely and waiting for the next gentle rainfall.

The arrangement of small round tables and chairs on the flag-stone patio was well used and set up for comfort. Inside the screened in porch was a larger, more unwieldy picnic table that they sometimes used when it rained. Mostly the family sat outside, as evidenced by the stubs in the candle jars from the night before, when his parents and probably Mia had sat and watched the sheet lighting while having a beer or two, and talking till it got quite dark.

There would be many more of those kinds of evenings, now that summer was coming on strong, and they could talk about bees and honey and lavender and the farmer's market and everything that made up his parent's lives, and Mia's, and his. Finn found himself overwhelmed by the thought of becoming a part of that in a way he'd never wanted to before, though whether this was for Artie's benefit or his own, he wasn't sure.

Finn led the way into the house from the porch, stepping into the comfortable family room that took up most of the front area of the house. There were two sprawling couches, a flat screen TV over the stone fireplace, a huge bookshelf along one wall, and a table in the corner where Dad did his crossword puzzles in the morning.

The other two rooms were the office, where Mom and Dad kept the books and dealt with marketing, and the enormous kitchen, which had the table they sat at and shared meals together. It was here that Finn went, right away, following his nose to find the source of the scent of vanilla and sugar, and hearing the babble of voices of his

Mom and Mia. He already had a smile on his face as he went through the door.

"There he is," said Mom, smiling as she came up to kiss him, her fair hair flying from her headband, her dangling earrings jingling, the smell of flour on her fingers as she clasped his face. "Our ghost hunter of the hour."

With a smile she turned him in the direction of the stove, where Mia, cheeks daubed with flour, was busy making her famous pancakes. After being scared to death that he wouldn't be able to get home to his own time, to see her there, doing what she normally did, almost brought tears to his eyes.

"Hey, sis," he said, coming up to bump shoulders. "Are you sure you're making enough?"

"Sure I'm sure," she said, smiling at their old joke about the time she'd made a double batch, except she'd actually made a quadruple batch. They'd ended up eating pancakes quite often for a month, thawing a little bit of batter each time, but keeping on with it because they'd quite run out of room in the freezer.

"Who's your friend?" asked Mom, from behind him.

Finn turned. Artie stood in the doorway to the kitchen, looking around him like he didn't recognize half of what he saw, and wasn't sure about the other half. Which made sense, only Finn shouldn't have left him on his own like that. Walking to Artie, Finn slung his arm around Artie's shoulders, regretting it a little when Artie twitched, so he let Artie go.

"This is my friend, Artie Larkin," said Finn. "I met him through ghost hunting. He needed a place to stay, so I brought him here. Artie, this is my Dad, Jared Keating, and my Mom, Hazel, and my sister, Mia."

Mom looked a tad surprised, her mouth open as though she was on the verge of saying something. Not that she would refuse Artie her welcome, no, but more on account of the fact that Finn had never brought anyone home before.

"Will he be sleeping with you or should I make up the fold-out couch?" asked Mom, as Mia continued with the pancakes, carefully turning each one while she listened with a cocked head, even going as far as tucking her dark bobbed hair behind her ear so she could hear better.

"I'm not sure," said Finn. His cheeks grew hot, and he felt Artie move closer to him, as though he didn't want to be separated. "Maybe we'll see?"

Right away, he knew he should not have hedged like that. He wanted Artie with him, didn't want to let him out of his sight, but you couldn't do that to a person, make them feel trapped or obligated. He needed to let Artie decide for himself what he wanted to be, how he wanted to be, since Finn had basically dragged him into the future without his permission.

"Sounds fine," said Mom. "It's easy enough to make up the couch, but for now, can you two set the table? I'll get Dad to make his famous coffee."

"I'm coming," said Dad, as he came into the kitchen, snagged his wife around the waist, and kissed her soundly. "I was just finishing that order for those new jars for the honey, you know, the squat ones."

"And the labels," asked Mom as she kissed him back, leaving flour on his mouth and cheek. "Did you order those?"

"Yes, and the special pens, too." Dad smiled and for a moment the two of them bumped noses as though they were quite alone in the kitchen. "Someone with a neater hand than mine can write out the labels though."

"I have a neat hand," said Artie, quite unexpectedly amidst the bustle the kitchen had become with all of them in it, gathering there as though there was no other room in the house.

"Yes, he does," said Finn, because although he didn't know if it was true or not, it was quite likely, seeing as how handwriting had been a thing back in the olden days.

"We'll put you to the test, then," said Mom. "Now set that table. Dad, make the coffee, while I help Mia with the bacon."

Easily put to work, everyone turned to their respective tasks, and Finn guided Artie to a seat so he could sit and look and take in a typical morning at the Keating house.

The sun was streaming past the back screen door, and while the day might grow warm as the sun rose, the kitchen would stay cool, as it was on the northwest side of the house. All the cotton curtains were drawn back to let in as much light as possible, and that, along with the good smells of cooking, had Finn wondering all over again why he ever thought leaving was a good idea.

To stem the flow of unanswerable questions, Finn quickly set the table, made sure there was cream and sugar for Dad's famous coffee, and got out the syrup and the cinnamon and sugar, already mixed in a tall castor. He unwrapped an entire stick of butter and placed it in the cut glass butter dish, and made sure there were enough paper napkins for syrup-sticky fingers.

Then, after getting out enough mugs for everyone, he sat next to Artie and reached to pat his thigh, for comfort. Artie reached back and, as he'd done in the car, covered Finn's hand with his own and held it there. He was still shaking, though only a little.

"It's going to be okay," said Finn, talking very low so as not to be overheard. "You're safe here."

"I feel safe," said Artie, equally low. "At least I think I do."

There wasn't much more opportunity to say anything more than that, as Mia brought over the heaping platter of pancakes and the plate of bacon, and Dad poured the coffee as Mom made sure all the burners were off. They all sat down and chatted normally, asking for the butter to be passed, and the syrup, and who was hogging the cream.

All of this was done without paying any extra special attention to Artie, as though they knew they were a bit overwhelming, which they were, in a way. But it was in a friendly way, as though they were on the verge of asking Artie to tell them everything about him, but were holding back to be polite. All this because, again, Finn had never brought anyone home before but it was about time that he did and they were glad it was Artie.

Finn fully expected that someone, Dad probably, would ask him about Artie, but for now, they were going on about things as though everything was normal.

"You like syrup on your pancakes, young Artie?" asked Dad, holding out the little tin container shaped like a Vermont farmhouse because, of course, Dad only wanted the best on his table. "Or cinnamon and sugar? Mia, pass that to me, would you?"

Mia, her mouth full of pancakes, and her eyes full of questions, obligingly passed the castor of cinnamon and sugar.

"You can have both, if you like," said Mom, looking at him gently. She must have realized that while Artie's mouth was open, he was overwhelmed by choice. "Try both, if you like, some of each on one half of the pancake. Then you can decide."

"Yes, ma'am," said Artie, in that polite way of his as he copied the motions everyone else was making, slathering on plenty of butter and, while it melted, pouring on syrup on one half, and cinnamon and sugar on the other. They all watched as he took a small bite of each, and when he seemed to favor the cinnamon and sugar half, Mia nodded her head.

"I knew it," she said, swallowing a mouthful of pancake. "He's a heathen."

Artie dropped his fork.

"She's only joking," said Dad. "She likes to pretend she only has the syrup, but I've seen her, oh yes, sneaking the cinnamon and sugar when she thinks nobody is looking."

Looking at Finn, Artie waited until Finn nodded, and then continued eating while the conversation flowed around him in the way it always had, making Finn feel a little more relaxed than he'd been since he dragged Artie through that door.

The farm was a good place, though it suddenly occurred to him that he could have ruined everything when he'd gone into the past, not just once, but four times. He could have changed time irrevocably, doing something that would change the farm, or the fact that Mom and Dad chose this life over another kind of life.

He made himself focus on the fact that the only change he could see was that the hotel had famous guests, rather than ghostly ones as a draw for customers, and they still seemed to be doing good business.

Everyone in the family seemed to remember that Finn had gone hunting ghosts at the hotel, but nothing else had changed.

Dad seemed to be the same, happy and full of energy, and Mom seemed her quiet self, watching the world with wide eyes. Mia, busy with her own interests at her tech writing job in downtown Denver, was happy with the as yet un-introduced Toby. The farm looked the same, and the long, upward sloping lavender plants were just as they should be. He'd keep his fingers crossed that truly, nothing else in this life, this world, had been affected by his impulsive rescue of the erstwhile ghost by the name of Arturo Larkin.

"I can help with the dishes," said Finn, as he scraped his plate clean.

"No, we've got it," said Mom. "Why don't you go for a walk, show your friend the farm. You two look as pale as anything, like you've both been cooped up in a box for far too long."

Finn had only been at the hotel for a few days, but it now felt like he'd spent a lifetime there, going in as a hopeful applicant to the Ghost Force team and coming out like he'd walked through a doorway and couldn't go back to his old dreams.

"Sure," he said, standing up, gesturing to Artie to follow suit. "Sound like a good idea?"

"Yes, please," said Artie, arranging his knife and fork in a careful way across the plate. "A walk sounds fine."

The expression on his face told Finn that Artie would be glad for a break from the friendly Keating family, and maybe he'd like to see the view from the top of the lavender colored hillside as well. There were so many things he could show Artie about the world that he now found himself in, but first he wanted Artie to be at ease, to know he was welcome. To feel safe.

CHAPTER TWENTY-SIX

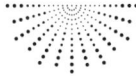

S tepping outside the tidy, white painted farmhouse, Artie took his first, deep breath of the day. The Keating family was lovely in a lively, jolly way that was almost overwhelming. But what did he know?

He'd never had a family of his own, never been invited to sit down to a casual breakfast at a table overflowing with food. Never had known what it was like to be emotionally embraced like that, as though he'd had the perfect right to sit down and partake of the bounty. He'd always felt like a beggar at a banquet, looking in,but never daring to knock. Now he'd had the first taste of what he'd been missing his entire life.

At his side, Finn made a gesture with his hand, as if to encompass the whole of the farm, which must cover many acres; as Artie scanned the horizon, he could only see lavender plants, and not any other kind that a regular farm would have.

"Let me give you the tour," said Finn, tugging on Artie's sleeve. "This is the house, and the porch, of course. And that smaller building is Mom's studio; we can go take a peek."

They walked along the flagstone path in the warmth of the sunshine, over to the small red-painted building that stood in the shadow of the larger barn, which was also painted red. Both buildings were trimmed with white, and as Finn opened the door, Artie leaned in.

There was a long table with tin trays and tin pots, half of which were painted. The large sketches of what was to be painted on the pieces of tin were leaning against the wall, with neatly arranged brushes and small pots all lined up and ready for work. There were also pieces of wood cut into the shape of hearts or trees or mushrooms, stacked on the shelves, waiting to be painted.

There were also several canvases leaning against the wall. Some looked blank, but the top one showed a grey cottage on a beach, done in soft colors.

"Your Mom's an artist," said Artie, with some reverence as he looked at the stillness and the creativity waiting to be brought forth.

"That she is," said Finn. "Her and Dad, well, they didn't want a regular life, didn't want to work in an office. I think they despair of Mia, working in a high-rise the way she does, but she seems happy so they don't pester her about it."

"So your Mom and Dad, they're farmers?" asked Artie, his head spinning a bit at all the options people in the future seemed to have.

"They're artisan farmers," said Finn. "That means they don't grow huge amounts of wheat or corn or whatever, but a small selection of things, like we do here—lavender and bees and alfalfa and painted things. It's a small life, but it's a good one."

"It looks like it is," said Artie, as Finn led him to the larger barn.

There, Finn showed him the bee smokers, the netted hats, the wooden frames for bees to build their wax homes in, and the newfangled honey press that Dad was going to try out soon. The whole of the barn was comfortably neat and organized, with everything someone might need to tend bees and gather honey. Across, on the far wall, hung several scythes on wooden pegs.

"What are those for?" asked Artie.

"We harvest alfalfa by hand," said Finn. "It's cheaper than having a mower, Dad says, and he likes it because it's quiet and gives him time to think."

"Do you know how to use one?" asked Artie, thinking it odd that with all the machines that were surely available this one man would prefer something that had been invented in the distant past. "Are you ever going to tell him about me?"

"I think I have to," said Finn, slowly. "I want to, I just want to do it in the right way, so he doesn't think I'm crazy. We're not a family that keeps those kinds of secrets from each other, and it's—well, it's hard."

"I'll tell him," said Artie, offering with all his heart. "If you want me to."

"We can tell him together," said Finn. "But let's give it a bit, I think. Unless you think—?"

"Let's walk," said Artie. "We can think of something as we walk."

On impulse, Artie curled his fingers around Finn's palm, wanting to comfort him, as Finn had done to him. Finn clasped Artie's hand, and they stayed that way as they walked out of the barn, closed the doors behind them, and headed along the flagstone path that led around the square, white beehives.

"We won't bother them and they won't bother us," said Finn. "I'm not afraid of bees, but they're still coming out of their winter state, and it's better to let them wake up gently."

Artie didn't have any experience with bees and was not a country boy, having spent all of his life in a city or town, with buildings all around and no green grass to be seen. Here, the grass was green and the sky was blue overhead. There was blue between the branches of the large cottonwood trees they passed under, as they headed around the beehives and down a small slope to a curved wooden bridge. This led them over a cheerfully burbling stream that, like the St. Vrain Creek in Harlin, was near to full at its bank with the spring thaw.

His shoulders started relaxing, and the back of his neck relaxed, too, as they walked hand in hand. He drew in deep breaths, enjoying the warmth of Finn's hand in his own, and sighed as the scent of lavender surrounded him as they stepped off the bridge and climbed the hill where the lavender grew.

Here there was no flagstone path, just the dusty narrow trail along the edge of where the fields began, and they walked up the slope till they reached the top. There, Finn waved over the rows and rows of lavender, as though presenting Artie with a gift.

"I don't know why I ever leave here," said Finn, almost to himself, as though the walk was calming for him, too.

"To seek fame and fortune, maybe?" asked Artie, thinking of how he'd followed that path, hoping that each new place would offer him a better life. And it did seem as though Finn had been blind, a bit, to leave all this behind him.

"Maybe." Finn was silent for a moment, then he drew in a breath and turned to Artie, clasping his hand tighter for a minute as he slipped his arm around Artie's waist to hug him tight. Then, much to Artie's pleasure, he did not let go.

"I came back for you—maybe I would have gotten stuck in 1912, but I couldn't leave you on your own. I don't want to say that I saved you because it makes it sound like I'm some big damn hero, and I'm not. But ever since I saw your photograph and read about you and how you died—" Finn shook his head and finally drew his hand away, so he could rub it along the back of his neck. "Ever since then, my application to the Ghost Force didn't seem as important as making a difference. Not as important as saving Daisy, and Ruby, and you. Isn't that strange?"

Not quite knowing what to say to this, as ghost hunting had been Finn's dream from the moment Artie had met him, Artie kissed Finn on the cheek.

"Thank you for coming back to me."

"You're more than welcome," said Finn, quite solemnly, and together they stood hip to hip for a moment, as though a promise had been exchanged between them.

Artie tugged on Finn's sleeve, and pointed to the other side of the hill from the rows of lavender.

"What's that?" he asked, pointing at the small house he saw perched on the hillside. The porch was supported by narrow beams, like an elegant bird about to take flight, and overlooked a small green and flower-bedecked creek that wended its way downhill.

"Oh, that?" Finn turned to look at it. "Dad wanted to do a bed and breakfast kind of thing, but the insurance was sky high, so he decided not to do it. It's maybe going to be for guests that we have over, though we can't make a business out of it. Which is sad, because the view of the sunsets from that porch is amazing."

Artie turned to face the mountains. The white-painted farmhouse was low in a dell, almost out of sight, making it so that the whole of the front range and the back range could be seen, with snowy peaks shining against the blue skies behind them. He'd never seen the mountains like this, never been in a spot where the whole world, horizon to horizon, seemed to open up and welcome him.

"It's beautiful."

His words barely stirred the air, but his body felt the reverence for such a view, and he shivered all the way through. Sensed Finn coming up behind him to embrace him, arms around his waist, the comforting warmth of a body next to his. Finn's body. Finn, who had come back for him after all, and who seemed set on giving up his dreams of ghost hunting just so Artie wouldn't be alone.

Could he really stay here in this time, with Finn and his family? Could he be allowed, at last, to be happy, to live in a world where young men like him didn't have to skulk about and hide their true selves? It seemed too much to believe, just as the view, the blue sky, and the snow-topped mountains were too beautiful to be real.

"You okay?" asked Finn, whispering in his ear, the words kind and soft.

"Can we go back to the farmhouse?" asked Artie. "It all seems too big, too grand—"

"Sure."

Finn's answer was immediate, as though there was nothing more important to him than what Artie needed from him. He'd never had anything like that before, never.

On impulse, there beneath the blue, blue sky he turned in Finn's arms and hugged him right back, inhaling the scent of the breezy bright morning and the secret perfume of Finn's hair. Sighed as Finn's warmth surrounded him. All of this, all of it—the farm, the sky, and Finn—surrounded him, pushing into him as though

245

promising happiness if only he would trust it enough to open his heart.

"We'll go back, and I'll show you the rest of the house." Smiling, Finn cupped Artie's face in his hands and kissed the end of his nose, as he seemed so fond of doing. "Would you like to sleep with me? I'd love it if you would. There are clean sheets on the bed, and plenty of room to cuddle in."

"I'd like that, but will we really be able to live at the farmhouse together like that?" asked Artie, struggling with this seemingly forgone conclusion, hardly able to imagine that he and Finn, together, would be welcomed with open arms.

"Sure." Finn nodded, almost to himself, as though he was utterly confident in this. "Dad's always urging me to make a life on the farm. He thinks it's the best life, and it is in a way. But I'd always thought I'd roam the Earth. You know, me and my van, hunting ghosts, making Youtube videos."

Artie didn't understand some of this, but he realized quite easily that because of Artie, Finn was giving up something he'd dreamed of doing.

"You should roam the Earth, if that's what you want," said Artie. He leaned into the touch of Finn's hands, and kissed him on the mouth, savoring the feel of doing this with the sun shining on his shoulders. "You shouldn't give up what you want because of me. I wouldn't want you to. Not ever."

"Oh, my sweet—" said Finn, pausing, his eyebrows rising, his dark blue eyes serious and sad as he looked at Artie. "That's been an issue with me for awhile. I do want to roam—we should roam together—but first we need to figure it all out, your papers, you and me together. You and me and the family. We have time. I'm not giving anything up, least of all you."

"But you're doing this for me." Artie's heart ached at the thought that anyone would want to do all of this for him.

"I went hunting for three ghosts," said Finn, smiling, his eyes now soft as he looked at Artie. "And I came home with just the one, the only one that matters to me."

Something warm and wonderful rose in Artie's chest, which now felt as though it was ready—ready for this, for Finn's arms around him, and ready for the idea that he could, at last, be happy. He just needed to trust that it would all work out. But that was hard.

"So, you won't ever leave me?" asked Artie, his voice very small. "Or what if I get yanked back?"

"You won't and I won't," said Finn, nodding, seeming quite sure. "It's only those stairs at the Harlin Hotel, and we won't ever go back there, okay? Besides, what does your compass tell you?"

Slipping his hand from around Finn's waist, Artie reached into his pocket and pulled out his compass. As he held it there in the flat of his hand with the sun shining down, the brass lid became warm in his hand, the tip of the dial sparkled.

It pointed directly to true north and not to Finn at all. Just like it should do, as though everything was back to normal. Only now, he was in the future instead of his own time. He needed to give the future a chance, to trust that Finn would always be there, and that the compass would always point north. Everything would turn out fine; perhaps it could be even better than that, if he just trusted that it would.

"Shall we go back?" asked Finn. He tugged on Artie's waist and clasped his fingers around Artie's hand, the one that held the compass, and looked at it in the sunlight. "You and me." Finn nodded. "We're going to be fine. Just fine."

"Okay," said Artie, half-breathless, expectation rising in him like bubbles of joy. "I'd like to see your room."

"Our room," said Finn. He smiled, eyes half-lidded, a sweet gleam of love amidst the blue. "You and me, we'll make it our room."

Together, hand in hand, just like a picture in a storybook, they walked along the dirt path, crossed over the little humped bridge as the blue and green water sparkled along the rocks, and headed back to the farmhouse.

CHAPTER TWENTY-SEVEN

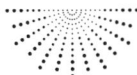

W hen the evening grew chilly, Mom and Mia went inside to get their sweaters, with Artie close at their heels, making himself useful by carrying in the tray of empty gin and tonic glasses. He'd already offered Dad his muscle and energy in scything the alfalfa, and in harvesting honey and lavender. He was full of willingness to help, though Finn thought it might be that he wanted to earn his keep so he wouldn't be thrown out. Not that that would happen, but given where Artie had come from, *when* he came from, it made total sense.

But now, Finn and his Dad sat side by side in the wooden Adirondack chairs, looking at the traces of sunset still lingering along the craggy edges of the mountain ridges to the west. Dad held a small glass with a single sip of whiskey in it, which Finn knew from long experience watching this ritual, that Dad was saving for when the last trace of light left the sky and all the stars started to come out.

To the south, if he turned his head, Finn could already see the sparkles and spritely lights from the sheet lightning, so common at this time of year. Had the lightning been part of his ability to go back through time? He had no wish to go back to the hotel and experiment, so for now he was going to say that the answer was that yes, it had.

"So, kiddo," said Dad as he scanned the darkening skies. Finn imagined he could see the last traces of purple dusk on his father's face, and closed his eyes so he could remember the moment forever.

"Yeah, Dad?" asked Finn, opening his eyes. He kind of wanted another gin and tonic right about then because the tone in his Dad's voice told him the conversation was just about to get a little serious. But if he drank more, he'd just blur his own feelings and wake up with a headache in the morning. And since he'd be waking up with Artie in his arms, there was no way he was going to ruin a moment like that. Or like the one that was happening now.

"You came back with two suitcases, one of which held your gear."

"Yes, Dad."

"You brought a friend with you, which your mother and I both agree is totally awesome. Your Artie seems like a great kid."

"He is, Dad," said Finn, quick to assure Dad about this. "He's a good guy."

"But here's the thing." Dad swallowed the last of his whiskey and then very carefully placed the small glass near the leg of his chair so it wouldn't get knocked over. "He's different. You can't deny that."

"No, Dad." Finn sat up, his hands between his thighs, waiting for Dad to formalize his thoughts before he spoke them out loud, which had always been his way.

"He's very formal and polite, eager to help, all of this is a fine thing. But—" Dad paused, and Finn could see a glimmer from his eyeglasses in the dark. "But I couldn't help but notice that he came with no luggage, no luggage at all. He's also wearing clothes that aren't what all the cool kids your age are wearing. Which leads me to believe that you kidnapped him from a cult, or—" Dad paused, raising his finger, as though making a point in a very carefully laid out argument, one that he'd been exploring in his own mind since the first moment he'd laid eyes on Artie. "Or there's something deeper to this story that perhaps, maybe, you'd like to tell me?"

Finn wanted to tell Dad the truth, wanted it so badly. He and Dad did not have secrets from each other, nobody in the family did, really. But he'd not thought the time for truth would come so soon.

"I need Artie here with me," said Finn. "So we can tell you together."

Dad tipped back his head and hollered at the house.

"Artie, come out here, please."

A second later, maybe even less than that, Artie opened the screen door, a quickly moving shadow, and came over to them.

"Did you want another gin and tonic, Mr. Keating?" asked Artie. "Mrs. Keating says she can make you another one if you want, or a whisky."

"You're not the waiter, Artie," said Dad, kindly. "And I told you already. The name is Jared. We're Jared and Hazel to you. Okay?"

"Okay, Jared."

"Now, sit down a minute."

"Yes, sir," said Artie in that polite way of his.

Finn could sense his apprehension, as if it had come time to pay the piper only Artie didn't have anything but the few coins in his pocket, a compass in the other pocket, and the clothes on his back. Clothes that Dad had easily recognized as not being normal.

Artie sat in the Adirondack chair next to Finn's and leaned forward, echoing Finn's pose as he clasped his hands between his thighs.

"So." Dad leaned forward, sitting like they were, though he propped his elbows on his knees and let his hands dangle. "Who would like to go first? You, Artie, are dressed like you came straight from one of those cults, and you have no luggage, which tells me you left where you were quite suddenly. And Finn, who brought you here, has spoken not a single word about his ghostly research at the hotel, has shown no excitement, has neither urged me to listen to his EVP recordings, nor has he mentioned his application to the Ghost Force, not even once. Something happened, and I'd like to know what that is. Care to share? Or are you going to leave dear old Dad in the dark?"

"I would never do that, Dad," said Finn, and he meant it. "I just don't know how to explain everything. It happened so fast, and I got wrapped up in it so hard—"

"I can imagine that it did," said Dad, laconic and casual. "But it's like you've thrown away all your old dreams, just like that. Poof." Dad raised his hands, spreading his fingers to demonstrate the sudden and odd transience of Finn's dreams. "That's not like you, my only son."

"No, Dad, it's not." Finn nodded, looking down at his hands in the dark, barely able to see them, though they were pale against his blue jeans. "I'm going to tell you the truth, and Artie's going to fill in anything I forgot. But you have to let me tell it the way I'm going to tell it. And you have to have an open mind, okay? Promise me?"

"I've got the openest mind this world has ever seen," said Dad, half laughing, half serious.

"Okay," said Finn, wishing he wasn't as nervous as he was. "Here goes."

He started talking, gently at first, quietly, not quite believing that he was telling this story out loud.

He told Dad about the Harlin Hotel, and how it had, at one time, in another universe, hosted three ghosts: Daisy McKee, Ruby Hopkins, and Arturo Larkin.

Dad opened his mouth to speak, probably to protest that the hotel only ever had one ghost, if that. Finn raised his hand to remind Dad that he promised to listen.

Then he went on, tracing the story through all of the important points. How he'd done his research and written up his notes on three ghosts, and how kind Mrs. Brice, the hotel manager, had been. How he'd gone with the ghost tour and had a good time, doing his best to stay out of the way. And how, at last, he'd gone down the stairs and opened the back door to the hotel, just in time to rescue Artie from Horace and Ricky, the bullies from 1912.

"1912?" asked Dad, breaking through the story.

"Yes," said Finn quite firmly, though Dad's eyes were as wide as a kid's on Christmas morning.

He told about how he'd not believed he was in 1912, but then, when he went back, the tableau at the hotel was subtly changed. He told how he kept rescuing Artie, over and over, and how, after he'd rescued Daisy, thereby changing time itself, he'd come back to a different reality.

His only concern had been whether or not he'd ruined everything, but the only thing that had changed was the fact that Daisy was no longer a ghost. Emboldened, he went back again, this time on purpose, and saved Ruby, and then Artie again.

"Every time I came back to the future," said Finn, his throat dry, "Artie had died an even more horrible death than the one before. I couldn't leave him there to die, Dad, I just couldn't."

"Of course you couldn't," said Dad, and though his words indicated that he completely agreed on this point, he sounded a little faint, as though the rest of Finn's story was knocking him for a loop.

"The stairway became a time portal, that's all I know." Spreading his hands, Finn looked at Artie and then at Dad. "It's like when I left I was in one reality, but now that I'm home, I'm four realities beyond that, four universes ago. But everything is the same except these few details: Daisy ended up with Maude, Ruby Hopkins didn't get run over, and Artie didn't die."

"Do you believe us, sir?" asked Artie, his voice very small as he huddled in his wooden chair, not having spoken at all while Finn was telling the story.

"I believe in other worlds, other possible worlds," said Dad quite slowly. "But never in my wildest dreams—"

"You do believe me, don't you Dad?" Finn scooted to the edge of his seat, his heart bursting with hope.

"You've never lied to me before, son." Dad bowed his head looking at his hands before lifting his gaze to look Finn right in the eyes. "And I don't think you've suddenly started now, but it's going to take me a while, I think. To think about it, to understand it."

"I wouldn't lie, either, Mr.—I mean, Jared." Artie was on the edge of his seat too, his body taut, his voice strident, breaking on the words.

"I would never think it," said Dad. He reached over and patted Artie on the knee. "You've got the most honest face I've ever seen in my life." With a laugh, Dad sat up, tipped his head back, and looked at the night sky.

Finn followed his motions, and Artie did too, until all three of them were lost in that moment of stargazing, focusing on the velvet blue black, sprinkled with bits of faraway light.

"I'm going to take you at your word, Finn," said Dad slowly into the silence. "But you know, it's funny. We bought this place back in the nineties, d'you remember?"

"Sure, I do, Dad," said Finn. "You were trying to show me those photographs last week, those old black and white ones."

"Still have 'em," said Dad. "Like to show 'em off from time to time, to remind me how we got here. Older couple. They wanted to sell and then they didn't, and then they did. They pulled stakes, sold us the farm, and went off to live in an Airstream on the Oregon coast somewhere."

"Why—" Finn paused letting the darkness settle over him and calm his jangled nerves. "Why are you telling me this, Dad?"

"Time's a funny thing," said Dad. "It races on and soon you find yourself forgetting the small details, except for one or two, like flashes of light in the back of your mind."

"And?" It was obvious Dad was trying to tell him something, but he had no idea what.

"Who sold us this farm?" asked Dad. "Do you remember?"

"No," said Finn. On impulse he reached over and took Artie's hand in his. Artie's skin was ice cold, so Finn lifted it to his mouth and blew on it gently, warming it in his palms.

"Their name was Hopkins-Smith," said Dad. He sat up. In the half-darkness, lit by the light coming through the screen door of the farmhouse, there was a funny little gleam in his eyes. "Ruby and Sam Hopkins-Smith. They must have been near eighty years old when they sold, but they were game for anything, you know. I hope I'm as spry as that when I'm that old."

"Years from now," said Finn, automatically, but now it was he who was cold. "Ruby *Hopkins*-Smith, you say?"

"Indeed I did." Dad got up and stretched, reaching for the sky. "It appears to me that this is the same little girl you saved. What if you hadn't gone back in time to save her? She never would have sold us the farm, back when we bought it, because the farm would have belonged to somebody else. Someone who didn't get run over by a Model T Ford when they were just seven years old. The question is," said Dad, looking down at Finn. "Which came first? You saving Ruby? Or Ruby selling us the farm because you saved her?"

"I can't Dad," said Finn as he stood up too. His throat hurt, and his chest ached. "I have been trying to figure it out, you know, the space time continuum thing, but it just goes round and round."

"It's a headache, all right," said Dad, giving Finn a quick hug. "But that doesn't make it less true. Right?"

"Right." Finn let go of Dad to pull Artie into their little circle, Artie who hadn't said an entire word once Finn started telling his story.

"You kept coming back," said Artie now, mumbling against Finn's chest. "I didn't realize that each time, I was supposed to have died, and would have, except for you."

"I would have kept coming back forever," said Finn. "Forever and for always. For you."

"Thank you," said Artie. "Thank you for everything."

"Oh, my," said Dad, a little laugh in his voice as he began to make a little joke, like he usually did. "Looks like I'll have an ex-ghost for a son-in-law. What will Hazel say? We will tell her, won't we?"

"Some day, Dad, for sure." Finn didn't feel up to telling any more stories, or thinking about time paradoxes right now. He just wanted to go to bed and hold Artie till they fell asleep in each other's arms. Then, in the morning, it would be a new day, and they would talk and learn about each other and walk among the purple and green rows of lavender while the bees buzzed among the fragrant petals.

"Tell you what," said Dad. "Let's get out those old black and white photographs, and you tell me if you recognize little Ruby, all grown up."

"Okay," said Finn.

"Okay," said Artie. He slung his arm around Finn's waist and seemed to pause as though waiting for someone to tell him he shouldn't. But nobody did because nobody would. At least not on the farm.

"And ice cream?" asked Finn as they headed into the house. "Artie likes root beer floats, I'll have you know."

"Ah," said Dad, leading the way, hurrying ahead. "I knew I liked you, Artie, from the moment I laid eyes on you. I knew it."

The automatic porch light came on over the screen door as they got nearer to the farmhouse. Artie jerked back a little, but Finn settled him with a hug and promised himself he'd do a better job of acclimating Artie, his ex-ghost, his old fashioned boyfriend, to the future.

CHAPTER TWENTY-EIGHT

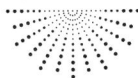

T he morning came with a soft gentle rain pattering outside the windows, keeping Finn's room in a low gloom. Artie tried to stay still, but it was hard. He loved the farm, loved being amidst the Keating family, loved it so hard, he'd barely been able to fall asleep.

And yes, there were all kinds of gadgets and gizmos that tended to turn off and on when he least expected them too. There were all kinds of noises and buzzers and alarms and all the kitchen equipment—each one strident, demanding attention. But this was the future Finn had brought him to.

This was the time and place where he was right now, because Finn had come back for him, over and over. Finn, who had risked being stuck in 1912, all because he cared for Artie. He used affectionate words and gestures. Had taken a walk in the park with Artie, because Artie had asked him to. Had dallied for a while at the ice cream parlor because Artie had wanted it. He had touches and words and kisses— all for Artie. Being pretty much everything Artie had ever dreamed of, were he able to express his affection and get affection in return. Which, in the future—in the *now*—was completely legal and accepted.

He clasped his hands over his chest, fiddling with the bedsheet while he waited for Finn to wake up. And thought about the black and white photographs Pa Jared had brought out to share with them.

He had them organized by year, and showed them to Finn, as he must have done in the past, wanting to share the experience with his son. Only last night, Finn had been quite attentive, and together they had gone through the photographs, looking for an image of Ruby as a young girl.

"There she is," Finn had said at one point, pulling the photograph in front of his father. "This is the same one that is in the lobby, though she's a famous guest and not a ghost anymore. That's her dog, Leo."

Pa Jared had flipped over the photograph that his son had never bothered to look at before, and read the penciled description. "Ruby and Leo, pure love, 1912."

"Does it prove it, Dad?" asked Finn, rushed and anxious, looking up at his father.

"I don't need proof," said Pa Jared, his voice a little clogged. "You told me it was the truth, and so it is. And, wow, just look at that cute dog. Did you save the dog, too?"

"We kind of did," Finn had said. "Though really, Artie was the one who picked Leo up to keep him from running around, so Ruby wouldn't throw the red rubber ball and end up in the street when that drunk driver came by."

Pa Jared was still for a moment, though Artie could practically hear him thinking that he'd research drunk drivers in Harlin in 1912, just to see what he could see. The whole family was like that, inquisitive, their minds always going, yet content to live a simple life that was more like what Artie was familiar with.

"You awake?" asked a sleepy voice from the space next to him.

Artie turned his head to look, and there was Finn, sweet as always, blue-eyed and rumpled. Dozily, Finn reached for Artie and Artie willingly went into Finn's arms, into the morning-warm closeness of him. This was where he'd always longed to be, only he'd never known it till now.

Finn kissed his nose, and Artie smiled, ducking his head as his cheeks warmed with pleasure.

"You know," said Finn, in a rather serious tone, though by this time Artie had grown used to the quiet joke beneath the pretend. "This is how mornings are going to go from now on, so you better get used to it."

"How's that, then?" asked Artie, doing his best to follow along with the gentle play.

"You waking up. Me holding you. Kisses. Maybe more." Finn waggled his dark brows, then reached down to adjust himself beneath the sheets.

Oh. Now Artie understood. He'd always ignored himself in the morning, pretending his cock wasn't hard against his belly. Most mornings, in the lodging house, there'd never been any privacy. Then, in Harlin, he'd always been worried someone would hear him through the thin walls, and so he'd gotten out of practice at taking himself in hand.

"Can we?" asked Artie. He kissed Finn's cheek and waited, as still as a mouse, for the answer.

"Provided neither of us is a screamer," said Finn with a laugh.

"What?" asked Artie, totally confused now.

"That's just someone who is loud during sex," said Finn, smiling as he traced the line of Artie's cheek as carefully as if Artie had been made of bone china. That was how Finn made him feel with every word, every touch, as though Artie was something rare and unique and special.

"My ghost," said Finn. "I'm glad you're not a ghost anymore, but that's when I fell in love with you. When I realized that unless I brought you back to the future, you'd always be a ghost to me. And I didn't want you to be. I wanted you to be real. To be mine."

Finn shrugged as though he wanted to relax his shoulders, blushing. And maybe he wanted to take back those words, those out-of-the-blue words that now settled in Artie's heart like a soft and protective blanket.

"You fell in love with me?" asked Artie, hope rising within him as he snuggled closer.

"Almost from the moment I laid eyes on your portrait," said Finn.

"And really, from the moment I met you, thought I didn't realize it, not fully."

"And now?" asked Artie. He tipped his head back to look up at Finn, to bask in the sweetness of that smile, to enjoy the moment they were in, warm and curled in each other's arms.

"Then," said Finn. "Now. Always. Can I kiss you?"

"Yes," said Artie. "You never have to ask, you know. Not ever."

"In the beginning, as we are, I think I do." The serious expression was back on Finn's face, making his eyes dark as he lowered his brows. "It's always better to be sure, in the beginning. Later, of course, I'll just have my wicked way with you any old time, right? And you can with me."

"I can?"

The images rose in front of Artie as though Finn had tossed him a bouquet of photographs, each one of them together, smiling, laughing, holding each other. Kissing. Tumbling beneath the sheets, their hands on each other, all over, their bodies entwined.

Mixed among this were the silent still times, the moments of looks and longing, of understanding. It was his imagination running wild; he'd kept such a hard hold on it for as long as he could remember that it was hard to let it have its way now. But he was going to let it, he was.

"I love you," said Artie. "Is that okay to say? I wanted to say it but I was worried, only you said it so—"

"Any time, any where," said Finn. He kissed Artie on the nose and then rolled toward him, pulling Artie into his arms, covering him with his body, but gently, with his weight on his own elbows.

"And now, may I have my wicked way with you?"

It was obvious that the answer was and always would be yes, especially since both of their cocks were pressed between their bodies, and Artie's blood began to race. Tingles danced up his spine, and he arched back as Finn kissed him liberally on the neck and down his chest. Down and down he went, until Artie gasped, finally figuring out what Finn wanted to do.

"I've never—" he said, panting, half sitting up. "I've only had hands, never anyone's mouth on me. But I've given blow jobs, you know," he added, wanting to be clear. "I've just never gotten one myself."

"Then it's about damn time," said Finn, growling, doing one of his pretends where he was angry about this, and meant to do something about it. "I'm your first in this, then, thank goodness."

Artie thought about the men he'd been with. Some men that Artie had known had only wanted virgins and had been willing to give Artie good money for it, but it had always felt sordid and unlovely.

As if sensing Artie's distress, Finn scooted up, straddling Artie's legs, placing kisses on his thighs, until finally he paused and looked at Artie.

"I don't care how many you've been with," said Finn. "I just care if you got used, or hurt, or someone did something you didn't want—"

"No," said Artie, shaking his head. "I never went unwilling, and I always drew the line when they wanted to do what I didn't want to do."

"And nobody's ever given you a blow job?" asked Finn.

"Never," said Artie. "Never till now, at least hopefully now."

"Yes, now," said Finn. "Absolutely now."

Finn bent down and pulled the sheets back and carefully unbuttoned the tiny buttons on Artie's cotton underwear. The night before, there'd been talk of taking Artie to the store to get him new clothes, but that conversation had melted into the darkness when everybody went to bed. Now, it was a pleasure to watch Finn manipulate the tiny, shell-white buttons, one by one, exposing Artie's chest, the dark-gold hair of his groin, his aching cock where it curled against his belly.

With a slight touch, Finn ran his nose along the hard curve of Artie's cock, and then, licked it and kissed it, all up and down, taking his time, making the surface slick. Then he kissed the tip, his tongue licking up the drop from the slit and, with a smile, began to suck Artie slowly down. Inch by inch, going up and down, irregular and fascinatingly slow.

Artie closed his eyes, tipped his head back, and sank into the pleasure. He let Finn's kisses and licks and sucks erase all the too-fast-to-enjoy encounters, the sour looks, the rain spattered and stinking back alleys of East Colfax. Every gesture, every pet, turned Cecil's betrayal —including the final one—into an invisible phantom that would soon vanish under the onslaught of Finn's affection, his love, his caring. His very presence.

With Finn sucking him down hard, now, even the fear and trembling that Horace and Ricky had left in their wake would soon become a memory and, under repeated onslaughts of such attention, would vanish into the sands of time, where they belonged.

As to whatever happened to Horace, and why on earth Ricky had not joined him in the final, most brutal attack, he neither knew nor cared. And what did it matter, when he had such a handsome fellow pushing between his thighs now, spreading his knees apart ever so kindly so that he could swirl Artie's balls in his fingers and blow gentle, soft breaths across wet flesh.

But it was more than that, much more. As Artie trembled while he came, Finn's hands were gentle on his thighs, petting him, soothing him. Ever aware of Artie, as though he was a delicate flower in need of special care. He'd always been this way, from the very first, treating Artie as though he mattered. With a cry, Artie pulled Finn on top of him and scrubbed at his eyes, and tried to slow his breathing.

"What is it, my sweet?" asked Finn, his voice soft but urgent in Artie's ear. "What is it, please tell me?"

"I just can't believe I'm here, that we're here together." Artie gulped and blinked away his tears so he could look up and focus on Finn properly. "I just can't."

"Well you are," said Finn with mock sternness, planting his elbows on either side of Artie's head, using his thumb to help dry Artie's tears. "You're here to stay with me. I brought you here because I wanted you with me."

"And I wanted to be with you," said Artie, though he knew it would be a while till he acclimated himself to Finn's world.

"And what else do you want?" asked Finn. "Ask. Just ask. Anything in the world."

Artie took a long slow breath and thought. He could have anything he wanted, anything. What he wanted, though, was right here in his arms. And Finn wanted him there, so what more was there to want?

Yet, he could see the brightness of Finn's expectation that Artie would ask for something and then Finn could move heaven and earth to give it to him. He liked that, it was true, though he knew he would want to be able to do the same for Finn in return.

As for the moment between them, the crumpled sheets, the sweat that was growing between their bodies, the way his cotton underwear was currently cutting into the crease of his thigh, well, if that was how it was to go each morning, he was fine with that. Quite fine, indeed.

He wanted to become a part of the farm, to help Pa Jared and Ma Hazel, to learn how to tease Mia and the as yet unmet boyfriend Toby. He wanted to help with the lavender and the bees and the alfalfa, to help the farm be as prosperous as it possibly could be. He wanted all of it.

And then his stomach growled.

"I should like pancakes, if you please," said Artie, doing his best to put a little laugh behind his mock demand. "And some more of Ma Hazel's good coffee, too."

"Now?" asked Finn, making a face, though it was a pretend frown. "Ain't I good enough for ya?"

"You are all that I need," said Artie. He cupped Finn's face in his hands and kissed him wherever he could reach, tasting himself on Finn's lips, enjoying the slight brush of Finn's morning beard. "You are all that I ever would need. I had no idea you'd come into my life, but I'm very glad you have."

"Thank you, my sweet," said Finn. Then he lurched from the bed, dragging Artie with him, one arm around Artie's waist, another searching for clothes they might wear. They shrugged into their clothes and Finn flung the bedroom door wide, letting in the cooler air from the hallway.

"Ma Hazel," shouted Finn as he stumbled down the stairs, making a joke of it. "We need coffee. Ma!"

Artie kept up as best he could, smiling the whole while. It was as though the future had hidden in the wings this marvelous family for him to share in, to be a part of.

Had he known, he would have been braver about moving from Chicago to Denver to Harlin. Would have been more bold to tell Horace to back off, and Ricky too.

There were dozens of things he would have done differently, had he known that this was how it was all going to turn out. And it had, marvelously. He had Finn, and Finn had him, and it was to be forever. Finn had said so. Finn who loved him. Who *loved* him and who he loved in return, and he could never want more than that.

———

The End

———

JACKIE'S NEWSLETTER

Would you like to sign up for my newsletter? Subscribers are alway the first to hear about my new books. You'll get behind the scenes information, sales and cover reveal updates, and giveaways.

As my gift for signing up, you will receive two short stories, one sweet, and one steamy!

It's completely free to sign up and you will never be spammed by me; you can opt out easily at any time.

To sign up, visit the following URL:

https://www.subscribepage.com/JackieNorthNewsletter

facebook.com/jackienorthMM
twitter.com/JackieNorthMM
pinterest.com/jackienorthauthor
bookbub.com/profile/jackie-north
amazon.com/author/jackienorth
goodreads.com/Jackie_North
instagram.com/jackienorth_author

AUTHOR'S NOTES

I wanted to write a ghost story. No, truth, I wanted to be a ghost hunter, so I watched a lot of shows about ghost hunting and scared the hell out of myself! I just cannot abide things that jump out at me, so I wrote this time travel romance about my brave Finn, who can talk to ghosts and who has a heart as big as the sky.

I have had some ghostly encounters, which is probably why the shiny idea to buy an EVP and a special camera to take pictures at midnight never panned out.

The encounter I remember with great fondness was when, after my own Nana died, she visited me in my bedroom. And yes, she came three times, each time showing up a fainter and fainter version of herself. I could feel she was checking up on me, making sure I was okay, and I remember assuring her that I was, and I thanked her for the cookie jar she left me, one of my most treasured possessions. (It's the same cookie jar that's in the story.)

The other encounter I had was when we had a memorial service for my Dad. He'd been in the Air Force, and so I had my brother in law read aloud the poem, "High Flight," as he had asked me to make sure happened, many years before.

When all the other parts of the service had been going on, it had been fairly quiet, but when my brother in law started reading, it turned weird. For one thing, a dog, all out of nowhere, started howling. He howled the entire time my brother in law was reading, and stopped when my brother in law finished reading the poem.

The other thing that happened, and I swear this is true, is that I saw the shape of my Dad form, as though he was standing there, right next to the podium. I blinked very fast, and looked, and there he was, a dark shape, his arms akimbo, like he used to stand. I looked away and blinked, and looked back, and there he still was, almost solid by that time. I stared at him and he looked at me - and when the poem was done, he went away, slowly, like a grey mist dissipating in the morning's sunrise.

Ghosts are real. I know they are.

A LETTER FROM JACKIE

Hello, Reader!

Thank you for reading *For the Love of a Ghost* from my Love Across Time series.

Please take a moment to write a review of *For the Love of a Ghost* on Amazon and Goodreads. Reviews help with the rankings of my book and can bring them to the attention of other readers who might enjoy them.

Best Regards and Happy Reading!

Jackie

facebook.com/jackienorthMM
twitter.com/JackieNorthMM
instagram.com/jackienorth_author
pinterest.com/jackienorthauthor
bookbub.com/profile/jackie-north
amazon.com/author/jackienorth
goodreads.com/Jackie_North

ABOUT THE AUTHOR

Jackie North has written since grade school and spent years absorbing mainstream romances. Her dream was to write full time and put her English degree to good use.

As fate would have it, she discovered m/m romance and decided that men falling in love with other men was exactly what she wanted to write about.

Her characters are a bit flawed and broken. Some find themselves on the edge of society, and others are lost. All of them deserve a happily ever after, and she makes sure they get it!

She likes long walks on the beach, the smell of lavender and rainstorms, and enjoys sleeping in on snowy mornings.

In her heart, there is peace to be found everywhere, but since in the real world this isn't always true, Jackie writes for love.

Connect with Jackie:

https://www.jackienorth.com/
jackie@jackienorth.com

facebook.com/jackienorthMM
twitter.com/JackieNorthMM
pinterest.com/jackienorthauthor
bookbub.com/profile/jackie-north
amazon.com/author/jackienorth
goodreads.com/Jackie_North
instagram.com/jackienorth_author

Made in the USA
Middletown, DE
16 July 2021